JOHN F. WATSON

A Journey Of Hope

To Sean
Best Wishes
John F. Watson

First published by Independent Publishing Network 2019

Copyright © 2019 by John F. Watson

All rights reserved. No part of this publication may be reproduced, stored or transmitted in any form or by any means, electronic, mechanical, photocopying, recording, scanning, or otherwise without written permission from the publisher. It is illegal to copy this book, post it to a website, or distribute it by any other means without permission.

This novel is entirely a work of fiction. The names, characters and incidents portrayed in it are the work of the author's imagination. Any resemblance to actual persons, living or dead, events or localities is entirely coincidental.

John F. Watson asserts the moral right to be identified as the author of this work.

Fourth edition

ISBN: 978-1-80352-222-7

This book was professionally typeset on Reedsy.
Find out more at reedsy.com

To every one of my family who encouraged belief. Also to my late father Fred Watson, a great wordsmith and marvelous storyteller who, possibly, never had the chance to follow his dream.

Acknowledgement

Many people helped in bringing this book to fruition and I would like to thank Richard Watson for the stunning sunrise photograph, Stephen Hughes, Leader of Art and Photography at Stamford Welland Academy, Bethany Watson for her computer and design skills and Alice Hannan for the giving of her precious time after school to help produce such a striking and attractive cover.

Also thank you to Nicola Chalton of Valley News who helped tremendously with publicity, Claire Griffiths from Botton Theatre for the supply of Victorian clothing and to Grosmont Writers Group for their knowledgeable, critical and humorous input. Finally, to David Fowler and Ren Yaldren from Farthings Publishing who also believed in the project and brought it to reality for me. Thank you all.

Chapter 1

Ruth's scream shattered the early morning silence. For a moment, her eyes opened wide, staring wildly, but still only seeing the vivid, terrifying images conjured up by the nightmare. Finally, her sleep fuddled brain slowly cleared to release her, once again, back into the reality of her small, but comfortable bedroom.

It never changed; the aftermath always the same, leaving her weak, trembling and drenched in sweat. But Ruth knew, eventually, she would learn to box it away, as she was forced to do with so many other dreadful memories of the past, banishing it to the far recesses of her mind.

Still visibly shaken, Ruth jumped out of bed, immediately rushing to the low window, breathing a sigh of relief, as no one appeared to be within hearing distance. Splashing cold water into a bowl, she gathered her senses, bathed and dressed, focusing on the day ahead, blissfully happy in the knowledge she would see Jim today. Out in the wild, open countryside, free as a bird to enjoy this bleak, rugged moorland which she now thought of as home and knew in her heart, whatever lay ahead, she would be loath to leave this small, isolated hamlet set in the very heart of the North Yorkshire moors.

Eagerly going about the daily routine, she rushed through to the kitchen to begin making breakfast for Jacob and Joshua, who were already out in the yard feeding the stock and preparing horses for the ever-growing number of passing travellers. Filling the kettle from the one cold tap set above the old soapstone sink, Ruth hurried through and hung it on the crane, swinging it over the now glowing peat fire to boil. Just in time, she thought, as the babble of voices outside grew louder, followed by the familiar click of the door latch and in walked the Reverend Jacob Thrall.

"Morning, Ruth. Another beautiful day ahead of us I believe. I hope you slept well?"

An authoritative figure with an effortless gait, immediately striding through to the kitchen to wash and dry his hands before returning to the room, his tall, angular frame just beginning to show signs of a stoop, his long white hair flowing out from underneath the broad brimmed hat which he quickly removed to hang on the back of his chair. A loosely buttoned shirt, scruffy at the cuffs and a growth of stubble around the strong chin added a grimness to his features, belying a benevolent nature. At this moment, no one could ever look less like a man of the cloth, only the white strip of dog collar betraying his choice of trade, as his normally sallow features remained slightly flushed from the hard labour outside.

Following closely on his heels came his son Joshua, of much stockier build and broader of shoulder, which his long golden curls almost reached. Ruth glanced quickly at Jacob wondering if he'd heard her scream earlier. Deciding the question was asked innocently she replied, "Beautiful indeed, Jacob; and yes, I slept soundly thank you," adding to the pair of them, "you two really can smell when breakfast is on the go, can't you?"

They seated themselves around the table in the meagrely, but comfortably, furnished room, Joshua already there, hungry as a wolf, carving hunks of bread from the loaf as Ruth brought the fried eggs and bacon to the table, slipping them onto each plate. Joshua smiled up at her, a mix of admiration and love for this girl showing clearly in the honest blue eyes as he asked, "I suppose you'll be away to see Jim this morning, Ruth, are you?"

"Might be," Ruth teased. "What if I am?"

"Well, don't forsake us men back at home just because you're going a-courting." Then added jokingly, "we can't be expected to look after ourselves for long you know."

"You were managing pretty well before I came along if I recall rightly, Master Josh."

"Yes, that might be so, but we've got used to having a woman about the house, spoiling us of late and would take badly to fettling for ourselves. Isn't that so, father?" He cast an enquiring glance across at Jacob as he said it.

"Now that's enough of that you two. Don't you ever stop chattering?" Jacob answered, rising from his chair, a hint of a smile playing about the lips, softening the grim features. Jacob had a feeling these two shared a secret. Not as lovers; he would certainly have spotted that. It was something deeper; something, Jacob believed, happened the night Joshua regained his speech. But however hard he tried, he could not even hazard a guess. He was just happy that they shared time together as if brother and sister.

"Aah, don't mind us two, father. Remember, I have a lot of catching up to do. Talking that is," replied Joshua.

"I realize that, Josh. Now, more importantly, will you be attending church today, Ruth?"

"No, not this week, Jacob. Although I hate to admit it, Josh shall be proved right for once," a sly wink crossing between them. "I'll possibly take a walk over the high moor toward Ralph's Cross to meet Jim, seeing as it is Sunday."

"Well, you know Jim would be more than welcome as well Ruth," he replied, an earnest look spreading across his ageing countenance, "but maybe in his own good time, eh?"

"Maybe. But you know what he's like," she said, a frown creasing her brow as she remembered the hardships Jim had encountered just to survive. "Sometimes he can be a bit stubborn."

A chuckle escaped from Jacob's lips as he pushed his chair back from the table, saying, "I remember someone else more than a little bit stubborn on such things just a short while ago. But time will tell, dear girl. Now, can I help you with the washing up before church?"

"No, I have plenty of time. Jim'll not be finished until at least ten," she replied brightly before looking him up and down, then mockingly scolding him for his shabby appearance. "Now, come on Jacob, it is time to get yourself tidied up and looking respectable. You cannot possibly go to preach in that state, the congregation will hold their noses as soon as you walk through the door. You two be off, I will tidy up and see you tonight."

"Very good, Ruth. I must admit it is a glorious day, so go and enjoy your time off and we'll see you back about teatime young lady. Bye."

After changing into their Sunday attire, father and son strode out, following the well-worn stone pathway laid for the early pack horse merchants who travelled these moors centuries ago, as it cleaved its way through the deep heather leading to the church, an old tin tabernacle that had clearly seen better days, in the distance.

Newly quarried stone stacked high on timber bases stood on either side in readiness for the building of a new church to worship when funds allowed but was proving a monumental task for such a small community. Ruth listened to their distant voices carrying to her ears on the light breeze, as they acknowledged the other religious followers of the village also on their way to worship, until finally fading into a world of silence.

On finishing the housework, Ruth ran upstairs and gathered her diary from the bedside drawer. It wasn't a real diary, more a small notebook, but very precious all the same, as it was given to her by her mother when just seven years old to help improve her writing skills. Flicking through a few of the early pages, she almost laughed out loud as she desperately tried to decipher the childish scrawl. Suddenly, and without warning, a stab of loss, loneliness and longing so deep it proved more painful than any wound of the flesh, savagely wrenching memories of the past from the box where she thought they were safely secreted away forever. The familiar prick of tears wet her eyes but, bravely, before they could form, she forced herself to turn to a brand-new page, fervently hoping that this first entry would mark a new start once again in her life.

Sunday, July 30th 1911

How I am so looking forward to the future. It is the only way. I cannot allow myself to look back and think what might have been and what I have lost. I can now begin to believe in a future I doubted would ever open up for me. I am actually

Chapter 1

feeling guilty about feeling so happy. Is that wrong? Surely not. I cannot forget the past, nor would I want to. It is now part of me. Part of what I am. I cannot forget the cruelty I have endured at the hands of others and I sometimes wonder on the fate of my father, although I have to admit to feeling nothing for him, no doubt hung by the neck from the gallows in York. I have heard nothing since he was taken to gaol. But also, I have not tried to contact him. Am I a heartless daughter?

I cannot forgive myself for some of the terrible deeds I have done over these past few years, but, with God's help and Jacob's, I have learned to put them away where they cannot harm me anymore, as long as I remain strong. I also feel happiness for Joshua, whose voice has returned, but I sometimes weep during a night at the loneliness and uncertainty Judge John Durville will be suffering at the whereabouts of his wayward son, Henry.

Pondering silently for a while, she closed the book with a sigh, holding it close to her heart, a feeling of melancholy passing over her. But, with a determination to look to the future, she pushed the macabre thoughts of the past from her mind, then returned the diary, before running out into the warmth of the bright sunlight, the heady aroma of newly mown grass drifting sweetly up onto the high moor, dizzying her senses.

The village was quiet, almost deserted as those not attending church were busy with hay making out in the fields. Looking down into the vast sun-bathed basin of the dale, Ruth spotted tiny pin pricks of figures with horse and cart, busily leading hay, while this good spell of weather lasted.

Ruth dragged her gaze away from the valley and acknowledged young Toby with a wave of the hand, as he desperately tried to lead a pair of horses back to the stable who seemed more intent on staying close to the stone watering troughs under the shade of the huge oak trees than returning inside. Running over, Ruth laid a hand on the bigger of the two, stroking the hard, smooth neck.

"Come on you two, don't be causing trouble for young Toby now. Let's have you back inside, eh?" the bright eyes of the animal studying Ruth closely before allowing itself to be led gently back to the stable with the other following. Toby was the eleven-year-old son of the blacksmith, who lived on the outskirts of the village and helped look after customers arriving for horses or stable hire on a Sunday, leaving Jacob free to attend and preach at his beloved church.

Mopping the sweat from his rosy cheeked face with a dirty old rag, he said, "I don't know how you do it, Ruth. A few words from you and they seem to understand. If I try that, they just seem to become more obstinate."

"Don't worry, Toby, you're coming along fine. Just continue talking to them and you'll soon have them eating out of your hand," and with that she put a couple of fingers to her lips and a shrill whistle brought Nell, her loyal dog bounding over in excitement, tongue hanging out, eager to be off on a long walk.

Toby looked on admiringly. "You said you would teach me how to whistle like that, Ruth. How much longer do I have to wait?"

"Before very long Toby as you are growing up really quickly now." Toby beamed after her as he waved his goodbye.

Ruth had never, ever experienced freedom and happiness such as this. It produced a warm glow that began slowly in her chest and just continued to spread out to every pore in her body. Oh, she couldn't explain it, not even going to try, knowing full well she must grasp it with both hands and enjoy it as long as it lasts.

Unable to suppress an impish laugh that rang clear and sharp across this vast open moorland she tried, unsuccessfully, to keep pace with the black and white cross bred collie that she saved from dying more than a year ago, the dog appearing to understand that this girl was her saviour, and hardly ever left her side.

Ruth, growing in height and strength, leapt with delight over the rough ground, the strong sunlight brightening her long, golden tresses streaming out behind her and on through the heather which would soon change to a brilliant purple hue as far as the eye could see. Not yet sixteen years old, the clear blue eyes and elfin features hid a troubled past, adding a certain maturity to her that belied her age. In the distance she spotted Jim striding out toward her. At the same time, Nell gave a loud yap of recognition, setting off at speed to greet him. Ruth followed minutes later, gasping for breath,

Chapter 1

instantly throwing her arms around the young man's neck, before planting a passionate kiss full on his lips.

Chapter 2

1895

Sarah and Patrick Brennan's baby arrived into a savage world already in poverty's cruel grip, as heavy rain lashed against the partially boarded up window of the small, dimly lit bedroom, the lone gas lamp struggling to provide sufficient illumination for what was turning into a desperate situation. But Mrs Bailey the midwife, oblivious to storm or lack of light, continued to work feverishly, knowing two lives, that of mother and child, were at risk. Everything now depended on her experience and skills learnt over many years of midwifery, as this labour was proving long and difficult. Her stout frame, bent almost double between the spread-eagled legs of Sarah was doing all she possibly could, willing and urging Sarah on to greater efforts. With no real headway being made, the old lady's voice became desperate. "Push Sarah, push. You must make one big push. We haven't much longer. You're weakening fast dearie. Please, Sarah," begging now, "for your child's sake, one final effort and it will all be over."

Doctor Evans stood to one side, stern faced, worried, due to the long, protracted birth. He expected difficulties.

Suddenly, a long, agonising scream from Sarah echoed chillingly around the low-ceilinged bedroom as, using every last ounce of energy, she finally gave birth to a new life. But at what cost? Drained with the exertion and

Chapter 2

the length of time in labour, she collapsed back on the bed, drifting into unconsciousness.

Mrs Bailey, cheeks aglow, even in the dull lamplight, whispered, "Sarah Brennan, be proud of yourself dearie, you have just produced a beautiful baby girl." At that very moment, a soft, tiny hand grasped one of Mrs Bailey's fingers, opened its mouth and began to scream, as if to prove what a healthy pair of lungs it possessed. Although bringing many children into the world, the birth of a new life always left her emotional. 'Must go with the job' she thought, eyes misting over as she set to work washing and cleaning the baby, all the while humming quietly to the child, who, after her initial outburst, quietened. Wrapping warm blankets around the new born and laying her in the cot, she busied herself tidying the bed to leave Doctor Evans to do his best for Sarah.

The Doctor had every right to be concerned. After several hours attending the birth, he realized Sarah had suffered internal damage and was unsure if he had been able to do enough for Sarah to survive. As dawn broke, he finally called Patrick Brennan into the room to deliver the grave news.

"Patrick, Sarah is still unconscious at present. I have administered a sedative to keep her calm and quiet so no further damage occurs, but I am not entirely sure she is strong enough to pull through. I have done all I possibly can; it is now in the hands of the Lord as to whether she will recover. I will return home to get some sleep and call back tonight to see if her condition has deteriorated. The next couple of days are critical. Mrs Bailey has promised to look after the child if you will make sure Sarah is kept comfortable and warm."

A frown creased Patrick's young features as he said, "I'll do my best to look after her, to be sure, but my nursing skills might not be up to scratch, Doctor."

"You can do no more than your best, Patrick, and we'll hope that's enough. Well, if that is settled then, I will leave you to it and hope for better news when I call again.

Goodnight for now."

"Goodnight, Doctor and thank you."

Doctor Evans gathered his bag and hat, and walked out into the dark, stormy dawn shaking his head, not only wondering what the chances were on mother and child surviving, but also for all the other luckless people struggling to cope in stinking, disease riddled areas such as this.

But Sarah and baby did survive. After seven long days hovering on the edge of life and death, Sarah's eyes flickered open. Only these eyes that had once sparkled with the enthusiasm and optimism of life for the future were now lack lustre, dull, sunk deep into skeletal features, her skin pale, the colour of parchment. The difficult birth had taken its toll. As Sarah lifted herself into a sitting position, Mrs Bailey entered the room cradling the baby, her round, ruddy face, beaming with delight when noticing Sarah, eyes open, sitting almost upright in bed.

"Ah, thank God you are back in the world of the living dearie, eh?" she said with a real sense of relief." If truth be known" she whispered, "I didn't think you were going to pull through but, my goodness, you have done wonderful. Now, I have just the tonic to put you on the road to recovery," and placed the baby gently by her side for Sarah to experience the first touch of her new born baby. "There you go, Sarah. See what a lovely child you've brought into this world, a real beauty. She really is going to be special this one. A real fighter, like her mum." There was no doubting the love that the old lady held for this child, it showed through in every way and a special bond had formed between the pair just in the matter of a week.

Sarah's arms folded softly around her new born, a wan smile of thanks for the kindness shown to her by the midwife and, from that very moment, a small spark of life began to light the lifeless, pallid features. Already it appeared that this little miracle bundle of flesh and blood would possibly fuse new energy into her body.

Chapter 3

The following months proved difficult for the young family but with each new dawn, Sarah brightened a little more. A faint glimmer of light began to filter through the dark, damning cloud of depression that had so blighted the emotional joy she should have experienced from the arrival of her baby. The constant tiredness eased and a trace of colour returned to the pale cheeks. Sarah found the effort of caring for Ruth, plus the housework, sapped her energy but it helped push her to greater efforts on the long, hard road back to recovery, thus allowing Patrick to begin work at the market again, easing the constant worry as to where the next shilling was coming from.

As for Patrick, he was heartily glad to be away from the confines of the house and the constant cleaning and feeding that he did not profess to be good at. But at least he had done his bit until Sarah was able to cope.

Unfortunately, the traumatic birth did leave a serious scar upon her health. The light, blonde hair that once turned many a head of the opposite sex, and of which she was so proud, turned grey almost overnight and her shoulders hunched forward, afflicting her with the stooping posture of a much older woman.

Doctor Evans, a kindly man, knowing full well the couple's circumstances, having visited regularly over the past few weeks, was determined not to embarrass the young couple by asking for payment, deciding to wait until such times as their fortunes took a turn for the better. On his final visit, and after giving Sarah a full examination, he delighted in informing her there was nothing to stop her from leading a normal life.

But before leaving, his face turned serious as he settled in the chair opposite her. After a few moments of awkward silence, he began to speak. "Now Sarah, before I leave, there is something I must say…"

Sarah held up her hand to silence him, certain the subject of payment was about to be broached.

Embarrassed, she took a deep breath, before saying, "Please let me stop you there, Doctor. I know what you are about to say and I do understand how lucky I am and so fortunate to be alive. I cannot thank you enough for all you have done, but I have been worrying myself sick about how to tell you this, because I don't honestly know how we will be able to pay your bill at present. If you could just grant me a little more time and, maybe, accept so much a month until I am out of your debt. That would be a burden lifted from our shoulders."

"Sarah," he said with a smile, taking her hands in his, "you are many things, but you are no mind reader, dear girl. Money is the last thing I want to talk to you about. I know payment will be made when you can afford. In fact, improvements are promised for this area and my God, let's hope the restoration of this whole area and all these dwellings takes place sooner rather than later. Until then, it is reward enough for me to see you and your daughter happy and doing so well after what you went through." This said with true feeling. "No, what I was going to say, and this is a far more important matter than money, is that it concerns your future health."

Easing back into the comfort of his chair, hands steepled together before him, he told her, "Now, you do realize that your remarkable fight back from near death is little less than miraculous, dear girl. This time!" He paused for effect, letting the fact sink in, before adding, "but in giving birth, your body suffered internal damage and, I'm afraid, you will never be the same healthy girl you were before your pregnancy. I'm sorry that I cannot do more. But you do have a life, and an active life at that, I might add. You also

Chapter 3

have a beautiful, healthy daughter. Now, what I am really trying to say and wanting to stress Sarah, is that I strongly advise against another pregnancy, as next time you may not be so lucky. I hope you understand."

A look of relief swept over Sarah. "I do understand Doctor and I will take your advice and count my blessings that I am still here to be as good a mother as I can be."

The Doctor studied her closely before giving his reply.

"Well, I'm sure you will be one of the best. By the way, have you chosen a name for the baby yet?"

"We have, we are going to christen her Ruth after my mother. She was a really kind, sensitive soul and I hope Ruth will grow up to be just such a person."

"Ah, Sarah," he said, "Ruth is a beautiful name." He frowned as if trying to recall some hidden memory, before adding, "an old Hebrew name, I think, if my memory serves correct. I'm sure the name Ruth does mean 'friend' or 'friendship,' so if she grows up with such a nature, which I am sure she will, it will just suit her fine."

He rose to leave. "Well, I must be going, Sarah. I'll see myself out. Please take care and heed my advice, young girl." Smiling, he picked up his hat and walked out. Sarah quietly watched from the window until his tall figure was swallowed up in the darkness of the alley, thinking how lucky she was to have such a kind man looking after their health at this difficult time.

Following the Doctors stern words was not as difficult as Sarah first thought, as after the birth of their daughter, Patrick seemed to lose all interest in lovemaking. Oh, she knew it wasn't just Patrick's fault. Although still enjoying moments of comfort and tenderness when their bodies wrapped together as one in bed, his strong arms holding her tight, once his touch became more than intimate, which, in the past had thrilled her so much, it now terrified her, leaving her unable to respond. Just the thought of anything more left her body rigid with fear. At least she thought, an almost rueful smile crossing her features, with the intimacy fading fast from the marital bed, it made it easier heeding the good Doctor's advice, making it unlikely she would ever face the complications of another unwanted pregnancy and another hungry mouth to feed.

Chapter 4

Even though the tightly crunched middle terrace house in Lady Peckitt's Yard was sparsely furnished, the Brennan family regarded it as home. A humble dwelling situated in a forgotten corner of the city of York, but a far cry from the genteel, historic character that the vast majority of the city inhabitants were accustomed too, or the rapidly rising number of visitors arriving daily, due to the popularity of the railways criss-crossing the country. Most were drawn to the city by its obvious centre of attraction, the ceremonial magnificence of York Minster. An architectural masterpiece, built well over a thousand years ago as an expression on earth of the Kingdom of Heaven, telling the story of Christian faith. But venture further away from the splendour of this building and soon the tidy cobbled roads and well maintained brightly painted houses steadily deteriorated into row upon row of neglected, terraced houses, squalid back alleys and street urchins, the hardships endured becoming obvious.

It was as if these living quarters were meant to be hidden away. A grim reminder of a past life last experienced more than a hundred years ago. A small part of the city left behind and forgotten, with no real place in this fast-changing world as the slums appeared to be sliding into oblivion as they dipped toward the River Ouse, maybe to be finally swallowed up by the mighty river. An area riddled by disease, poverty, poor sanitation and water pollution, the stench of rotting garbage and the smell of death cloying the air and clinging to the very fabric of every dwelling, searing the nostrils of any strangers foolish enough to venture near.

The community itself also seemed to have become accustomed to such dire conditions, adapted to it; unable to extricate themselves from this way of life. In fact, so often had the promise and expectancy of a better life been dashed, they now stoically accepted this as their place in society.

But Sarah did not accept, would not accept that it had to be this way forever. There must be a better life ahead and looked with determined optimism to the future fervently hoping, in a year or two and with hard work, better times lay ahead. In fact, even with living conditions such as they were, Sarah counted herself lucky, as her home did have the benefit of two bedrooms, many families were surviving in just one room.

Directly outside the back door, a narrow, stone paved alley ran the length of the street and although the main structures were suffering from cracked and crumbling brickwork, the heavy timber struts crossing the width of the alley assured they stayed upright. It also made a great playground for many of the children, scrambling and climbing among these heavy beams until chased away by angry residents.

With no spare money for repairs, broken window panes were boarded over with bits of old timber, or even cardboard in some cases, anything laid to hand, in a desperate attempt to keep the elements at bay.

Rotting window frames turned to a softer pulp with every passing winter and the dark stained, sagging pan tile roofs, close to collapse, placed more pressure onto already pregnant walls. All were in urgent need of repairs, but progress of the supposedly Better Housing Bill passed upon these dwellings as unfit for living accommodation was proving slow and laborious.

Sarah knew in her heart that only when these houses were demolished, only then would regeneration take place. This would create more work and more work would lead to better wages, releasing many families from this relentless treadmill of destitution. But the cogs of the ruling bodies refused to be rushed, oblivious to the difficulties these families were enduring and so the years passed with only broken promises of improvement.

Chapter 4

With Ruth approaching school age and Sarah gaining strength, it became easier to escape the confines of the tight narrow alleyways and constant stench of midden piles, especially on beautiful summer days, to enjoy the simple pleasures of walking along the robust, formidable fortress walls encircling the city, delighting in stopping to watch the bustling activity of men working on their brightly coloured boats on the banks of the Ouse, the soft orange glow of the sun turning the mighty river into a rippling ribbon of molten gold. These moments Sarah cherished, precious time spent with her daughter, watching her grow. On returning home, often exhausted but happy, from such exertions, Sarah would flop in a chair to sit quietly, while Ruth fussed over her as only young children worried about loved ones can and always trying to take care of her mother's comforts.

But poverty did not display such feelings, never once slackening its ruthless grip. Although struggling to make ends meet, Sarah somehow managed to keep enough food on the table for the family, often going hungry herself, making the excuse she had eaten earlier. Never would she have her family, especially Ruth, her own flesh and blood, suffer the pangs of hunger in their bellies which she knew others were enduring. Through the harsh weather of winter gone, she had seen with her own eye's families reduced to breaking up furniture to throw on the fire, such was the problem of merely surviving.

Chapter 5

With every passing day, Ruth began to question Sarah on the world about her, curious of her surroundings, of the shabbily dressed, homeless people, now only caricatures of their former selves, dragged down by such a cruel shortage of money. They frightened her, even with her mother alongside, as they roused on a morning from sleeping rough in doorways or under bridges, covered only by ragged blankets or cardboard boxes.

As Ruth snuggled down into the comfort of her own bed one night, she surprised her mother by inquiring, "Why do some people choose to live out on the street mother? Why don't they go home?"

Sarah, not expecting such a question, tried her best to explain. "Well, Ruth," she said, bending to give her a hug, "it isn't as if they choose to sleep outside but, you see, not all families are as lucky as we are. Although we don't have much money, we do have a special love that binds us together. There are some who may never be lucky enough to share such an experience and many others, through no fault of their own, will never have the money to escape from this poverty. Some even have their children taken from them as they cannot afford a roof over their head, relying only on the workhouse for food and survival."

Sarah knew what the young girl was thinking as a frown creased Ruth's

Chapter 5

brow before she asked worriedly, "Will we ever have to go to the workhouse, mother?"

"Never. Not as long as I have breath in my body, Ruth," Sarah told her convincingly, giving Ruth another hug for reassurance and comfort. Then brightly. "No, we must be patient. Once this promised house restoration begins, we could be rehoused in a year or two and living in a much better place. I'm sure it will be a great improvement for everyone." These reassuring words appeared to settle Ruth's curiosity, the subject never surfacing again.

Soon, the excitement of school occupied Ruth's mind as she quickly made new friends. Only the short-tempered old Headmaster Mr Bridges frightening her, never lacking in finding an excuse to shout or smack the children, even if caught for something as frivolous as chattering. But as Ruth had an inquisitive mind, plus holding a deep desire to learn, she became a favourite of Miss Benson, the English teacher.

Miss Benson, a strict forty-year-old spinster, possessed a kindly outlook toward all the children in her care and soon spotted potential in Ruth for her exceptional knowledge on the English language and her reading for such a young age. Aware of Ruth's background and well knowing the area where she lived, Miss Benson realized it would be an uphill struggle for the young girl but felt in her heart, that as a teacher, she should try to encourage her as much as possible, Ruth appearing quite keen to learn, especially in her English lessons. On several occasions, when the large brass bell rang out to signal the end of the school day, Miss Benson would peer over the top of her black rimmed glasses perched on the end of her nose and ask, "Ruth Brennan, if you can spare a few moments of your time before rushing off home, I think we should retire to the library for a while."

"Yes, miss. I would like that," Ruth would reply, a ripple of pleasure running through her on hearing these words, relishing another chance to enter this silent, whispering world of knowledge. Row upon row of books lining the walls from floor to ceiling, just waiting to be read. And the smell on entering. Such a distinctive smell. Mustiness, leather and ink all combined, Ruth thought. When sliding a book from its dusty slot on the shelf, she knew a treasure trove of stories awaited her with every turn of a page.

Studying the many shelves of children's books with a quizzical eye, Miss Benson explained which she thought suitable reading. "Remember my words, Ruth Brennan.

Study hard, learn a good command of the English language and there are many opportunities on offer. For girls as well as boys, I might add, and as you grow older, the world will become your oyster dear girl, always in demand," passing the chosen books over to Ruth. "Now, I suggest you take these and read them in your leisure time and then when you have finished, we will discuss the importance of these stories."

"Thank you, Miss Benson." Ruth was already brimming with joy and looking forward to returning home and, at first chance, running upstairs to her bedroom to enter a world of adventure and excitement, transported to the faraway places described in such vivid detail on every page.

Determined to learn, Ruth was also developing into a strong-willed character with a very inquisitive mind and although loving her schooldays, she also enjoyed the freedom and fun of weekends. As Lady Peckitt's Yard was close by the bustling Saint Sampson's Square, Ruth often ran through the maze of alleyways, whatever the weather, to where her father Patrick worked, helping out on a market stall, selling fruit and vegetables. On hearing her shout, he would bend down, sweep her into his arms and swing her clear of the ground, greeting her with, "Now, Ruthie me darling, have you come to run errands for me?"

Once her breath returned, she would say crossly, "Don't call me that, father, you know my name is Ruth. I have come to help but if you tease me, I will go play." His wide boyish smile would open up, softening the hard, weathered features, the coal dark eyes dancing with a humour that Ruth did not fully understand. But the older girls and ladies did, which always assured him brisk business at the stall. As weekends were particularly busy Ruth, and her close friend Meg, loved the chatter and excitement, running errands, delivering bags of vegetables too heavy to carry for some of the older customers. On returning home, bright eyed with pleasure, a few pennies clasped tightly in her hand, she would show Sarah. "Look what I

Chapter 5

have earned today, mother."

While at the market later than usual one Saturday, Ruth noticed the throng of people gradually drifting away from the market stalls to gather round an array of brightly coloured flags fluttering gently in the late afternoon breeze at the very centre of the square. Inquisitive as ever Ruth asked, "Can I go and see what is happening over there, father?"

Patrick glanced across to see what all the fuss was about.

"Ah, that's just the Salvation Army preaching their holier than thou outlook on life to the lost souls of this world." Ruth, head on one side, gave him an inquiring look as if expecting more, so he added. "Aye, take no notice girl, they'll fill your pretty little head with more blarney than all the Irish put together." His eyes flashing angrily as he turned back to his work.

Ruth was quite surprised by his sharpness, the first time her father had ever shown any resentment to religion or the word of God. Soon, blood red banners circled their chosen patch, while several men quickly erected a platform. Immediately a young man, in matching black and red uniform, jumped lightly up onto it and began to speak. Eager to learn more Ruth slipped away from the stall, running over to join the gathering crowd, finally winkling her slight frame to the very front where she stood, arms behind her back, looking up and studying the man closely. Not much older than her father, Ruth thought, although he was clean shaven, apart from a thin, dark line of a moustache on his upper lip matching his jet-black hair plastered tight to his scalp. A generous, friendly smile beckoned the crowd to come closer.

The man spotted Ruth watching intently. It was not often he had the attention of children in his audience and he would make of this chance. Catching her eye, he dropped to one knee, and as if speaking directly to her but with a voice that he knew would resonate across the square, he began to speak fluently and passionately... *"and I quote from the good book, Luke 18, verse 15 to 17, 'and they brought unto him also infants, that he would touch them: but when his disciples saw this, they rebuked him. But Jesus called them unto him and said, 'suffer little children to come unto me and forbid them not, for of such is the Kingdom of God.'*

Verily I say unto you, whosoever shall not receive the kingdom of God as a little child will by no means enter it.'"

He paused, allowing his words to take effect, then sprang quickly to his feet, spreading his arms in one expansive gesture, as if to grasp every single one of his audience in his embrace and in a distinctive booming voice for one so young, shouted, *"Listen to me now when I say we must learn to love our brothers and sisters, love our fellow companions. If they wrong us, forgive them. Show compassion to those who have suffered misfortune. Let the love from your heart spread. Reach out to each other. Remember, no matter how far down the slippery road of sin we travel, there is always redemption if willing to believe in the one true God."*

His preaching carried a strength, powerful and thought provoking and held the crowd, had them clinging to every word uttered and they responded loudly to his sermon. "We believe, Preacher," they cried. At this he threw his arms heavenward again and proclaimed loudly, *"Hear us Oh Lord we pray."* The crowd, in unison, instantly echoing his words, "Hear us Oh Lord we pray."

Fascinated, Ruth stood open mouthed at this powerful oratory, never experiencing anything like it before. Oh, she had learnt about God and Jesus from early morning assemblies at school and certain stories had grabbed her attention when reading from the Bible, but this was the first time ever in witnessing such an authoritative preacher and was surprised at how anyone could wield such a spell over so many people. And not even in a church or chapel, out in the open air in a public place. This was her first real encounter with the power of a religious faith.

Finally, the sermon over, the crowd began to drift away and Ruth returned excitedly to the stall to tell her father about the preacher.

"He was very good, father. I heard him say, 'the meek shall inherit the earth.' She screwed her face up in concentration.

"What did he mean?"

"Well, to be sure I am not well read on the Bible, but I believe it says always turn the other cheek, then good will come of you and everything will fall into your lap. What he wouldn't preach up there on his makeshift pulpit was

Chapter 5

if there is such a thing as an all-seeing God, who works miracles, why did he not save the millions in Ireland who starved to death? Why are we still suffering in a povertystricken world here and now?" He bent down, level with her face. "I'll tell you why! Because there is no one up there listening! No one to help the likes of us. I know from experience. If we don't do it ourselves nothing will pour forth from the heavens above and if you are ever fool enough to turn the other cheek, you will surely stay downtrodden for the rest of your life; trampled underfoot with never a backward glance from the do-gooders and Bible bashers of this world. They are far too busy looking after their own interests, with no thought at all for the millions of starving people that they preach about helping. And this includes your young preacher man spouting off on his platform."

Ruth, sensing the anger within her father, decided it best to go play and ran off to meet her friend, vowing never to raise the subject of religion again.

Patrick, noted for a sharp temper in his youth and often in trouble for violence and fighting, appeared to calm down considerably with the responsibility of marriage to Sarah, followed by the birth of Ruth and succeeded in keeping a tight hold of emotions when sober. But there would be no room in his life for a God who had never once shown him the door to a better life. Never looked the side he was on, fighting every inch of the way through life. Everything he owned, which, he had to admit, didn't amount to much, was won by him alone. He remembered only too well the many times, as a young boy, his mother dragging him to church by the ear, chastising him for such a blatant lack of faith. But, even after all these years nothing had changed his belief. To him it was voices in the head. "Cranks, every man jack of 'em," was his stock reply.

Chapter 6

Life settled into a continual day to day grind for the young family and inevitably, responsibilities, shortage of money and the constant deprivation began to tell on Patrick. At just twenty-two years old and was, in his own mind, still a relatively young man who should be out enjoying himself, not someone festering at home, wasting his life away with never two pennies to rub together. He realized he was now paying the price for his irresponsible, and impetuous, hot headed nights of passion with Sarah and suddenly found himself trapped in a marriage with a child. Trapped in a spiral of want, privation and destitution from which he could see no escape.

Becoming restless and unsettled at home, the excuses to Sarah came thick and fast as to why he spent more time with Ben Miller and friends in The Neptune, a public house nestled between the butchers' shops of the Shambles, than he did at home. Sarah was not oblivious to the change in him, knew in her heart things were beginning to go horribly wrong between them. No one understood better than her that the difficult birth had aged her terribly, never regaining the same high spirits she possessed as a girl, or when first married. But, above all, Sarah was a fighter and wanted more than anything for her marriage to work. If not for herself, for Ruth's sake.

With patience finally running out, Sarah decided she had no option but

Chapter 6

to confront Patrick and try to make him see sense. The deep worry lines etched across her pretty features told their own story and one night as he made to go out once more, she decided to confront him.

"Patrick, what is happening between us? What am I doing wrong? You never spend time at home with Ruth and I any more. It seems you would much rather spend money in the public house that we can ill afford, while I continue to scrimp and save every way I can to make ends meet. I know things are difficult and I am not the same healthy girl you married, but you must know that I love you deeply. More than words can ever say."

Patrick ran a hand through his unkempt hair, a knot of guilt tightening his stomach, his eyes flicking away from Sarah, unable to meet her steady gaze. He answered brusquely, waving his arms dramatically in the air.

"Of course I'm not tiring of you. Damn it all, sure it's not too much to ask to go see my mates now and then, especially after a hard day's graft, instead of being stuck in here with you nag, nag, nagging at me all the time."

"But Patrick, I don't nag all the time and it isn't just now and then, it's a regular occurrence." Her voice began to rise in anger as he tried to place the blame on her. "You know well enough we haven't the money to waste on drink. This is the major reason why things are hard for us all as a family."

Now, glad of an excuse to vent his frustration, his temper flared and with eyes black as night he turned on her, spoiling for an argument. Sarah, for the first time in her life felt fearful, the full force of his anger spilling out as he hissed in her face.

"Well, it's all my fault now, is it. Nothing to do with you or your poor bloody housekeeping, eh?" His voice rising, he would not be stopped. "I thought it wouldn't be long before you brought the drinking into it. Well, if you think I'm just going to sit here and have you lecture me like some little kid on how I should live my life, you are mistaken. I'm going out."

Without waiting for an answer, he rose from the chair flinging it backward with all his might away from the table with a loud clatter. Sarah quickly crossed the room and bravely stood barring the door, staring defiantly back at him. Patrick waited for her to move, but she was not about to back down. Quick as a flash, his right hand struck her hard across the face, the slap resounding like a gunshot in the small kitchen. Startled by the sudden ferocity, she stepped away from the door, holding a hand to her now reddening face as without a word, he stormed out into the night, slamming the door shut so hard it rattled the broken panes of glass in the old window.

Sarah, fighting back the tears, the shock and the pain of the sudden assault frightening her. Trying to contain her own anger and emotions, she finally collapsed into a chair to stare into the dwindling embers of the fire as if the answer to their problems may lie in the flickering flames. Deciding not, she wiped her eyes and with a sigh, wearily raised herself from the chair and made her way up the creaking stairs. Before retiring to bed, alone once again, she peeped in to check on Ruth as she did without fail every night.

Thankfully she was fast asleep, not having heard the disturbance. Still seething from Patrick's cruel, callous comments and behaviour, knowing she was doing everything possible to save money at every turn, keeping the home clean and tidy, with a hot meal most nights for Patrick and Ruth to come home to. Deep in her heart, she honestly believed Patrick would eventually see reason and turn things around. But her optimism was unfounded as their relationship went from bad to worse, the arguments over Patrick's drinking and the lack of finances becoming more frequent.

Chapter 7

Food brought from the stall proved a life saver for a time and next-door neighbour Aunty Moll was very good, popping home-made cakes in once in a while which helped out, but it would never be sufficient, Sarah finally falling into arrears with the rent, dreading the knock on the door from the rent man. After making numerous excuses over the last few months, she had to resort to hiding away like a common criminal in her own home, whenever he called, waiting for hours in silence until certain he'd lost patience and moved on. Sarah knew full well this was only delaying the inevitable and they would soon be kicked out in the street.

It was now public knowledge that Patrick spent all his time and money on drink and Sarah eventually reached the limit of her patience. A slave in her own home, no longer able to hold her head up in the street. The frequent slanging matches brought the sharp Irish temper and cruel streak to the surface in Patrick and even those who thought they knew him well, gave him a wide berth. Living under the same roof, Sarah could not, finding no escape from the pain and distress these drunken binges caused.

As the drink steadily dragged him down, eating away at his very soul, the money once spent on family now fuelled his urge for alcohol. He aged before their eyes and Ruth, although only nine years old, she was still mature enough to understand that the father she loved was becoming distant, unreachable. The straight shoulders hunched, the firm jaw became slack, the once sharp, dark eyes that so entranced Sarah in the early days of courtship, became haunted, frightened, as if sensing control of his very life was beginning to slip away. Realizing he needed help, Sarah used everything in her power to try and ease this man she loved out of this ever-spiralling downward cycle as his whole life had now centred on where the next drink would come from and the lower he sank into these drunken stupors, the more wretched he felt and so the beatings began, sometimes severe enough for Sarah to fear for her life.

After the violence, the story was always the same, begging forgiveness, swearing it would never happen again, their tears mingling as she cradled him in her arms, while trying desperately to understand how a person could cause such hurt to the ones he supposedly loved.

Upstairs, alone in her room, it became a regular occurrence for Ruth to bury herself deep in bed, pillow clasped tightly around her head trying to nullify the shouting and cursing on his return home. Too frightened to venture down, Ruth lay in the oppressive darkness, heart thudding in her chest until a welcome silence reigned, only then gaining relief as sleep finally gathered her in its embrace to rescue her from this wretched, miserable sadness.

Ruth dreaded rising on a morning in fear of what she might find, often the hideous bruising distorting the caring features of her mother telling its own cruel story more than words could do. With heart aching, she would rush to her mother's arms, a feeling of utter helplessness in knowing she could never ease the suffering and pain.

It could not go on like this. As Sarah sat waiting nervously for Patrick to arrive home late one night a stab of fear shot through her as she heard the click of the latch lifting and her worst nightmares were realized. The staggering hulk of her husband, in a frighteningly drunken state, stumbled into the tiny kitchen.

But Sarah had suffered enough and had made up her mind. She spoke quietly, before Patrick had chance to speak.

"Patrick, Ruth and I are leaving you. We cannot go on living like this. I

Chapter 7

have spent the last two years frightened for my life. You have changed into a monster. We are more than three months behind with the rent and will soon be evicted." She pointed to her bruised and battered face. "Look at me!" her voice rising with emotion. He lowered his gaze, the guilt evident. "Look at my face from the last beating I endured." Tears began to streak down the purple patches of her cheeks, the once pretty face crumpling in anguish, the reality almost bringing her to her knees, so sorry that it had to come to this.

With a finality she did not feel, she told him. "I have packed our belongings and we are leaving tomorrow. We will be better off in the workhouse than living here. I am not having Ruth damaged by seeing such violence." Defiance showed in her face and she managed to stay calm, but the tremor in her limbs betrayed her. Stubbornly she carried on. "I will not have our child brought up like this. I cannot, and will not, stand the beatings a moment longer." With that she turned to walk away.

It took a moment for the words to register through the thick fog addling Patrick's brain. Then suddenly he lost all sense of reason, violently lashing out, the back of his hand catching Sarah full on the side of her jaw, cracking like a whiplash in the silence of the kitchen. Her head whipped sideways, and her light frame was sent sprawling across the room, her head crashing into the table under the window with a sickening crunch. Her body dropped like a stone, blood pouring from the deep gash that split her forehead wide open and lay inert on the floor, not a muscle moving. Patrick just stood, motionless, staring at the lifeless body of his wife, not fully comprehending the enormity of his act.

Eventually, something in his booze-riddled brain clicked and sprang to life, realization of what he had done sinking in. Falling to his knees, he gently held her in his arms, mumbling through heart wracking sobs, "Sarah, Sarah, speak to me. I'm sorry. I'm so sorry." Then, when no response was forthcoming, he threw his head heavenward and a long, anguished howl broke the deathly silence of the small room.

Lying in bed, pillows scrunched tight, Ruth still heard the muffled sounds, but dare not venture down, fearing the worst. Finally, as silence reigned, she drifted off to sleep.

Next morning, as the sun broke through the flimsy curtains of the tiny bedroom, Ruth awakened to the sound of people chattering excitedly outside her window in the street below. Dressing quickly, she ran downstairs and straight into the arms of a burly policeman.

Gruffly he said, "Now then, steady on there, young girl," as he quickly looked round for help, not sure what to do with one so young. "Didn't anyone know this child was in the house? Help me someone, please take her next door, away from all this," roughly handing her over to Aunty Moll, the neighbour who first raised the alarm. Gathering the hysterical girl into her arms, she carried her away from the heartrending scene, but not before the young girl witnessed the traumatic scene of her father kneeling, in a daze, still cradling the stiffening body of her mother lying dead in a pool of blood. Already, another policeman was moving in to shackle him with handcuffs, an image Ruth would never forget. Aged just nine years old, her life would change dramatically. And forever.

Chapter 8

Patrick Brennan sat, head in hands in the small, grey painted brick cell, a broken man. Everything lost through abuse of drink, stupidity and a violent temper. A loving wife, a beautiful child, his only child and a livelihood that he'd worked so hard to build. All gone in one sudden flash of anger.

He expected the gallows awaited him. In fact, it would be a release from this pit of despair he wallowed in. He seemed to recall, earlier that week, or it could have been yesterday, someone came into his cell. Could it have been his solicitor? Could have been anybody for all he knew. He wasn't sure. Hadn't even listened to what was said. He couldn't think straight anyhow. Maybe it was just a dream, he thought as days and nights congealed into one. He slept, ate, emptied the slops, only exercised because forced to do so, otherwise he never left the cell.

Patrick let his head slump forward to stare vacantly at the floor, when the door clanked open and a pair of wellpolished shoes appeared in his vision. A voice said, "You can leave us now warden, I just need a word with Mr Brennan on this case."

"Right you are, sir," and with that the door clanged shut again.

"Now, Mr Brennan, we have met before, but you may not remember me. My name is Jack Devlin and I will be representing you when your case comes before the court." He waited a few seconds. Patrick didn't respond. He tried again. "We need to talk Mr Brennan. Do you feel ready to talk, to answer a few questions on what happened that night? I know it will be difficult, but you must face it sooner or later."

Patrick slowly raised his head, forcing his gaze upward, away from the polished shoes to study the man. Well dressed, carrying a briefcase, hair receding and just beginning to grey at the temples. But there was something about the features, a grittiness around the strong set of the chin, wrinkles around the eyes, and the hands, they were hard working hands. Maybe not now, but these tell-tale signs showed of a different upbringing. Definitely different lifestyle from the job he was in now. Resignedly, Patrick nodded his agreement.

"There is no need to go over the details again, unless your version of events has changed. If it still stands, we go for a plea of manslaughter on the grounds of mental instability. This may just save you from the death penalty. We haven't long Mr Brennan; the case is next week and I now know the Judge will be John Durville. A hard man, but fair. We need to show the court, and the jury, the remorse and pain you are suffering to stand any chance of you escaping the gallows. Do you understand?"

Patrick's head fell to his chest and Jack went and sat by his side. "Patrick, I know what you are going through. I am from a similar background to yourself. I suffered the torment of a broken home, resulting in serious trouble with the law, leading to a lengthy prison sentence, from which I took the opportunity to study law and make my way toward a better life. Please," he urged, "do not spurn this last chance you have of staying alive. If we are lucky, and I am not promising anything, the sentence may not be too long. For God's sake man, if nothing else, think of your daughter. If she has to bear the brunt of her father hanging from the gallows and losing you as well as her mother, what is that going to do to her?"

Patrick sobbed quietly, his shoulders shaking with grief. Jack gave him time to control his emotions and eventually Patrick lifted his head to the steady gaze of Jack.

"What do I have to do?" he asked.

Chapter 8

"You stand up before the Judge and jury, tell them exactly what happened that night, nothing added, nothing left out. Leave the rest to me and pray that John Durville and the jury, are about to be lenient."

As Jack got up to leave, he turned and added, "you can begin the process by tidying yourself up, getting washed and shaved and presenting yourself as a respectable human being. Believe me Patrick, I know what I am talking about. I have been there. I am your only chance."

Patrick rose from his bed, offering his hand, the heart felt words creating a feeling of trust toward this man. He would do as he asked. Jack Devlin was not promising the impossible, but as he said, there is a chance he may just escape with his life. At this present time Patrick wasn't sure which was the best option because, these last few days, if the guards had left anything in his cell by which to take his life, he knew for a fact he would have finished it.

Jack rapped sharply on the cell door for the prison guard and when the door opened, he turned, speaking quietly.

"Don't forget, I will be with you all the way on this Patrick and I will do whatever I possibly can. See you on trial day."

Patrick Brennan was tried and sentenced at York assizes and as Jack promised he supported him all the way. In fact, the heart-rending speech, delivered in his final summing up of this dreadful case, stunned the jury with its brutal honesty, many moved to tears, on how a life of poverty and deprivation can affect lives in the most serious of ways imaginable.

Judge John Durville received the decision from the foreman and studied it, a scowl crossing his face as he stared hard at the Foreman of the jury, before asking the question, "And this is the decision of you all?" The Foreman replied, "It is your Honour."

The Judge nodded to the man on his left and instantly the man's voice boomed around the hushed courtroom.

"The court please rise for the verdict."

There was a shuffling of chairs as the court stood. Patrick, with Jack's help, raised himself with difficulty just willing this to be over, the thought of the noose being placed over his head dominating his thoughts. John Durville's spoke clearly and audibly to the once again silent courtroom.

"I have studied the verdict handed to me. I can only say I am shocked. It is unanimous and I have no option but to abide by you, the jurors, and your decision." He turned to look directly at Patrick. "Patrick Brennan, you are found not guilty of murder, but guilty of manslaughter." At the very mention of not guilty, Patrick's legs gave way but Jack quickly held him upright until sentence was passed.

The Judge carried on. "I believe you have the man by your side to thank for being spared the death penalty and a fifteen-year gaol sentence will give you chance to come to terms with the terrible deed you carried out. That will be all. Court adjourned."

A buzz ran through the packed gallery as Jack murmured quietly, "Patrick, it's all over." He was shaking him by the shoulder. "This is unbelievable. Do you understand, you are going to live? A fifteen-year sentence. With good behaviour you could be a free man in ten years, still with a life in front of you."

Patrick, overcome with relief and hardly able to speak, his voice cracking with emotion, managed to say, "Jack, I don't know how to thank you. I have no money that I can pay you. I have nothing left in this whole world to my name."

"Do not worry on that score. There is a fund available that handles my payments, to defend those who cannot afford a lawyer. It worked for me, it can work for you, Patrick Brennan. Now go, do your time, then show everyone, including me, you are not a beaten man. Take care, Patrick." "You too, Jack. I know it is a long time from now and I am not sure I will, or can, survive but I will fight hard to not only get over the past, but also live with my crime and maybe, one day, I may have a daughter who will find it in her heart to forgive me.

Chapter 9

With no living relatives to care for Ruth, her home was immediately boarded up and her mother's elderly next-door neighbour, known as Aunty Moll, took her in so she had a roof over her head.

Although no real blood relative of the family and, as good hearted as she was, after just a few weeks it became impossible for the old lady to keep them both. Her heart was heavy as she told Ruth the news that she could no longer afford to keep her and the only option was for her to be placed in the Orphanage at York where at least she would be fed and looked after.

Next day, at the crack of dawn, her few meagre belongings packed in a small case, a policeman came to collect her. Ruth desperately tried to hang on to Aunty Moll, before being wrenched away by the apparently embarrassed officer at having such a young girl sobbing and crying in his care. Roughly gathering her into his arms, he lifted her into the seat at the front of the cab and jumped in alongside.

"Drive on," he ordered. "To the Orphanage." Never another word spoken, the silence broken only by the clatter of hooves and the muffled sobbing from Ruth. Drawing up outside the austere building, the policeman said, "Here we are, young lady. You will be well looked after here, they'll see you don't starve." While he banged his fist on the huge wooden door, he held tightly onto her arm, so no escape was possible, until the door swung open to be confronted by a stout, grizzle faced old lady peering from behind it.

"Another stray for you, Miss Wade," he said, before bundling Ruth through the door and stalking off, unable to get away quick enough, leaving Ruth terrified and numb with shock. The old lady looked her up and down.

"You can stop the crying, girl, that won't help here. Come with me," she ordered in a brusque voice. Ruth tried to do as the old lady bid. Her eyes, once wet with tears, now widened in trepidation, as she followed the stooping figure, the tap, tap, tap of the old lady's boots on the stone flagged floor, echoing along the length of the long, gloomy corridor. They passed numerous doors leading to other rooms at either side before pausing at a smaller one which she unlocked from a bunch of keys slung round her ample waist and with a hefty shove from her shoulder the door creaked open. A musty, unused smell swept past them into the corridor. Miss Wade turned to Ruth and continued to speak in the same abrupt manner. "This is the only available room left in the whole building. It is usually only used as a storeroom, but in emergencies such as this, it is useful. This will be your room for now."

Ruth surveyed the room with saddening heart, taking stock of her new surroundings. A row of shelves down one side were crammed with dusty old boxes and tins piled high on top of one another showing it still to be a stock room, allowing only a tiny gap between them and the small iron bedstead pushed tight against the opposite wall. A battered old table with a jug and wash bowl alongside hardly gave her enough room to turn around. Miss Wade's gravel voice brought Ruth back to reality.

"You will have everything you need. Keep it tidy and when the bell rings you come for your meals. We assemble for breakfast at eight o clock sharp and you will be told what to do then. What is your name, girl? I shall need it for assembly later."

"Ruth, Ruth Brennan."

"A bit of Irish in you, eh. Well, let's hope you haven't been born with a fiery Irish temper or we will have troubles. We are very strict here." With that remark from the old lady ringing in her ears, the door slammed shut

Chapter 9

and she was gone.

Ruth had shed so many tears, she felt unable to weep any more, nothing left in her body to give. She sat on the bed, grief stricken and terribly lonely but, deep inside, an unexplainable steely will began to take hold as if realizing to survive she must be strong despite her age and try to forget everything that had gone before. This was the beginning of a new life for her.

As the old lady had told her, crying won't help and with all tears shed, Ruth lay down on the bed. The mattress stank of urine and stale sweat but at least it was dry. Quietly studying her room, her home now, for how long she did not dare think. The bare brick walls made the room dark and dingy and with only one small gas light hanging from the rafters, she was not going to be able to see very well but she had no reading material anyway, so that hardly mattered. The window, such as it was, placed high in the wall, let in a small amount of light but only added a sinister feel to the room. She curled up on the bed and began to rock to and fro in anguish, unsure what to do or how she would possibly survive. All she knew was that everything she had in the world was contained in the little black suitcase hastily packed by Aunty Moll before being brought here.

Suddenly, a gentle tap on the door startled her. Thinking the old lady had forgotten something, she was surprised to see the door slowly squeak open and a crop of tousled black hair topping a cheeky face peep in.

"Hey up, I'm Jim," he whispered, holding a finger to his lips, asking her to speak quietly. "We'll have to be quiet. If they find me in here, we'll cop for a beating. I just wondered if you were okay? I spotted you coming in." He appeared quite cocky and chirpy with a smile that appeared to split his young features in two. He was older than Ruth and the first friendly face encountered since forced to leave home.

"Hello," she whispered this as asked. "I'm Ruth Brennan. Where am I, Jim? Is this the Orphanage or the workhouse? I shouldn't be here but I have nowhere else to go. My mother is dead and my father is in prison. I heard one of the policemen say he will hang for murder. I'm so frightened." She began to tremble, as once again her thoughts brought the stark truth crashing in around her. The happy, reasonably comfortable world and family life had now been snatched cruelly away from her in a matter of days.

The words came in torrents with someone to talk to. Then the tears that she thought no more, streaked her pretty face once again. Jim reached out tenderly, gently, holding her close.

"Hey, come on, Ruth, don't cry," he coaxed, "dry those eyes," busily fishing about in his pocket, before finally pulling out an old rag of a handkerchief and handing it to Ruth. She tried hard to do as Jim told her. "They're a heartless crew in here, but they make sure we don't starve. They feed us, in a fashion and as long as 'ol hatchet face' thinks we are sticking to the rules she leaves us well alone. Anyway," he said, sticking his chin out, "she knows I'm almost big enough to give her a good hiding now, so she doesn't much bother me. Stick wi' me and you'll be okay."

He held her at arms-length and the sparkle in his eyes added new hope to this desperate world she found herself in. Jim sounded very confident, acting in a manner much older than his years. Ruth didn't feel like smiling but she actually found it funny when he said he thought he was big enough to thrash the old lady. Although older than Ruth, in stature he was not much bigger. His trousers were for a much larger boy and were held up with a piece of string. His shirt and jacket were patched and his boots, also tied with string, slopped around skinny legs.

"Come on, cheer up." The cheeky grin flashed across the grubby countenance once more and in spite of her fears, Ruth forced a smile back at him. "That's better. Now, what do you think of your room. You're lucky. I know it's only a storeroom but you are all on your own. I'm forced to share with six other kids and most of 'em snore terrible and stop me getting me beauty sleep." He crinkled his face into a look of disgust before breaking into his grin again. "Come on, I've brought you a candle for night time. We're not supposed to have these, so you better just use it when all is quiet." He fished about in his pocket, until bringing a small stub of a candle into view and a few matches. "Okay, I'll light it, that'll make you feel better."

The candle sputtered into flame and Jim held it in front of his cherubic features, conjuring up what he thought the sound a ghost would make, then laughed.

Chapter 9

"Jim, don't do that. You are scaring me."

"Sorry. Just trying to cheer you up. There's no such thing as ghosts you know."

"I know that. It's just I feel so lonely. I have no one now. Please, don't leave me, Jim," and she clung to him. Jim put his arms around her again, feeling very grown up as Ruth rested her head on his chest.

"Aw, there's no need to worry now," he whispered in her ear. "I'll look after you. You'll be okay. Once the bell rings, I'll take you to the Hall if you drop in alongside me." Ruth clutched him so tight he had to tell her she was crushing him.

"I'm sorry."

"That's okay. I liked it really. Oh, one other thing. Watch out for old Jeffers, the school master. He likes pretty young girls, he does."

Ruth grabbed him again, this time around his scrawny waist, then noticed the ever-ready smile, the toothy grin and his bright, dark eyes mocking her. She pushed him away, playfully, annoyed with herself for listening to him.

"It's not funny, Jim, whatever your name is. Don't you dare try to frighten me again." But she was glad of the comfort he had brought to her.

"I'm gonna go now, Ruth. If they catch me in here, they'll lock me in my room, so I'll sneak out and see you when the foods out. Now, remember what I told you, don't be frightened." He winked at her as he left and the room suddenly seemed brighter, as if a small ray of sunshine had broken through to light this utterly dark, miserable world in which she was now forced to live. Ruth began to think that with Jim as a friend she may just survive this dreadful time. But she had no way of knowing just what lay in store for the both of them.

Chapter 10

Staying quietly in her room Ruth was suddenly brought out of her morbid thoughts by the loud clanging of the bell sounding along the corridor, closely followed by the clatter of feet outside her door. Opening the door slightly, she peeped out. Children of all ages walked past in single file, girls on the left, boys to the right, Jim motioning, but not speaking, for her to quickly drop in behind a tall, gangly girl at the other side of the corridor. They entered a large, dusty room, open to the high rafters supporting the roof. Long trestle tables were set out in rows, with long wooden benches for the seats, the children all gathering and standing to attention in line behind their respective places, again the girls separated from the boys at the far side of the room.

Huge pans of steaming food, set on the front tables, were being ladled into dishes with chunks of bread and Ruth followed the tall thin girl in the queue. The food looked no better than pig swill but it did smell good. Ruth couldn't remember the last time any food had passed her lips and felt faint with hunger, thankful for anything put before her. When all were seated at the table, Ruth cast a sly look around at the other children, who were also stealing curious glances in her direction. Many had their heads shaved, girls as well as boys, some stained a disgusting nicotine brown from the treatment of Iodine in an effort to counter the contagious fungal infections

Chapter 10

of the scalp, such as ringworms and nits, spreading. Others just sat grinning inanely, apparently happy in their own little world.

Not a word uttered from anyone while eating, only the scraping and clattering of plates breaking the silence. Old 'hatchet face' and Jeffers the school master prowled between tables, their sharp, evil eyes flitting this way and that, watching keenly for any sign of trouble. After this socalled meal, Miss Wade called each name in alphabetical order and each child answered. When finished, Miss Wade called Ruth to the front. She edged nervously forward to stand in front of the old lady.

"This is Ruth Brennan children, brought here this morning because unfortunately, she is homeless and rather than having young children roaming the streets to cause trouble this is why the Orphanage began and still exists. And, as you can see there are many, many children who need looking after. She will learn your names as she settles in to our routine. This is your uniform, Ruth," she said, handing over the small bundle of clothes, "and it is up to you to keep these clean and serviceable at all times. Is that clear."

"Yes, Miss."

"Now I want you all back in the school room for first lessons in ten minutes. Dismissed."

A scurrying of feet as they walked back to the rooms, and after Jim made sure they were not being watched, he took Ruth aside.

"Well, that's it for grub until teatime now, Ruth. I'll see you at lessons and tomorrow we'll mebbe have more time to talk again." Hesitating, he added, "if you want me to, that is?"

"Oh, I do, Jim. I would like that." And with a cheery wave, off he went to his room.

As Ruth changed into the so-called uniform, a dull grey ankle length gingham dress and a supposedly white pinafore and bonnet, she tried hard to collect her thoughts, all the while wondering about Jim and the other luckless children. It was an awful place to be, but she was no longer on her own. Through this experience, Ruth believed she had found a friend who would help see her through the worst and she began to wonder, had Jim suffered like her? Did anyone know, or even care where he was? Was there anyone out there to love him or worry about him? All these thoughts rushed through her mind as she fought to understand how it had all gone wrong.

Ruth found this life thrust upon her hard, her emotions raw, ragged with anger and grief at the sudden loss of everything she held dear as she tried desperately to reconcile herself with this regime. But somehow, an inner resolve she never knew she possessed took hold, giving her the strength to cope even if it was just one day at a time.

Later in the week Jim came to her room after scrounging some old clothes for her to wear, so she, as he told her with a sly grin, didn't have to wear the 'uniform' when they escaped the confines of the Orphanage.

"If you wear those dingy old things, they'll have you straight back in here and ol' hatchet face will make you suffer." Ruth didn't say as much but was glad there was no mirror as the trousers, although better than Jim's, were still a bit ragged and finished just below the knee. The shirt and jacket were too big, but when pushing her blonde hair up inside the baggy cap to hide it from view, she knew she could easily be mistaken for a boy. A tingle of excitement rippled through her at the mention of the word 'escaping', even just for a day.

"Eh, you really are a sight for sore eyes," remarked Jim when he first saw her dressed in them but she knew from the sparkle in his eyes he still liked what he saw. They became close friends over the next few months, and Ruth really did try to take her learning seriously, especially her English lessons and tried to stay out of trouble, but one incident showed the strength and independence that Ruth was beginning to feel.

Alfie, a tall, rangy boy for his age, cornered Ruth when on her own in the kitchen preparing potatoes one day. He sauntered in, "Hello, Ruth, I'm Alfie. Settling in okay, are you? Want any help?"

"No thank you, Alfie." She glared at him. "You know I will manage. Now if you don't mind I must get these finished." Ruth didn't like the way his fishy eyes surveyed her and turned her back on him. She shivered slightly, hoping he didn't notice. She didn't see the sickly grin spread across his pock marked features revealing a mouthful of decaying teeth until he strode

Chapter 10

round to stand directly in front of her. Trying to take no notice, she carried on, but he let one arm slowly encircle her waist, tipping her chin in the air with the other.

"I see you and Jim are getting on pretty well. Are you allus this friendly with everyone you first set eyes on?" and then pulled her tight to his body. So tight she could smell his foul breath. Ruth's eyes narrowed. Still holding the knife in her hand which gave her courage, she hissed at him through clenched teeth so no one else could hear.

"Let me go, or I will give you such a smack and then scream for Miss Wade and tell her you attacked me."

His pale features turned even whiter, realizing she may do as she threatened and took a step back. In that instance the door flew open and Jim burst in, eyes blazing angrily. Not one to wait for explanations, he quickly grabbed Alfie by the shoulder, swung him round and hit him square on the jaw, sending him sprawling. Alfie toppled backwards, arms and legs flailing, among the pans, sending them clattering onto the stone flagged floor. Jim bent down, his face bright with anger, only inches from the dazed Alfie.

"Don't you ever try that on again with Ruth, or I will really give you what for." Dazed, Alfie tried to get his legs working properly as he staggered upright and ran out of the door without a backward glance.

Ruth was shocked at the violence. "Jim, what do you think you are doing? I had it under control. Don't you think you should have asked first before knocking him down?"

"Well I wasn't about to let him, err, you know, err, touch you or anything like that you know. I'll not let anyone pick on you."

"Oh Jim, I know you did it for the best reasons but flying into a rage and lashing out at everyone will only get you into more trouble. Sometimes it would be much better to think a little more."

Jim's face darkened even further. "Huh if that's all the thanks I get, I'll not bother next time."

"Jim, that's not what I meant. But I have seen the damage fists can do to people. I am grateful because he did frighten me but I don't want you to be in any further trouble with Miss Wade in case they send you away."

His sudden burst of anger left him, his countenance lighting up, when realizing Ruth was not mad at him. He knew he was guilty of having a short fuse and although picked on by the bigger and older kids because of his tiny frame, he could more than hold his own when it came to fighting. And fight he did. Usually the culprits mocking him, copping the worst of it, slinking away with bloody noses from his flying fists. Jim didn't know what a backward step meant, no matter who, or what he faced. This attitude, Ruth soon realized, was born from the fact he knew no other way of surviving but to fight everyone, especially authority. Meet things head on and suffer the consequences later if need be. Ruth could see he would always stand his ground and now, more than ever, she needed someone strong alongside her. But she had also witnessed what anger and a violent temper could lead to.

Jim reached for her hand, concern showing on his young face. "I'll never let anyone push you about, Ruth. We haven't had the best of starts in life, you and me, but some are a lot worse off than us, you know. If we stick together, we can face anything. Anything, or anyone, whatever they throw at us and one day we'll be free of this stinking place, out in the big wide world." He spread his arms in an expansive gesture. "Then they'd better watch out." The gaptoothed smile brighter than ever.

How could Ruth's resolve not be strengthened when faced with such optimism for the future, when they actually did break free from their surroundings. This was only temporary according to Jim.

Chapter 11

As time passed their friendship blossomed and, as ever, Jim had an answer to everything, knowing a way out of the old building and they soon made the most of it. Originally built as a school, with house attached for the head teacher to be always on hand, but over the years the building had fallen into disrepair due to shortage of money and neglect. While still an imposing building, the once red brick facade was now dull and crumbling due to its age and the acrid, smoking chimneys. The steeply pitched roof had many broken slates with patches blown off altogether and when the rain came, the drip, drip, drip of water hitting the old tin buckets in the loft, echoed around the high timbers of the building, sounding like distant chiming bells to the children. And it was their job to keep a check on these and empty before they overflowed. High wrought iron railings, rusty with age, encircled the yard and the broken panes of glass dotting the large lancet windows did nothing to keep out the bitter cold. A large pot-bellied stove that glowed a cherry red during the colder winter months stood in the middle of the classroom providing the sole heating for the whole of the Orphanage.

Ruth found it hard to cope with this harsh, strict environment, a life she hated but knew in her heart that one day, she knew not when, she would escape the confines of this soul-destroying place and find happiness. But at present, all other thoughts of happiness were swept aside as she concentrated on just surviving. With Jim's friendship, the Orphanage became, if not her home, a place of shelter where she was fed and kept off the street.

Schooling, if you could call it that, as every lesson was carried out by an old man called Mr Jeffers, who the children mocked terribly. His authority counted for nothing as he continuously spent his time shuffling about between the rows of desks trying his utmost to keep order. But whereas his authority wavered under the torrent of abuse from the children, Miss Wade could not be trifled with as easy, ruling the school with cruelty and a sharp tongue.

Although Jim and Ruth sat at opposite ends of the school room, Miss Wade's beady eyes missed nothing, knowing full well Jim had taken Ruth under his protective wing and it was in the early morning religious service that Ruth's troubles began. There was no escaping. Everyone had to attend and reply when their names were called.

Miss Wade ruled this lesson no differently from any other, striding along the rows of singing children, glaring at each in turn. Jeffers manfully tried to keep up and hit the right keys on the out of tune organ, the children hiding their amusement every time a wrong note was played, especially if Miss Wade was in sight. Suddenly she stopped in front of Ruth, waving her arms dramatically for quiet, ordering Jeffers to stop playing.

"Why are you not singing, child?" she scolded.

"I do not know the words, Miss Wade."

Miss Wade's eyes flashed and Ruth knew she was in trouble.

"Not know the words? How long have you been in this establishment? A year or more isn't it? Every thought, every word of the Lord should be imprinted in your heart by now. We should all know and learn the true meaning of the good Lord above.

Ruth's chin jutted out in determination to stand her ground. "Well I don't, and I have no intention of learning them," she said defiantly.

Miss Wade's features suddenly took on the hardness of granite, her eyes alone meting out the pure hatred she was feeling toward this young upstart of a girl. Her stooped frame suddenly straightened to its full height as she

Chapter 11

hissed,

"May God strike you down you young, worthless slut," spittle flying from her mouth such was her anger as she spat the words out. This proved too much for Ruth. The anger, fear and abuse suffered over the past year boiled over as she confronted the old woman head on with never a thought of the possible consequences.

"God," she hissed the words, her body rigid with anger. "God. There is no God in my life. Never has been. There is no God to look after me. If there was, would he have had my drunken father beat my mother to death to leave me homeless and an orphan. Dragged to this stinking hovel where you make us work our fingers to the bone, scrubbing floors, cleaning rooms, washing dishes. Don't you dare talk to me about God. If He exists let him strike me down now." These last words screamed out as Ruth flung her head back, as if searching for a sign of this divine being up among the dusty old rafters of the building, waiting for a flash of lightning to strike her down. A deathly hush descended the room, the class dumbfounded. Even Jim was lost for words, his mouth hanging open as if catching flies.

Ruth brought her gaze down and, in that instant, 'hatchet face' swung her hand to collide with Ruth's jaw, sending her sprawling backwards over the desks and chairs, stars shooting through her brain.

"Blaspheming young hussy. How dare you take the Lord's name in vain in this house," she screamed. Eyes bulging, she grabbed Ruth by the throat where she still lay, head spinning. Her grip tightened on her windpipe and Ruth began to claw and fight but she was no match for the woman's great bulk. A red mist swam before her eyes and was near to passing out when the pressure eased, the weight of the old lady's body lifted from her. As Ruth's vision cleared, she saw Jim and another boy with their arms around the old lady, grappling with her as she tried to shake herself free from their vice-like grip. Ruth was still shaking from the sudden attack but she had not finished with 'hatchet face' yet.

Voice shrill with fear she screamed after her. "You are mad as well as evil, you old witch. I hope you rot in hell for what you make us suffer in this awful place." Ruth's head was still spinning, but her senses were returning.

The old lady had stopped her struggles and the two boys released their grip and let her go.

"I have not finished with you, young lady. You dare to question my authority. Your life will not be worth living."

"There is nothing more you can do to make my life more unbearable. I shall come through anything that you can do, so do your worst." Ruth manfully tried to control her limbs and her voice, remaining utterly defiant. Jim looked on, admiration clear on his cheeky countenance. The old woman stormed out and the children crowded round Ruth to see if she was all right. No one had ever stood up to her like that they said. Not even Jim. A certain satisfaction flowed through Ruth. She did not regret her actions but knew she would suffer. But, there again, sufferance had become second nature to her these last awful years and the punishment meted out for misbehaving children shocked Ruth in its brutality.

Even for minor offences 'hatchet face' made sure they endured beatings in front of the whole class who were ordered to stand and watch. Miss Wade carried these punishments out herself, believing Jeffers not of a strong enough character to administer such pain to young ones. Ruth knew it was only a matter of time before she would eventually be brought to task.

All the children stuck rigidly to a rota of jobs to be done each week and every Tuesday morning it was Ruth's duty to clean the kitchen. When Miss Wade came to inspect, she accused her of not being thorough enough on scrubbing the kitchen floor. Ruth knew what to expect, having witnessed the thrashing of other children with the cane for misbehaving, or sometimes just for the simple fact of bed wetting.

"Billy and Alfie, carry the bench to the front of the class room," she ordered. "Ruth Brennan has not done her work properly on the kitchen floor. She is a conniving little slut that thinks she can get away with laziness and needs to be taught a lesson." Miss Wade reached up for the long cane kept on display above her desk. Grasping it in both hands and bending it almost double to test its pliability, she swished it down in a few practice strokes, a gleam in her eye and a wicked smile pulling at the side of her mouth as if relishing what was to come.

Chapter 11

"Step forward, Ruth Brennan," the old lady ordered. Ruth's mouth dried, no saliva left due to fear, her breathing quickening in prospect of the pain she was about to endure, wondering if her strength of will would see her brave enough to handle it. Walking slowly to the bench, she heard the words, "Bend over, girl." Sinking to her knees, she did as she was bid and bent over the bench. She then suffered the greatest indignity of her skirts lifted high above her waist before suffering the long agonising wait prior to the whistle of the cane cutting though the silence. Suddenly, a muffled thwack as she felt it cut into the tender flesh of her buttocks and the top of her legs. The old lady waited for the pain to bite before delivering the next stroke, each more painful than the last. With great effort, no more than a gasp escaped Ruth's lips with each lash of this destructive weapon.

Once finished, Miss Wade, nostrils flared and breathing hard from the effort, hissed the words, "Let that be a lesson to every one of you who misbehaves or think they can shirk their duties. Now get back to work and not a sound from any one of you." Shamefaced, they all trudged back to their desks, leaving Ruth trying, unsuccessfully, to rise to her feet. Instantly, Jim ran forward and helped lift her upright. Striding up to him, Miss Wade screamed in his face.

"What do you think you are doing, boy? Get back to your desk this instant." Jim's face twisted with such hate for this cruel, evil woman he could almost taste it. Straightening up, still clutching Ruth to him, he leant close in to the old lady and whispered menacingly in her ear.

"Don't you ever dare touch her again, or any of us with that cane, or I will beat you to within an inch of your life with it. Now, get out of my way, I am taking Ruth back to her room!" and he began to escort the unsteady girl back to her room.

Miss Wade realized he meant what he said and shuffled off, but not without a muttered, parting shot. "You've not heard the last of this."

The injuries sustained from the beating were not only to the flesh, severe as they were, taking weeks to heal before Ruth could walk without pain. But they did heal. The scars to her mind cut deeper and would stay with her forever. After this incident, due to Jim confronting Miss Wade, Ruth never once saw the cane used in anger on any child again and apart from trying to keep a distance between them and setting the pair as many horrible tasks as she could think of, the old lady realized, after this incidence, it was impossible trying to break their spirit.

Life settled into a humdrum routine over the next few months, Ruth trying desperately hard to learn a rudimentary education from the teachings of old Jeffers. But she had to admit, the beatings and the morally destroying nature of the Orphanage did mean that more lessons were learnt from Jim when school was out. She knew it was wrong but Jim persuaded her that this wrong- doing was only temporary and it would help them both eventually escape from this place.

They became a team and although against her better nature, Ruth soon learnt the art of thieving, prowling the market stalls and shops, mainly where fruit was on display. Jim explained how easy it was. "Right, Ruth, you nip to the back of the stall, catch the owner's attention while I grab a couple of apples off the front, okay?"

Ruth looked at him incredulous. "I can't do that, Jim. What do I say to him? I can't just go up to him and ask him the time of day, he'll know something is on."

"Nah, he won't. Trust me. Just give him that nice smile you give me," he said, eyes sparkling with amusement, "it'll be a piece o' cake. C'mon, it works a treat, I often do it. Just watch this." He walked jauntily around the front of the stall. This was the braggart coming out in him, showing off, always trying to impress other people but, this time, Ruth knew it was especially for her benefit.

Wandering nervously to the back of the stall she plucked up courage. "Hey, mister, can you let a poor street urchin have a couple of apples? I haven't eaten today. I'll do some jobs for you."

The man turned, peering at her and said, not unkindly, "Now, how do you think I could make a living if I kept giving apples away to young rascals like you. I would soon be out of business. Now be off with you, afore I call the police."

Ruth saw Jim, quick as lightening, snatch the apples and run off. "Okay,"

Chapter 11

she replied, but on turning away, a shout from the assistant reached her ears.

"Hey Jack, that young ragamuffin just pinched some apples. I'll soon get him for you."

The stall holder grabbed the man by the arm and whispered an aside. "Don't worry mate, it's only a couple o' bob gone astray. That's young Jim from the Orphanage. He's pretty well known around here. Every time he filches something, I don't let on I've seen him, cos most o' these kids don't have much going for 'em."

Ruth heard all this but decided not to mention it to Jim. She couldn't bear to see his confidence crushed. What the stallholder said was right, he doesn't have much going for him in this life. In fact, none of us orphans have much to look forward too. But that wasn't quite true at present, as deep down, her stomach rumbling with hunger, she was really looking forward to sinking her teeth into her share of the spoils.

But small crime leads to more crime and over the summer months their escapades became more serious. In a very short time, she developed into a quick and nimble street urchin, prowling the streets of the City, picking the pockets of the rich and well to do who, with not too much prompting from Jim, she had also come to despise because of their wealth and way of life.

With her dainty features, a growing confidence and precocious manner developing due to circumstances forced upon her, even at such a young age, and dressed shabbily, she was beginning to catch the eye of the opposite sex, Jim quickly teaching her how to gain advantage from this.

Biding their time until Miss Wade and Jeffers had their days off and when the gullible Mr Baldwin took over, Ruth felt the same bubble of excitement creep up on her whenever she discarded the old grey uniform and pinafore that they were forced to wear and changed into the old clothes that Jim had brought on her arrival. They knew then they would experience freedom, even if just for a day.

Often, the pair, giggling with exuberance at the thought of these adventures ahead would sneak away, not through the securely locked doors of the building but through a small, undiscovered cell type window in the basement.

Due to their skinny frames they could just manage to wriggle through and enjoy almost a full day away from the confines of the Orphanage.

When not at the table at mealtimes the other children would make excuses for them, telling Mr Baldwin, who was always one for a quiet life, that Jim and Ruth were not feeling well and this was accepted.

Once outside they ran and ran until, gasping for breath, they reached the better areas of the City. At just twelve years old Jim's attitude had not softened. If anything, he had developed into a more aggressive, in your face, lippy youngster as he grew older. But he would often study Ruth with sidelong glances when she was unaware, the thumping lurch of his heart uncomfortable in his chest as he knew, even now, he would always fight for this slip of a girl by his side.

On their early attempts they were almost caught as Ruth proved clumsy, nervous and frightened, but within a few months her technique proved quick and as near fool proof as possible. All spoils were kept hidden, until they soon had a tidy sum put by. Mostly their thieving targeted fruit stalls and bakeries because they were starving, often taking fruit back to the other children for keeping quiet and covering for their whereabouts.

But, like all criminals, the more successful they were, the greedier they became. Their favourite ploy starting with an argument, Jim suddenly hurling Ruth into the path of a gent chosen earlier as easy pickings, with such force, that taking his watch, wallet or any possessions became a cakewalk. Even though dressed in rags, with her slight build, blonde hair and pale complexion, the victim would inquire if she was hurt. Ruth would assure them she was fine and off they would go on their way, minus belongings, none the wiser. As their rooms were checked for signs of food or money, Jim had a hiding place in a disused cellar down one of the alleys in the Shambles.

He stumbled upon it quite by accident after fumbling a job and was chased long and hard by the man, finally managing to lose him among the many narrow walkways. Luckily Jim knew them off by heart. He realized fortune had favoured him this time, as panic gripped him, he was forced into taking an unknown alley and heart thumping, hoped it did not lead to a dead end. Quickly trying the first door he came to, it opened. Breathing hard, he

Chapter 11

dashed inside and shot the bolt across from the inside. The shouting and footsteps approached outside and someone rattled the door, but finding it locked ran on. Jim, still gasping for breath, finally heaved a sigh of relief and slumped in the corner.

Panic over. That was a close call. Not until things quietened down, did he dare venture out.

Since that day and with two of them now, Jim's confidence knew no bounds, doing as many as three or four pockets a day. Different areas, different surroundings but always where Jim knew the ground. Their takings mounted. But, unknown to them, their notoriety had spread, they had been noted.

On a cool summer evening just as shops were closing blinds and locking up, but still a bustle of customers to make it easier, they did a last walk up the street, their appointed man already picked and ready for the taking. Jim performed his customary shove and Ruth's hand whipped straight to his open jacket inside pocket to lift the wallet. Suddenly, her wrist was grasped in a vice like grip. A spark of fear ripped through her at the realization she had been caught.

"Run, run!" Ruth shouted at Jim, and he set off like a whippet, threading his way so quickly through the busy street that Ruth soon lost sight of him.

"Got you, young lady. We've been watching you for some time but you have always been too clever. You have learnt your trade well. I think you and your partner have been causing a lot of bother. Let us see what the police have to say about this, shall we." And never slackening his grip upon her arm, he almost had to drag her all the way to the police station before handing her over to a PC Brent who was not too happy about having his conversation with a lady warder rudely interrupted.

Ruth knew she was in deep trouble but, at least, Jim had got away with all their previous takings without being caught. All this would be needed when they escaped this wretched way of life. Although, at present, there appeared a much bigger threat in her life to worry about as she was not taken back to the Orphanage as expected, but to the police station where the Sergeant took her age, name and address, before taking her down to one of the cells. As the door clanged shut behind her, Ruth shuddered at the sound, reality sinking in on what had happened. The stench from the many unwashed bodies, open sewers and rotting rubbish permeating the cells made her want to wretch and she began to wonder whatever was to become of her.

Was this just another step toward finishing up in the gutter. Fighting back tears, she realized that in the last two years her life had turned upside down. From being a happy, carefree schoolgirl who liked nothing better than helping her father out on his market stall, to being locked up alongside hardened criminals in a stinking, rat infested cell.

Chapter 12

Jim took off like fury as Ruth shouted at him to run. He ran, like lightning, but not before turning to catch a glimpse of her as she struggled to break free from her would be victim's clutches. Nipping and darting through the back alleys, his other pursuer stood no chance of catching him and with beating heart arrived at the Orphanage. Squeezing through the narrow gap he replaced the frame and no one would be any the wiser just as long as he could reach his room without being seen.

He had no idea of the time but the cloak of night was drawing in and he knew every room would be checked to see if all were inside and lights were extinguished. Taking his boots off, he crept past the snoozing figure of Mr Baldwin slumped at his desk, finally making it to the safety of his room. Willing his thumping chest to settle, he undressed quickly and jumped into bed, pulling the sheets up to his chin just in time, as voices echoed in the corridor outside his room. Listening intently, the sound of footsteps stopped outside his door and the latch clicked open. Jim recognized Mr Baldwins voice.

"As you can see, Sergeant, all are accounted for every night as we check every room."

"Well, you don't seem to have kept an eye on the young girl we have just caught and she will certainly tell us who her accomplice was."

"I can't understand how she slipped out without us knowing," said Mr Baldwin, "but we will certainly keep an eye on her from now on."

"Oh, she won't be coming back here. It's the cells for her."

Jim died a little inside on hearing these words.

Shocked, Mr Baldwin said, "Surely, you cannot lock a girl of her age in alongside hardened criminals, Sergeant? Think of the damage it will have on such a young mind." "Too late for that. She is in serious trouble and for damage to her mind, I would think it's the best place for her before she drags more young ones into trouble."

Jim kept his eyes tight shut, willing his body to stay motionless, never moving a muscle, as he felt more than heard them come close and peer down at him to check if he really was fast asleep. Eventually the door clicked shut and Jim opened an eye to make sure all was clear. He couldn't believe he had got her into such trouble with the law. He'd never thought of it as that serious. In fact, he never, ever thought they would be caught.

After grasping the seriousness of it, he realized he must get a message to her somehow. The night dragged through as he kept dozing off, but the nightmare sight of the man hanging onto Ruth's arm woke him in a sweat. Jim was actually relieved when the thin shafts of sunlight pierced through the small window, heralding the break of day. Dressing quickly, he was all ready and waiting when the time came to be called for breakfast and for Miss Wade to address the children.

"We have bad news this morning, children. But not surprising news. We have had the police round." Gasps from the children. "It appears Ruth Brennan was caught picking pockets close to the Shambles area. This is a serious offence and she is now in gaol." Another gasp, before she continued. "Her accomplice got clean away." As she said this her eyes fastened on Jim. "But I am sure she will inform the police who it was and I will find out eventually. Let this be a lesson to you all." Chatter began between the children.

"Quiet please," she barked, her features hardening by the minute, gimlet eyes spearing into each and every child. "I knew she was a troublemaker from the moment she arrived. A blaspheming young upstart like her has

Chapter 12

only one way to go. To Hell." Defiantly, her voice lowering for impact, she uttered, "let me tell you again, if you spurn the words of the Almighty, no good will come of you, so listen to the teachings of the Lord."

Jim listened but didn't hear a word. He was already planning a way to get in touch with Ruth. If he went himself, there was every chance he would be recognized, so someone else would have to take the message. But what then? That's not going to get her out of trouble. Jim lifted his head as his name was called out.

"Yes, Miss," he replied.

"What do you know about your new friend's escapade, Jim?"

"Nothin', Miss Wade. I were tucked up in bed, like all good children should have been." The sarcasm was not missed by Miss Wade.

The old lady eyed him keenly for a few seconds before saying, "I do not believe you for one minute but I will leave it for the present until I receive more information. Now, eat your breakfast."

The sloppy, grey gruel splashed into their dishes and Jim forced the slime down his throat, the knot of guilt in his stomach almost bringing it back up again. Sat next to Billy Hunter, he took the chance to pass a note across and whisper to Billy, asking if he could take it to the police station. Billy's eyes widened in terror. "You 'spect me to go to the old plod. Not on your life. They might lock me up thinking I was in on it."

"Course they won't, you're nothing like me at all. They'll have my description. I can't go."

"You should have thought o' that beforehand, Jim," said Billy.

"I'll make it worth your while. We have a good stash put by, cos we were going to run away. I'll share some of it with you if you'll help me." A light switched on in Billy's head, his face brightening, immediately asking, "Well, that's different 'innit. What do you want me to do?"

"Go to the station, tell 'em you're her brother or somethin' and you need to see her 'cos you're worried about her, then slip this note to her somehow, so she knows I'm still here and haven't run away without her."

"Right, I'll do it, but tell me where the stuff is first."

"You think I'm soft in the head, Billy. I'm not letting you in on that. I'll bring it round to your room tonight. Do you want money or valuables?"

"Money, stupid. You know they search our rooms and if they caught me with stuff like that I'd soon be in clink." His face took on a sly look, before asking, "how much?"

"Plenty," replied Jim as they gathered their plates, stacking them on the huge table before commencing their lessons for the day.

Chapter 13

After a frightened, sleepless night, the very next day Ruth was ushered out of her cell by who she thought must be a female officer. A big, burly woman with short cropped hair and dressed in an overly tight-fitting uniform, led her through to a small dark, oak panelled office at the end of another corridor, with tidy stacks of papers placed upon a central desk. When ordered to sit down, Ruth did as she was told, taking a seat in one of the chairs while the female officer stood alongside, never speaking. Ruth heard the slow methodical thud of heavy footsteps approaching. They seemed to take forever. Suddenly a figure that seemed to fill the room appeared and sat at the desk, his heavy jowls dropping onto his collar, reminding Ruth of a bloodhound. After a few minutes silence he lifted his head and a droopy set of eyes rested directly on the woman, never once recognizing Ruth was in the room, and said. "What have we here, Evelyn?" as if talking about a piece of dirt that had been left.

"Another waif and stray, sir. The city is full of 'em at present. They can't keep an eye on 'em at that Orphanage. Big trouble if you ask me. This one's a pickpocket. Pretty good by all accounts."

"Yes, thank you, Evelyn. I don't want to hear anymore."

"Yes, sir. Thank you, sir."

"Would it be possible for you to take her back and let the Sergeant know

A Journey Of Hope

what's to be done with her? I'll fill in the paperwork. That will be all, Evelyn."

Evelyn tipped her head in Ruth's direction as much as to say, "come on, I haven't got all day," and she was marched back out of the office and returned to the desk where the Sergeant sat. Raising himself from behind the desk, Ruth took more notice this time. He was a tall, skinny man with a wisp of hair across his top lip like a dirty mark that needed washing off and long, black hair brushing the back of the frayed white collar of his shirt. His uniform slopped around his bony frame as if two sizes too big for him.

He strode to meet them as Evelyn asked, "Can you keep this one here a few days Arthur until such time as she goes to court." The words hit her like a punch to the stomach; appearing in court could only mean one thing. Gaol.

"Yes, will do. Can't see this one causing bother, she's not the size of two pennorth o' copper," and with that he rocked back on his heels, laughing heartily at his own stab of what he thought was humour.

Evelyn gave him a cold stare before saying. "Well she's in your hands now, I'm going."

"Right, young lady, come with me and I will see if I can find you a nice little corner cell away from everybody."

"What's going to happen to me? Am I to be thrown in prison?" Ruth dared to ask, the tremble in her voice betraying fear.

"Well, that depends on what you did, and what the Judge thinks. He might believe you didn't do it, dearie," laughing again with great gusto at his own joke.

Sergeant Porritt genuinely seemed to be enjoying his moment of authority, his high-pitched voice reverberating along the dark brick tunnel leading to the cells, dragging Ruth behind him and shouting, "Everyone must clean their cells from top to bottom. All beds must be made. Make sure all slops are taken out. All prisoners to be washed and ready for inspection standing to the front of their cell for Judge John Durville to make a prison inspection at 9 a.m. on the dot tomorrow morning. Is that clear?" There were a few mumbles along the corridor of steel, the guard presuming everyone was in agreement.

Chapter 13

Brandishing a jangling bunch of keys, Sergeant Porritt finally came to a halt at one of the steel barred doors and inserted one into the lock, swinging the door open for Ruth to enter. Quickly ushering her into the tiny, dingy cell, the door slammed shut with a loud metallic clang, causing a shudder to run through her as the noise reverberated around the passageways of this pitiful building, jolting her to the reality of being locked away as a criminal. Sergeant Porritt, head on one side, studied her for a second or two, before quickly turning on his heel to return to reading the paper upon his desk.

Chapter 14

Ruth, a hollow feeling in the pit of her stomach and at her lowest ebb, had no idea what lay ahead. What she did know was definitely a court appearance and possibly a prison sentence facing her. The thought turned her legs to jelly and she sat on the bed to save herself from falling but there was no Jim knocking on the door to save her in here.

The one good thing, although missing him terribly, Jim did make good his escape and she was sure he would find a way to contact her, or, maybe get a message to her. Not wanting other prisoners to hear her weeping, she muffled her sobs among the bed covers that smelled strongly of carbolic soap. They were rough on her skin but at least they were clean.

Somehow, she knew not how, she had to find the strength to see this through. There were no other options at present. Finally, sleep came to the rescue of her troubled soul and not even the scurrying of vermin could keep her awake. But a restless night ensued, tormented by the nightmare of a human hand on a long twisting tentacle weaving slowly toward her through the barred cell, tightening on her arm like a vice, suddenly jolting her awake, sweating and shaking.

After enduring the long silent hours of night, the dull greyness of dawn began to filter through the barred window, letting a small amount of light into the dark cell and voices from the early shift workers outside could be

Chapter 14

clearly heard. So, the prison must be close to a busy street. Ruth washed the sleep from her eyes with water from the small bowl on the washstand, rubbing her skin until sore in an effort to feel human once again.

She remembered the inspection and wanted to make a good impression if that was possible. Time dragged slowly by and the noise from the street grew louder with the clattering of ponies and traps and boisterous shouts from young boys on their way to school. Aren't they the lucky ones. If only I could be free and a schoolgirl once again but, as quickly as the thought emerged, she forced it from her mind, not allowing herself to dwell on what she could not possibly have. With the minutes ticking slowly by, Ruth had no idea of the time but knew it must be nearing inspection if schoolchildren were on their way to school.

Sudden activity at the far end of the corridor signalled something was about to happen, so Ruth stood, as requested at the front of the cell, everything tidy as asked for. Her clothes were scruffy but she couldn't really do anything about that. At least she was washed and clean, her short blonde hair, urchin like, but shiny and smooth in the shards of sunlight filtering through the high barred window. She stood and waited.

Eventually Ruth heard the outer door open and pushing her face close to the cold bars of the cell door she could just see to the top of the corridor where a giant of a man strode forward, a black cape flowing from his broad shoulders. Ruth's heart sank. He looked more like the devil than a Judge. Dressed from head to toe in black, even top hat and cane were black, only a sparkle of silver tipping the end of his walking cane.

He began firing questions at the desk Sergeant who appeared quite flummoxed by this man and his abrupt, forthright manner. Apprehensive, she watched as the big man turned and marched toward the locked steel door sealing off the top part of the gaol. Ruth backed away from the door, not daring to look but she heard the footsteps coming closer. On arrival at her cell, the big man hesitated, staring, not at Ruth, but above her head into the cell. Then he asked the Sergeant, "How old is this child?"

"I cannot say for definite, sir. I shall have to check the paperwork"?

Before Porritt had a chance to answer, Ruth blurted out.

"Twelve, sir."

A sudden shiver ran through her as he bent forward, slowly lowering himself to bring his piercing black eyes into direct contact with hers. With great difficulty, the innocent blue eyes of Ruth stared defiantly back, even forcing his gaze to falter. He then proceeded to appraise Ruth up and down, from under the heavy black, beetle brows.

Eventually, after what seemed an age, he enquired, "What is your crime, young girl? That is, if you are a girl?"

"I am indeed a girl," Ruth replied indignantly, "and my crime, if you can call it a crime was pinching. I was forced to pinch so I didn't starve to death." After a moment's pause for that to sink in, she added, "sir."

The cold eyes again held her for a second longer trying to weigh up if this young girl was just giving cheek.

Suddenly his booming voice rang out "Where the devil are you, Porritt? Who decided to put this girl behind bars? Would it be PC Brent or would it be one of the Detective Inspectors if they were in plain clothes?" Porritt had slunk quietly back to his desk but as the big man shouted, he came running.

"Er, I'm not sure who made the arrest but it was PC Brent and Evelyn who brought her into the station and handed her over. That's all I know, sir."

It was now Porritt's turn to witness those twin orbs of jet as the Judge rounded on him, hissing, "Do you not know the law, Sergeant? Young children cannot be locked up with hardened criminals at this age. You will not hear the last of this, Porritt. Do I make myself clear?"

"Yes sir, of course, sir," Porritt said pleadingly, "but what else could I do? Evelyn from the Trust seemed to think it was okay, so I just locked her up." The poor man's face had turned ashen in this fiery onslaught but Judge Durville had already begun walking away, not stopping or inspecting other prisoners or cells. He'd seen enough and stalked out.

Chapter 15

The next couple of days proved a living nightmare for Ruth, the hours dragging by in agonising slowness. The cells were damp and depressing, the nights long and cold. Many times, the other prisoners would rattle the bars of their cage or scream out in terror in the middle of the night and the prison food was a meagre portion of bread along with a watery soup. It kept them alive but that was all.

On the third day, Ruth received a visitor, Jim managing to smuggle a message through with Billy Hunter, the boy from the Orphanage. Billy was a tall, spindly legged youth, always wearing a slightly vacant look coupled with a violent nervous twitch of the head every few seconds. He, otherwise, had a pleasant countenance, topped with patchy brown hair which he scratched incessantly due to a large, unsightly ringworm that stretched from forehead to ear. Arriving at the gaol, Billy's nerve began to let him down, making the nervous tic more noticeable than usual. On approaching the front desk and coming face to face with Sergeant Porritt, he could hardly keep his head still, finally spluttering out, "Hello, Sergeant. I'm Billy. I've come to see my little sister. I heard you got her locked up in here, so I've brought her some food." He held the bag out for inspection. With his other hand he scratched at his scalp. Porritt stared at him, then shrank away from him, fearful that any of the flaky bits of scab coming from the boys violently shaking head, or nits for that matter, might land on him, or even jump across the close space and infest his hair. He quickly took a step backward, well away from the boy. But Porritt dare not be anything but thoroughly efficient and on his guard after the Judges visit, so he grabbed the packet off the boy at armslength, peered inside, smelt it, before handing it back, quickly turning on his heel and unlocking the door leading to the cells, then waved the boy through.

"I've brought you some food, Ruth," Billy said in an overly loud voice, making a big show of pushing the contents through the bars, while slipping a note into her hand. Ruth's spirits lifted instantly on sight of Billy and eagerly grabbed the two crusty sandwiches, talking as she did so.

"Oh, thank you, Billy, I'm starving. The food is like pig swill, worse than the Orphanage and that's saying something. Is Jim still there and if he is, will you tell him I'm okay though and not to worry. It is miserable and cold and I don't know how long I will be in here but please tell him I miss him, won't you."

"Course I will, Sis," he said loudly, then in a whisper, "Jim says he's got everything planned for when you get out. He said you would know what that meant. He daren't come in here as he might be recognised." Billy kept whispering out of the corner of his mouth, "the notes from him." He then broke into a louder voice for Sergeant Porrit's benefit. "Well, I'll have to go now, Sis," he boomed, then winked in what he considered a conspiratorial way but it appeared to Ruth as if it was just part of his nervous twitch. She couldn't help but smile despite her circumstances. "Mebbe see you tomorrow," he said, turning and hurrying up the long passageway to the open air.

Once outside, he gasped out with relief, also grabbing a lungful of fresh air. He felt sorry for Ruth but God, he really was relieved to be out of that stinking place. Now he began rubbing his hands together in expectancy at the thought of how much Jim would have in store for him. It had better be a tidy sum for the agony he had just gone through.

Chapter 16

Once Billy had left, the loneliness clamped around Ruth again, leaving her with only thoughts of Jim and what he would be doing. But, although on her own, she now had the scrap of paper and opened it up to try and read Jim's scrawl that passed as handwriting.

Sorry Ruth, no good at writing. My fault. Should have known we were pushing things. Will wait for you and run away. I'll get a job. Got to be better than this. This place stinks without you. Miss you. Jim

Ruth read and reread the letter, clasping it close to her chest as if it was Jim himself. She knew now this scrawny boy with the cheeky smile had touched her heart and a warm glow began to spread through her body once more. *There is somebody who does care what happens to me.*

The very next day, Porritt appeared at Ruth's cell, clean shaven, a nice clean shirt and hair trimmed above the collar. Ruth, after a fitful night's sleep, awoke at the crack of dawn and immediately made the bed. She had also washed and tidied her cell.

"You look very smart, Sergeant Porritt," she remarked.

Porritt was taken aback and lost for words for a few seconds. Not many complimented him on his appearance.

"Ah, yes, well, ah thank you," he finally managed to stammer, running his finger around his collar as if too tight. "Now young lady, I have just received some good news. You are to appear in court this very day. Seeing as that you are too young to be held in prison, the Judge will see you and decide on your fate. Now have you got all your belongings." Ruth glared at him. "I have nothing but the clothes I stand up in Sergeant. You should know that. I came in with nothing."

Although not a family man, his heart went out to this feisty young girl, battling against the odds and his features momentarily softened.

"Erm, of course. I'm sorry, my dear." He unlocked the door and ushered her out. "As you will have gathered, I'm not used to dealing with children. Usually hardened criminals I deal with. Different kettle o' fish to children, you see." Embarrassed, he again ran his finger on the inside of his collar as he struggled to find the right words.

Ruth made it easy for him. "Don't worry, I understand, Sergeant."

The Sergeant walked her to the door where Evelyn and a two-horse carriage waited patiently on the roadside for her. As she walked to the carriage the Sergeant shouted after her, "Good luck, Ruth. If I can help you anytime, let me know. I might not be able to do much but I'll try. You know where to find me."

"Thank you, Sergeant, I will remember that." And with that Evelyn grabbed her elbow and lifted her into the cab and without a word they made their way to the court house. The court house had a façade of creamy white stone shining bright in the early morning sunlight and the fancily decorated portico, supported by four huge Corinthian pillars covered the beautifully polished marble steps leading to the entrance. Ruth studied the imposing frontage and thought the Georgian style windows gave the building an appearance of many sets of eyes staring imperiously down, not only upon her but on all the more unfortunate people of this world.

Evelyn led her through the huge oak doors, once more Ruth having no option but to follow like a servile dog, taken she knew not where. They entered a very elaborate but very cold room where Evelyn told her to wait until called for. Doing exactly as she was bid, she settled on the long wooden bench, the tension building with every passing minute. After what seemed hours, the court usher shouted her name. Ruth looked enquiringly at Evelyn.

Chapter 16

"Follow that man," she ordered, nodding her head in the direction of a smartly dressed, bald headed fellow standing in the nearby doorway. Ruth was still dressed in the old cast offs that Jim had given her that made her look more like a boy than a girl. As Ruth neared, he looked her scornfully up and down before turning and strutting away with a brisk step, ordering her to follow him.

This time Ruth entered a larger, inner sanctum of the building, much more forbidding, with chairs neatly placed down either side, the dark oak panelling on the walls creating the same claustrophobic feel of a prison to her.

Seated behind a very ornate balustrade and raised on a platform at the head of the room were three people and she recognized Judge Durville instantly. With heart hammering to be free of her chest, Ruth thought they must surely be able to hear it in the deathly silence that pervaded the room.

The person to Judge Durville's left spoke first. "Name please?" he asked in a kindly tone.

"Ruth Brennan, sir." Although trying to sound confident, the tremor in her voice betrayed her. On the mention of her name, Judge Durville raised his head and studied her more closely, the name Brennan ringing bells somewhere in his memory but for the moment he just couldn't think why. Shaking his head, he let it drop back down to his papers in front of him.

The man on his left carried on. "How old are you, Ruth?"

"Twelve, sir."

"You were caught stealing, pickpocketing no less, in the Shambles area of York. Is that correct?"

"Yes, sir."

"What have you got to say for yourself?" Ruth tried her best to halt the shakiness in her voice and keep her legs still as she answered.

"I am sorry, sir. I did steal. But the food given to us at the Orphanage is like pig swill. Oh, we eat it. We have to, to stay alive but if I hadn't suffered the loss of both my father and mother I would not be here. I was dragged there by a policeman when my Aunt Molly could not afford to keep me." The anger began to pour from Ruth as she carried on, "we are treated like dirt by everyone; even the teachers at the Orphanage are cruel and beat us with canes when it is not our fault but no one ever sees this. Nobody cares about our troubles. All of you sit here with full stomachs and return home to your families, everything just perfect. You don't understand how we suffer. Not just me, all of us, in that horrible place." Ruth didn't realize but her voice had risen in this sudden outburst, the familiar prickle of tears welled up at the back of her eyes again. Unable to stop shaking but fighting hard to retain her dignity, she managed to keep the tears at bay.

Ruth watched the Judge carefully as his head slowly lifted from the table, those black eyes studying her once again. Again, she did not buckle and met his gaze until he lowered his head.

The man on the left spoke once more as if he hadn't heard her tirade.

"You had an accomplice, I believe?" A lead weight landed in her stomach. Oh, how could they ask that? She could not, would not split on Jim. Couldn't.

"No, sir."

She felt rather than saw the three pairs of eyes raise from their paperwork and rest on her.

"I believe you may have misheard the question young lady. I will ask again. Did you or did you not have an accomplice, Miss Brennan?" The voice had taken on a firmer tone.

"Yes, sir," she answered, barely audible in the large room. "That is more like it. What was his name?"

"I can't tell you that because I didn't know it. I only knew him as Archie. I slipped out of the Orphanage one day and met up with him on the street. He was hungry and we decided to steal some money to buy food. We are forced into it by the way we are treated." Ruth was pleading now, hoping they would understand, telling them again, "the food we get would hardly keep a cat alive," her voice trailing off as she finished, "and we thought we could buy some food with the money."

Three sets of eyes bored into her. They knew she was lying but she stuck to her story and even, at one time thinking she might faint, will power alone kept her upright. The three administrators of Justice fell into a huddle whispering and occasionally glancing across in Ruth's direction, while she

Chapter 16

continued to stand, legs aching, apprehensive and frightened at the outcome of the blatant lies she had uttered.

After what seemed an eternity, Judge Durville beckoned Evelyn back into the room and asked her to return Ruth to the waiting room. Studying her closely, Evelyn appeared to notice Ruth's distressed state for the first time. Sitting her down, she disappeared for a few minutes before returning with a glass of water and a sandwich which Ruth accepted, glad that she did as the hours ticked slowly by. Eventually, the door swung open and in strode Judge Durville, his huge presence almost blotting the light from the room. Sitting down beside her, he spoke in a low, gravelly but not uncaring voice and enquired if she had recovered from her ordeal in front of the Magistrates.

"Yes, thank you. The lady brought me a sandwich and a drink of water and I've stopped shaking."

A glimmer of a smile plucked at the corners of his mouth, admiration for this plucky young girl growing by the minute.

Speaking slowly, he said, "After discussing your case with my two knowledgeable friends we have decided that it would be useless putting you back out on the streets, or even sending you back to the Orphanage, if what you tell us is true. No doubt you would just fall in with your accomplice again, so I am going to offer you a position which, if you show yourself capable and trustworthy, may give you a chance to redeem yourself from the foolhardy lies you told us in court. I understand your sense of loyalty and commendable though it was, it was still lying."

Ruth could not believe what she was hearing. Was he offering her some sort of a job, or had she misunderstood him?

"Thank you, sir," was all she could mutter.

"Have you anything to take with you at all. Is there anything from home or the Orphanage that you may need." The mention of home brought a huge lump to her throat but, grimly hanging on to her composure, she said, "I have a few things still at the Orphanage but I don't ever want to spend another night there, or in that terrible gaol."

"Well, that's settled then, I shall have someone pick your belongings up," he said, easing his bulk out of the chair. "Evelyn will call a cab and take you to my house and we will have a better talk when I have more time." Drawing a gold pocket watch out of his waistcoat pocket, he glanced at it.

"It is now almost four p.m. I shall be back at my residence at five, or just after. Evelyn will see you safely to the door and then you must ask Bella, the maid, to show you to your room."

"Thank you, sir. I will not let you down." This said in almost a whisper. It was all she could do to keep her emotions in check as relief flowed through her veins at not having to return to the stinking gaol or the cruel words and beatings of Miss Wade at the Orphanage, a warm feeling spreading through her that she had not experienced since Jim held her close.

"Yes, Ruth, I do believe you will try your hardest and that is all I ask." With those words, he turned and walked out of the room.

Evelyn, waiting patiently and with her ear to the door, jumped back just in time as the Judge departed. Poking her head round the door, she said, "Who's a lucky girl then. I heard what the Judge said. He must have taken a liking to you, letting you off the hook like that. Thinks you're worth a second chance, eh? Right, come on, look sharp, we haven't got all day. I want to be back home for my tea at five. We'll hail a cab." And with that she rushed Ruth out into the busy street, Evelyn striding out onto the cobbles putting her considerable bulk in front of a passing cabbie, so he had no choice but to stop.

"Thank you, kind sir," she said, then hastily pushed Ruth up into the cab before following her inside. Now squashed together in the tiny space, she shouted to the driver "Number ten, Darwin Court, please, cabbie." Ruth stared out of the cab window wondering just where she was as the beautiful black horse clattered along these unknown streets, soon leaving the modest houses and streets behind.

Eventually the appearance and architectural structure of the houses changed and they entered into a large crescent shaped road, surrounded by a beautiful grassy park area lined with lime trees, the sunshine bursting through onto the dazzling white curve of houses. Ruth stared open mouthed as the driver drew to a halt. Evelyn jumped out and paid the driver.

Ruth still sat inside. "Come on, out you get, young lady. We are here." She

Chapter 16

took both Ruth's hands in hers and bent to her height. "Now, I don't mean this nastily but I hope I never see you again, 'cos you see, that will mean you've kept your nose clean and made a go of it and I really hope you do. You deserve it." For good measure she could not help but give this young slip of a girl a big hug. "Good luck and goodbye," and with a cheery wave she walked away without a backward glance, her job done.

Chapter 17

The carriage driver didn't drive quickly away and seemed quite kind and well mannered, not looking down his nose at her at all. Taking her arm, he escorted her up the steep stone steps. Ruth, holding on to the fancy wrought iron railings stood on the top step and faced the huge front door, painted a brilliant white, with the highly polished brass numerals of ten shining bright in the strong sunlight.

This appeared, in Ruth's eyes, to be a mansion. Having being swept along by incidents she had no control over, she was really struggling to cope with such a turn of events. She had no idea what was going to happen, or what was expected of her. These were the first deeds of kindness shown to her since the traumatic loss of her parents over two year ago, although she could not help but notice the turning of heads from neighbours as they swept past in their starched dresses and bonnets, parasols spinning daintily, staring at the scruffy little urchin stood at the entrance of this beautiful building, then quickly turning away, noses in the air. Ruth had too much on her mind to be upset by such uncaring people; she was more concerned in what lay ahead and why the Judge had taken her out of prison.

Whatever the answer, she would face up to it. It couldn't be any worse than what she had already endured. The door swung open silently to the lightest of knocks from the cab driver and a sad faced young maid, dressed in an

Chapter 17

immaculate black and white uniform ushered her through to the entrance hall, where the cabbie took his leave, taking Ruth by the hand to wish her luck.

"It appears you may not now be fighting a lonely battle, young lady. Maybe Lady Luck has decided to shine on you for once."

"Thank you, I hope so," and the light and optimism that had once shone bright in Ruth's life began to glow again and along with it, an inner belief that she may just see this through somehow.

"I am often in the area taking the Judge to and fro on business, so he will keep me informed on how you are getting on in the near future. One day I may pass by and see a young lady walk down these very steps dressed in all her finery and hail a cab. Who knows, that lucky cabbie may just be me." Sweeping his hat from his head and bowing deeply from the waist in an exaggerated manner, he gave her a cheeky wink of the eye before dashing back out into the street. Ruth smiled after him, not really understanding these slight flirtations coming her way.

Chapter 18

Ruth studied her surroundings. A huge, wide staircase with carved balustrade rising to a first landing where a large, elaborate chandelier, sparkling brighter than any cluster of diamonds could, hung from the high ceiling before a second flight disappeared up to the next floor. Dark oak panelling covered the lower half of the walls and old paintings hung above with fancy gilded, gold leaf frames lining each wall on the ascent of the staircase to the first landing and upper rooms.

The maid tapped on the first door in the hall, jumping back sharply as a piercing voice called out, "Enter." Opening the door gently, the maid entered, immediately stepping to one side, allowing Ruth to walk forward and she was slightly shocked by the sight of a wizened old woman sat in a large chair behind the desk, writing.

"Come in, girl. Don't be frightened." Her voice was scratchy, short of patience. "You may go, Bella". The maid backed quietly out and closed the door. Ruth's throat had turned to parchment. Her legs were, once more, quite unsteady, not obeying her as she would have liked. As she stood in front of the polished mahogany desk, she felt her feet steadily sinking deeper and deeper into the thick pile of the pale blue carpet. Eventually the woman raised her head and asked, "What is your name?"

"Ruth. Ruth Brennan." Her voice hardly above a whisper. "Speak up,

Chapter 18

young lady. My hearing is not too good." Her head cocked to one side as if suffering from a permanently cricked neck.

"Sorry ma'am." Ruth cleared her throat and repeated her name.

"What business have you here, Miss Brennan."

"Judge Durville sent me." Ruth's mouth was dry and she hoped the Judge would soon be here to convince this woman she wasn't lying.

"Did he now, and for what reason? Did he tell you?"

"No, he just said he may be able to help me."

"Did he just take you off the street or were you caught for some misdemeanour?"

"I'm not sure I understand what you mean."

A hint of a smile from the old lady as she explained. "Were you in trouble with the law?" Ruth remained silent, wondering if she should be brave and give a truthful answer.

"Well?" The old lady brought her steely, pebble grey eyes to meet Ruth's with an enquiring stare. Ruth decided no more lies.

"I was caught on the street for pinching."

"And what makes you think I will want a thief in my house?"

"I'm not a thief." Ruth said defiantly.

"Well, you admit you were pinching. Is that different from thieving?" she asked.

"Well, yes. Quite a lot different. I have no option but to pinch to survive. My father killed my mother and is now in gaol. Or, he may have been hung for all I know. I have no relatives or anyone to look after me and I was taken to the Orphanage where they beat many of the children and starve us near to death."

"And that is why you break the law?"

"Yes."

"Do you know who I am?"

"No, but I think you must be Judge Durville's wife. He sent me here."

"Yes, you did tell me before. Quite an observant young girl aren't you."

"Yes."

"Spirited as well."

"Yes." Although very nervous, Ruth was not about to show her that and she was pleased the truth was out. Rising unsteadily from her chair, the old lady reached for the two sticks beside the desk and walked round behind her. Ruth kept her head ramrod still, staring directly ahead.

"Right." A pause before she carried on. "Ruth, what would you say to living here?"

"Why would you want me to live here?"

"You didn't answer my question," she said sharply. "Would you like to live here, in this house?"

"What are my choices?" Ruth forced the question out, knowing full well her choices were not good.

"Well, as I see it, you have the Orphanage, gaol or back out on the street."

"I would very much like to live here. I know Judge Durville took me out of the prison because of my age but I don't really know what is going to happen…" her voice, shaking, tailed off to a whisper.

"Let's not worry about that. I think my husband may think you will be able to fill the role of personal maid. Would you be able to do that? Personally, I don't think you will be strong enough but we would have to see, wouldn't we?"

"Yes, Miss, I'm sure I could. I'm stronger than I look."

A smile formed on Mrs Durville's lips, deepening the wrinkles of the walnut hard features into a grinning caricature figure that reminded Ruth of carved gargoyles staring out from churches, but the smile did help add a certain softness, making her appear almost human.

Years of pain had etched these deep furrows into this once aristocratic face and the crooked back and hands like gnarled oak were testament to a body riddled with arthritic pain.

"Good, good, then that's settled. You can bring your belongings in and Bella will show you to your room."

"These are my belongings, Miss," Ruth answered, then remembered, her face brightening, "although I do have one or two things of my mother's which Judge Durville did say he would try and pick up from the Orphanage."

The old lady's eyebrows arched as she stood and surveyed this small,

Chapter 18

dishevelled but brave young street urchin, silently admiring her demeanour and also her open defiance. She had nowhere to go. No one to turn to, but still she did not buckle.

"Very well," and she turned to the door and rang a small bell in her hand. She waited a few seconds and was just about to ring the bell again when Bella scurried into the hallway. "Ah, there you are, Bella. Would you be kind enough to show Ruth to her room. Tiffany's room I think will be suitable." Staring at Ruth as if sizing her up, she carried on, "there will be a choice of clothes in the wardrobe which should fit, although maybe slightly on the large side but you will soon grow into them. That will be all."

Ruth's head whirled about her. Not only whisked out of the stinking hole of a prison but away from the Orphanage as well, into this mansion to be a personal maid. For what reason? Yes, the old lady is ill and struggling to walk but surely a man of the Judge's standing could have a choice of any number of people to employ who were qualified for the job of personal maid. What made him choose me, she thought.

Chapter 19

Although young and quite innocent, Ruth was not foolish enough to think there would be no payback but decided that if she were to keep her wits about her, she would tackle that problem when it arose.

These thoughts were whistling through her head as Bella led the way upstairs to the bedchambers. Ruth lost count of the number of rooms before arriving at her bedroom, where she was ushered inside by Bella. The room was enormous, larger than the whole of the terraced house she had lived in as a child. Two tall Georgian style windows dominated the wall overlooking the back street. The room had more furniture in it than Ruth had ever seen and the four-poster bed, festooned with lime green drapes surrounding carved oak newels promised comfort unheard of in her entire life.

Again, from the high ceiling hung an elaborate chandelier and the highly embossed paper covering the walls proved soft to the touch, Ruth experiencing the feel as she ran her fingers over the surface.

A smell of polish pervaded the room and everything shone as though someone, Bella maybe, had just been busy. A large dressing table, again beautifully carved with swivel mirror and hairbrushes laid at one side stood to the front of one of the windows. Bella fluttered busily about, opening

Chapter 19

the wardrobe to display a choice of clothes. Ruth gasped in surprise. This was pure luxury, but a hard knot of fear began to form in her stomach that she could not shake off.

"Bella, what is going on? Why has the Judge taken me out of prison?"

Bella, slightly older than Ruth, maybe fourteen, fifteen years old and of a similar height and hair colour but whereas Ruth was sharp and nimble, Bella appeared quite slow moving, a worldly weariness shrouding her young frame, the pretty face drawn tight and pinched, as though burdened with worry. Blue eyes that should be sparkling bright and full of vitality were dull, lack lustre, never once lifting from the floor, the blonde hair pulled back and tucked under her maids cap.

"I'm sure I don't know, miss," she replied but not once did her head lift to make eye contact, as if hiding a furtive secret of some kind. As Bella turned to leave, Ruth strode to the door. "I hope we can be friends, Bella, you and I?" Bella stared as if in a trance at the ground.

"Ring the bell if you want me, miss. Oh, I nearly forgot, the bathroom is at the end of the landing." This said as she tried to squeeze past, Ruth eventually standing aside to let her pass.

Ruth locked the door and sat on the bed to ponder her future and these opulent surroundings. Finally, her thoughts returned to Jim, wondering what he would be doing now. Lessons would be ending and they would be lining up for their meal. With a sigh, she stripped off her dirty, smelling clothes and splashed some water from the jug into the washstand, before remembering Bella's information about the bathroom. Quickly, she found a dressing gown in the wardrobe and throwing it on opened the door and peeped out. Not a sound. Nervously and trying desperately not to break the silence in this huge house, she tiptoed ever so quietly along the bare boards on the wooden landing. Entering the bathroom, she could not believe her eyes. Never having seen a proper bathroom before, amazement spread across her features at the size of the cast iron bath and the gold-plated taps placed centre stage in the room. Brightly patterned towels were draped over the back of a green brocade chair sat in the corner and along the opposite wall a pedestal and wash basin stood, with a flushing toilet to the right of the door. Ruth knew, even at her young age that luxury like this could only be enjoyed by the very wealthy and would remain only a dream for most people.

Locking the door Ruth decided to risk turning the hot tap on and after a moment or two of gurgling, steaming water gushed forth and she tentatively dipped a foot over the side, before totally submerging herself into the steaming water. Enjoying the luxury of the moment, she began scrubbing herself, trying hard not only to erase the smells and horror of prison away, but thought also that if she scrubbed hard enough it would rid her of the awful memories of the last two years.

It was impossible, the memories remained. They would always remain. But that is all they are. Memories. The only way now is to try and put everything behind her and move forward. How long she spent in the bath, Ruth had no idea, luxuriating in the steam and the heat, before, finally and reluctantly, she let the water drain away.

There was no doubt she was growing up fast. Drying herself off, she rubbed so hard until her skin glowed, then suddenly caught sight of her reflection in the full-length mirror stood in the far corner of the room. She studied herself. Never in the past having chance to be a vain person, she was shocked at the transformation. The once skinny body was beginning to fill out, even though living on scraps. Oh, she could still see her ribs, but her breasts were forming, the legs lengthening. Running a brush through her short hair, she posed and preened in front of the mirror before donning dressing gown to return to her room.

Now she must choose a dress suitable for… suitable for what? She had no idea what was expected of her. Skimming through the dresses, they would all fit her. But who did they belong to, or who were they intended for?

Chapter 20

Doubts crept into her mind, spoiling the initial delight she had felt. Pretty gowns, dresses, shoes, bonnets, ribbons of every colour adorned the shelves. Shocked, Ruth stood and stared until the chill of the day brought goose bumps to her flesh. After the horrors of prison, feeling the smooth, silkiness of the underwear against her skin and the warmth of the gowns was heaven.

Standing once again in front of the long mirror, Ruth felt uncomfortable, out of place. The ragged urchin had disappeared. No, Ruth thought, I'm still the ragged street urchin underneath that nobody wants. A new outfit of clothes cannot take that away. But she had to admit, the reflection shocked her, only the short-cropped hair belying her background.

The ringing of a bell brought her back to reality. Peeping out through the door and down the staircase, she noticed Bella with trays of food disappear into one of the rooms which she presumed must be the dining room. Her stomach churned, having eaten nothing but the sandwich that Evelyn had brought her earlier and night was now closing in. Tip toeing downstairs, Ruth sneaked a look through one of the doors in the hallway. It must be the library. Every wall shelved and stacked with books.

"Looking for something to pinch, Miss Brennan?"

Ruth jumped back as the Judge loomed into view. As she turned to face him, a look of disbelief spread across his countenance, the colour draining from his features, leaving the jet-black eyes in the now pallid face like luminous pools of water. He rubbed his eyes and stared again.

"What's wrong, sir? Haven't you seen a young girl before?" Ruth asked.

"Yes, yes," he said, flustered, "but I was just so shocked at the change in you. I can't believe it. For the better I might add. Your previous... er, uniform did nothing to flatter you, but I see you have found something that suits you perfectly. A really good choice, Ruth." He was now beginning to regain his composure. "Come, we shall have dinner." At that moment Bella passed with a tray of hot food that smelt so good, Ruth nearly snatched it from her such was her hunger.

"Bella, would you be good enough to set another place alongside my wife and I for dinner. Ruth will be eating with us."

"Of course, sir," Bella replied, almost mechanically.

"Follow me, Ruth." And he strode off down the long hall until opening a door on his right. The dining room, with its floor to ceiling windows, was moderately furnished, the large table and candelabra set out to take centre stage. Knives, forks, spoons, so much cutlery, Ruth was unsure which to use first. Serviettes set alongside small plates with bread rolls and a bottle of red wine already uncorked. Ruth could not believe her eyes, but, after suffering so many setbacks, she knew she must be always alert to any dangers that may crop up in the future.

Judge Durville's wife was already seated, hunched up, at the table, her sticks within easy reach alongside her chair. The long grey hair which had been tied back when Ruth met her was now almost waist length, passing like waves over her shoulders, while the dull grey eyes, staring out of pinched features, took in Ruth's new appearance.

"This is Ruth, Miriam. She is going to look after you for a while."

"I know that, John. Ruth and I have already met. She arrived here before you, remember. But I don't see how this slip of a girl can look after me. She isn't the size of anything."

"We shall talk about it later," John said with a finality that clearly meant the conversation was finished as far as he was concerned. Noticing Ruth's

Chapter 20

uncertainty, John pulled a chair back from the table and motioned for her to sit down as he began to pour the wine.

The meal was eaten in silence, apart from the chinking sound of knives on plates and although Ruth tried not to rush, she was so hungry that she wolfed the food down, only looking up on finishing to notice John watching her closely. "When did you last eat, Ruth?" he asked. The clock was now striking seven.

"Evelyn brought me a sandwich today, sir, then before that it was yesterday morning. I am sorry if I appear bad mannered but I was so hungry, I felt ill."
"Did you enjoy the meal," he asked.

"Yes, sir. That is the first proper meal I have had in years." Bella came to take the plates. Ruth stole a glance in her direction but Bella never acknowledged her.

John eventually broke the long silence. "I hope you like your room Ruth and if there is anything you require let me know."

"The room is fine, sir. There is nothing more that I want. I would like to ask that you be patient with me for a few days until I know my way about and what is expected of me and I will do my best. If you will explain my duties for tomorrow then I should like to go to my room as it has been a very long and exciting day."

"Very well. Your day will begin at six thirty to be ready to help Mrs Durville dress at seven a.m. Bella will see to all meals. Your duty is to see that my wife is kept warm and anything she needs I leave it to you as I will be working. As you can see, you will of course be at her beck and call, but in return, as Miriam is a retired school teacher, she will give you all the education you need and more if you are willing to learn. Sunday, once a month will be your day off when you can do as you want once Mrs Durville is up and dressed. Is that understood?"

"Yes, sir," and with that Ruth left the table and retired to the quiet solitude and sanctity of her very own room.

Chapter 21

Once in the privacy of her bedroom, Ruth leapt onto the huge bed and lay out at full stretch, still not quite able to grasp the magnitude of what had happened. As darkness crept in, a light tapping on the door brought her back to reality and jumping off the bed, answered the knock. Bella asked if she could lay the fire ready for morning. Smiling, Ruth welcomed her in, swinging the door wide to let her enter. While Bella placed the paper and kindling in the open grate, Ruth asked, "How long have you lived here, Bella?"

"All my life," she replied.

Shutting the door and almost in a whisper, Ruth said, "Do you know where I was before I came here, Bella. I was in prison for pinching. I was a pickpocket. Why would the Judge take me out of prison? Surely not just to look after his wife. I am only twelve years old. I barely know how to look after myself, let alone an old lady who is almost bedridden. Don't you find it strange Bella?"

"Not for me to say, miss."

"Why are you so unhappy here, Bella. I can see it in your face. You're frightened and nervous. What is wrong? Can't you see I want to be your friend?"

"You cannot help me. No one can."

Chapter 21

"If you don't tell me I can't help. But sometimes just someone to talk to is better than nothing. I remember I had a friend in the Orphanage called Jim and when I had no one to turn to, he became my true friend and we would sit and talk and make plans for the future, how we were going to escape the cruelty, dirt and poverty. We planned to run off into the wide world, away from all the cruel people who were making our lives a misery and make our fortunes to live in a mansion like this." She cast her eyes around the room. "This is a mansion, a castle, a fairy story."

Bella turned to Ruth with a fierce intensity, almost hissing the words. "You have come to an evil place. You must not stop here. It is not what it seems." Ruth's skin prickled on hearing these words.

"If it is evil, Bella, why do you stay? Tell me please, Bella I have a right to know," Ruth begged her.

Bella began to sob and through the tears she said, "I have no choice, I have to stay. My mother used to work here before her death. She died when giving birth to me, and the Durville's, through a sense of duty I suppose, have kept me ever since."

"You must be happy here then."

"Happy. You think I'm happy. I have no life. I'm a prisoner here. Oh, they keep me and feed me all right but he has punished me for years. I shouldn't be telling you this. I will get into trouble. Promise you won't tell?" Her gaze once more lowered to the carpet. Ruth's eyes widened in disbelief.

"I promise I won't tell. I will help you. I told you so. Is it the Judge who is doing these wicked things?"

A knock at the door. Bella leapt from the bed like a startled animal, holding a finger to her lips, frightened that Ruth would betray her.

"Are you in there, Bella." Judge Durville's voice.

"Yes, sir, just laying the fire. Almost done," then in a whisper to Ruth, "please don't tell." And with that she rushed to the door and was gone.

Undressing, Ruth chose a nightgown from the wardrobe and lay in the comfortable bed and her thoughts wandered to Jim. What will he be doing? Will he be lying awake thinking of me? He won't know where I am, or what has happened to me. After mulling it over in her mind, she decided the first chance that arose she would find her way back to the Orphanage to see him. And with this uppermost in her mind, succumbed to the luxury of the bed and the warmth of the room and drifted off into a deep sleep.

Chapter 22

At six a.m. Ruth was wide awake, having slept soundly all night and was soon ready to help Mrs Durville and it was only now she began to worry just how useless the old lady's limbs really were and if she would be strong enough to manage her. Creeping quietly downstairs, the house as silent as a grave, Ruth tapped quietly on the door and heard her call, "Enter."

Ruth dipped a curtsey on entering, hoping it was the right thing to do. The old lady sat up in bed and barely had the strength to swing her scrawny legs over the edge.

"Bring me my clothes, girl," she ordered.

"My name is Ruth if you don't mind. How would you like to be addressed, Mrs Durville? Should I call you Mrs Durville, Madam, or My Lady?" Ruth said this as she went to the huge wardrobe to take her clothes out, feeling the grey, sunken eyes following her.

"Confident young thing aren't you? Madam will be fine." Ruth stole a quick glance through the chink in the curtains and noted the sun rising. "Seeing as it is going to be a bright, sunny day, I think these will look nice on you. Come, let me help you get dressed then I will plait your hair, like my mother taught me." After the effort of dressing, Miriam sat breathing hard. It had tired her. Ruth also found it hard work, almost having to do everything for her. While recovering Ruth took the comb and brush from the dressing table and began to brush the long grey hair until it was as soft as silk in her hands, hoping against hope she could remember her mother's teachings. It seemed such a long time ago. A stab of longing for the past seized her young heart, her eyes moistening as memories flooded back of when she used to sit and brush the silken hair of her mother. Fiercely fighting her rising emotions and the everthreatening tears, she knew she could not afford to dwell on the past. Only the future mattered now.

The old lady's hair shone silvery bright in the early morning sunshine by the time Ruth had finished and she coiled the long plait into a bun. Grabbing the mirror from the dressing table, Ruth proudly showed off her handiwork. The thin lips split into a smile that seemed more a grimace of pain than a smile to Ruth, before she gathered her sticks from the corner of the room.

"Come, we will go down for breakfast." More an order than an invitation. Ruth realized she would have to be very careful, not being used to so much food, living mainly on bread and water for the last couple of years or more. As Miriam entered the dining room downstairs, John remarked on how well she looked and appeared pleased with how Ruth had coped. Again, the meal was eaten in complete silence with only the clatter of plates as Bella cleared away. Then Miriam spoke directly to Ruth.

"Come, Ruth, we will retire to the library where you can read to me."

"My reading may not be good enough but I will try my best, madam."

"I will help you, child, if you stumble." She was beginning to soften and show a certain kindness. And kindness was something that Ruth had not witnessed since her mother died.

They made their way slowly to the Library and once there Miriam pointed to a book half open on the cluttered table by her chair. Ruth began to read, hesitantly at first, then, gaining in confidence, found she needed very few corrections from the old lady and felt very pleased with herself, thankful of her early interest in reading at school. After a while Miriam's head rolled to one side and long painful sighs whistled forth through the thin lips, so while peacefully asleep, Ruth took the opportunity to study the room.

A large desk littered with papers stood toward the back of the room, with

Chapter 22

a writing pad and brass ink stand alongside, along with a couple of glass paperweights, while Miriam had chosen her favourite high-backed chair facing the fireplace in which to drop to sleep. There was more writing material and a pile of books placed here on a small table within easy reach for her. Wandering over to the numerous rows of books that lined the walls from floor to ceiling, Ruth found many to be old law books, most of them it seemed unused now as a film of dust had settled on and around them. But with careful study of each book spine and plenty of time on her hands, she did recognize some which would make suitable reading for herself, already thinking she must ask Mrs Durville if she could borrow one to take to her room.

Chapter 23

The clatter of horses' hooves and the noise of early morning activity as the day came alive, drew Ruth to the slightly open window facing onto the main street. Still quite in awe of her sumptuous surroundings, she gazed out, amazed at the splendour of the sweeping crescent of houses, and the park opposite adorned with blossoming trees across the way, the entrance of which could be gained through a wrought iron archway and heavy metal gates just across from the front entrance of where she now lived. Far in the distance, the unmistakable outline of the Minster, standing proud and stark on the skyline.

Finally, dragging herself away from the window and returning to the book shelves she lifted a book from the shelf and began to read to pass the time until her employer roused as she was still sleeping soundly and quietly at present. Ruth could not believe how her fortunes had changed so dramatically and intended to do her utmost to keep the old lady happy and enjoy this time to herself for as long as it lasted.

In the peaceful silence, she heard the front door open. Maybe Mr Durville forgot something, Ruth thought. Peeping out of the library, she secretly hoped Bella would hear but she was busy in the kitchen. A young man entered. Tall and quite handsome in a foppish sort of way. Slick black hair, drawn tightly back, cravat at the chin and tight fawn coloured breeches and

Chapter 23

with highly polished knee boots it made Ruth think he was a man of the gentry. Carrying a cane and top hat, he was just the sort of man that Jim sorted out as a target for easy pickings. Ruth tried to dodge back out of sight but was too slow, the man spotted her, ordering her to stay where she was, before sauntering over. It was more of a swagger really. His eyes swept over Ruth from top to bottom.

"Come here, girl. Do not hide from me." An air of arrogance about him that set Ruth on edge.

"I was not hiding from you, sir. I just came to see who was making all the noise. Madam is asleep."

"Who are you and what are you doing here, may I ask?" This said in a sneering, contemptuous voice.

"You may ask. My name is Ruth and I work here looking after Mrs Durville."

"Since when?"

"This past week."

"On whose authority?"

"On Judge Durville's authority."

"He found you in the gutter no doubt?" He took his cane, lifted it to Ruth's chin, tilting her head back as if surveying horse flesh, slowly striding around her before coming back into view.

Ruth's flesh crawled. There was a look in his eyes that frightened her and for the first time, she backed away and she somehow knew what he was thinking. Knowing she would have to make an excuse to be rid of him she said, "I will have to go now as Madam may be awake, sir." Ruth turned to enter the library. He was quicker and blocked the door.

"Do you not want to know who I am, or what I am doing here?"

"None of my business, sir. Now, if you will please step aside, I have to see to Mrs Durville."

He stepped aside and with a sigh of relief Ruth entered the room and turned the key. She did not want to come into contact with him again.

Ruth was kept busy for most of the day with Miriam and her only chance in catching Bella on her own was when she entered her room to lay the fire for next morning.

"Bella, did you see the man who called this morning?" Bella's face lost its colour and she busied herself with the paper and kindling. "That is the master's son, Henry."

"I bet he's a nasty piece of work, I don't like him at all, Bella. He frightens me." Ruth was studying Bella's reaction and noticed tears spring to her eyes.

"What is it Bella? Is this the man you're afraid of?" When Bella refused to answer, Ruth became persistent and faced the young girl. Finally, Bella flung herself into Ruth's arms and broke down in tears, the full sordid story finally gushing out as the flood gates opened to a torrent of words.

Bella had fallen in love with Henry and he had taken advantage of her vulnerability by assuring her they would be married as soon as she was old enough. She knew it was wrong but she really believed he loved her. Henry had told her more than once never to mention their love as she was underage and he would be thrown out and be cut from his father's inheritance and then there would be no chance of marriage. Frightened for her well-being, Bella went along with the affair, secretly enjoying the short moments of stolen passion when Henry called, as he introduced her more and more into his world of illicit sex. She never saw him any other time.

Ruth held her close, rocking her as you would a baby and eventually the sobbing subsided but Ruth continued talking in a soothing voice, stroking her hair and wiping away the tears until Bella's body ceased its trembling.

"Please, you must not breathe a word of this to anyone Ruth. Do you promise?" Ruth nodded. Bella continued, "I have been going to run away many times but I had nowhere to go. I didn't have the courage, Ruth." Bella sat on the bed, the two girls still clutching each other. Although Bella had control of herself now, she was a pale ghost of a figure that appeared lost. Ruth knew the feeling only too well and her heart went out to her.

"Oh, Bella, running away is not going to help. You have got to tell someone. You will never keep it a secret forever. What about the Master? I'm sure he will understand if you explain what has happened."

Bella snorted with laughter "What! When I march in and tell him I'm going to marry his son. I don't think so!"

Chapter 23

"But we have to do something." Ruth screwed her eyes tight as if to concentrate harder in search for a solution but to no avail. "Anything would be better than the suffering you are going through at present, Bella. We have got to come up with a plan of some kind. Did he touch you this morning?"

A whispered, "Yes, but it's not that he forces me, Ruth. Oh, you won't understand, you're too young. I want him too, even though I know it's wrong but when he touches me, I can't help but do it with him. Every time afterwards, I feel like killing myself for being so weak but I haven't even got the courage to do that."

As Bella told her story, Ruth realized just how much she herself had matured in the last couple of years. But then experiences suffered had made her learn quickly to survive and although not experiencing anything with men like Bella she began to wonder how it would feel.

"You do realize he has no intention of marrying you Bella, he is just leading you on."

"I do now. But for a long time, I believed him."

Ruth was wide eyed in amazement at this girl, only slightly older than herself, knowing what to do with a man. But there again, maybe she didn't know, as Henry would be worldly wise and be the teacher, knowing what to do. Ruth was thoughtful for a minute as Jim came to mind and she felt a warm feeling inside. She pushed these thoughts and strange feelings to the back of her mind.

"We need more time to think, Bella. How often does he call?"

"Maybe twice a week, sometimes three times, always during the day when the master is at work and the old lady is asleep."

"Right, here's what we will do. And for this to work, you must keep out of his way and not allow him near you. He is a worthless toad and you are better than that, Bella. Now listen to me, we carry on as normal the next time he calls. Make sure you are busy or out for the day, even if you have to hide or sneak away somewhere. I shall try and keep Miriam awake for longer. But you must be strong Bella. It won't work if you fall into his arms every time he calls. Promise you'll give it a try."

"I will. Now I have someone to help me."

Ruth smiled. Her plan seemed workable, for a time at least. Bella smiled back, relief clear on her face.

"Thank you, Ruth. I do feel better now that I know I have someone on my side."

Chapter 24

Ruth managed Miriam very well for the next few days as all she really wanted was help in bathing and dressing, her hair brushed and plaited, a little bit of pampering and reading to until falling asleep.

Ruth even found time to pick flowers from the garden when venturing out to run errands during the day. These she placed in a vase found on top of the book shelves, creating a beautiful aroma to the room which Miriam was delighted with and decided it should be done at least once a week.

The constant reading, which Ruth enjoyed, brought her education along as Miriam helped her with the understanding and meaning of words. Miriam also focussed on opening Ruth's eyes to the larger world with geography and history lessons. It proved better than any school lessons with one to one teaching and Ruth, her brain taking in as much information as possible, loved it.

Having been totally engrossed with her education and also committed to the care of Miriam, then on top of that Bella's troubles, Ruth suddenly realized her first day to herself was almost upon her and began planning excitedly as to how she could possibly make contact with Jim again.

Bella worked on a Sunday so it would not be possible to ask her to do it and, anyway, Ruth so wanted to see Jim herself.

The only possible way to do it safely would be to find her way back to the Orphanage, if she dared, and sneak in hoping to spot Jim. But then, she may not have to sneak in. Who would recognize her now, dressed as she was in such smart new clothes. No, I will march up to the front door and ask to see my long-lost brother Jim, even if it is 'old hatchet face.'

That night Ruth retired early to bed but the excitement of what lay ahead kept her awake, tossing and turning until the early hours of the morning.

Chapter 25

Across the landing, Bella also lay in bed, an open book by her side but unable to concentrate on reading. A knot of uncertainty lodged like lead in the very pit of her stomach, such was the frightening thought of what lay ahead. An involuntary shiver rippled through her body each time sleep threatened, as a realistic image of a hooded, but faceless figure of a young mother dressed in rags, hunkered down on her haunches to protect against the cold of the day, cradling a new born baby in her arms, forced onto the streets and begging for scraps from passers-by to stay alive.

Bella tried every way possible to push these morbid thoughts from her mind but nothing worked. With sleep unlikely, she rose from the bed and settled herself in the easy chair by the fireside, trying hard to think rationally on a way to figure out a solution.

Running a hand over her stomach, she could not be sure if it was her over active imagination or was there a life growing inside her? Maybe there was a slight swelling, causing a tautness of the skin. All she knew for certain was that if she was pregnant, if left longer it would soon begin to feel a part of her.

In quieter moments such as this, her thoughts ran riot, finding it impossible to think straight, apprehension clouding her troubled mind at what lay ahead. But she also felt relief after confiding her secret to Ruth.

What did worry her was the uncertainty that she may not possess the courage to free herself from Henry's Svengali like grip, because, in truth, he did terrify her, appearing to gain sadistic satisfaction in witnessing her suffer. The memory of the last time they made love crawled into her consciousness. There was no tenderness, no gentle caressing of her body, no whispered endearments saying he loved her. After a quick check to make sure they would not be disturbed, Henry quickly stripped the clothes from her body and forced her down onto the bed, before satisfying his lust, leaving her weeping, feeling hurt, used and dirty. She tried to cling to him, to hold him, yearning for him to say, "I love you, Bella," but only suffered the humiliation of him pushing her away and stalking out.

But now it was more than just the disdainful and degrading way Henry treated her. She had become listless and tired, the strength draining from her body. All chores were becoming an effort now, the days long, hard and laborious, whatever her tasks. How long should she carry on? More to the point, how long before someone noticed?

If a doctor were to be called in, how could that be explained? She had already lumbered Ruth with the truth of Henry being her secret lover, it didn't seem right to burden her with more, especially after the life she had endured. Oh, if only she was as strong as Ruth. But she wasn't, she realized that.

In the back of her mind Bella knew the only way out of her predicament, if she was bearing Henry's child, was an abortion. She'd heard of places where you could go and that, as far as she could see, was her only option. The money wasn't a problem for her as she had that saved and secreted away. Even if it cost everything she had, it would be worth it.

Finally, praying and hoping her nerve did not fail her, Bella settled on this as her plan, and feeling more positive on what she would do, she clambered back into bed.

But then, maybe there was another way. What if she told Henry? He may know a way out of this. After all, he would not want a prison sentence hanging over him, or even a scandal. Whatever, the decision would have to be made soon, before it became noticeable.

Chapter 26

Jim was also finding sleep difficult as he lay in bed racking his brain and trying to think of a way to get in touch with Ruth. He hadn't heard a dicky bird now for well over a month, but that was understandable, as when Billy returned with the message telling him that she missed him, she did add that he'd better be careful as the police were still on the lookout for him. Jim had paid Billy to once again take a note to the prison, but this time the information was that Ruth had appeared in court and nobody knew quite where she had gone, or what had happened to her.

So, over the next few days, Jim tried working out how to escape the Orphanage for a few hours each day so he might have a chance of finding something out. At least he could scour the streets in the hope of seeing her, but deep down he knew he was going to need much more help if he was to be successful. She could be anywhere by now. But who could he turn to? Billy had mentioned to him that he thought Sergeant Porritt looked a 'bit shifty' as though he might take a bribe if shown some cash. It's worth a try, he thought. It is risky, but that's what I'll do, I'll risk the police station.

Next day when classes finished and all was quiet Jim wriggled through the grating and quickly made his way through the back streets that led to where his secret hoard was stashed away and pocketed what he thought would be enough cash and made for the Police Station. Many times he nearly turned and fled but, with thumping heart, he plucked up courage and knocked on the large blue door. The hollow echo of footsteps sounded in the big entrance hall, the door creaking open just enough for a face to appear and mutter, "What do you want you young ruffian? Clear off before I give you a clip round the ear." It was Porritt.

"Sorry to bother you, Sergeant, but I thought you might be able to help me. I'm trying to find the girl that was locked up in here about a month since. She's my sister you see and I can't find her anywhere."

Porritt opened the door wider, continuing to study this ragged little boy closely. "You're not the same one that called last time," he judged after a while.

"No, that was my younger brother." The lie came swiftly off Jim's lips.

"Hmm. Well, yes, I do remember her as a matter of fact. Sweet little thing. Had a rough time of it by all accounts. I don't know what happened her but, she'll come through, she seemed like a fighter." He turned as if to walk away.

"I have some money if that'll help," offered Jim. Porritt stopped mid stride, turned back and bent down so he was face to face with Jim.

"How much?" he whispered.

"A shilling," said Jim holding the coin in front of the officer. Porritt made a grab for it, but Jim was quicker.

"Not until you tell me where she is."

"You crafty little sod. Erm, well, I suppose I can tell you. I remember Evelyn came to collect her for a court appearance in front of Judge Durville and he would be passing sentence on her. So, as she couldn't come back here and she isn't at the Orphanage, he may have sent her to the workhouse. That's the only other place I can think of. You could ask the Judge."

"But I don't know where he lives. And another thing, if I turn up on his doorstep like this, he might lock me up."

"Well, for another shilling I have his address," said Porritt, now holding the upper hand.

"You greedy old git." Jim scowled, annoyed that Porritt had got the better of him as he ferreted another coin from his pocket and held it up.

"He resides at Number 10, Darwin Court, toward the better end of York,"

Chapter 26

Porritt said pompously, "but if you don't have any luck, pop back tomorrow as Evelyn will be in and she will definitely know what happened."

"Eeh, thanks, Sergeant. That's really good of you," and with a cheeky grin Jim handed the money over. He felt happier than he had ever done since Ruth was caught. He turned away with a spring in his step and a tuneless whistle on his lips as he made his way through the now busy market stalls, slipping a couple of apples into his pockets along the way. Well, all this detective work was tiring. He needed to keep his strength up, didn't he?

Chapter 27

Jim sauntered over to the nearest hackney cab stand, where he stood, hands in pockets, just hanging about within earshot of where the customers were heading. It required patience and some restraint on his part, but he was in no rush. Sooner or later he knew someone would ask for somewhere close to the Darwin Court area. If nothing else Jim was knowledgeable about certain areas of the city of York and soon his patience paid off as a well to do couple sauntered up to the driver. "Could you possibly take us to 20, Darwin Court please, cabbie."

"Right you are, sir." And the driver promptly swung the door open for the lady to step inside. Jumping back atop the cab, the driver picked up the reins and with a rattle of carriage wheels and jingling of harness they were on their way. Once on the move, Jim quickly sneaked in behind it, leaping onto the small running board right at the back and then hung on for grim death. Well out of sight of the driver, he kept his eyes open for any policemen. After ten minutes Jim's arms were almost dropping off, aching with the strain and hoping they would soon be there. He couldn't hold on much longer.

He'd heard about the posh area of Darwin Court, but had never been there before and he now noticed the buildings getting brighter and higher, the streets cleaner. The men wore top hats and the ladies were in brightly

Chapter 27

coloured hooped skirts that swished about them as they walked. No rubbish littered the streets here and Jim realized he was entering a totally different world from the one he was forced to live in.

On hearing a shout from inside the cab, "I believe the next road is Darwin Court, cabbie," Jim thought it time to jump off. As the horse slowed to a walk, Jim dropped lightly to his feet behind the cab and straight away wished that his clothes were in a better state as people began staring at him.

But his resolve stiffened, he had come this far and was not about to back down now as he entered the wide crescent shaped row of houses that was Darwin Court.

Bolstered with excitement in the hope of finding news about Ruth, or, if he was really lucky, maybe seeing her again. Lost deep in thought, Jim finally raised his head and there before him, in highly polished brass, shining boldly in the bright sunlight, the number ten. This was his destination.

He drew a quick breath as he noticed the smooth, clean sandstone steps with the wrought iron railings leading up to the entrance. Large windows, with lace curtains at every one, towered above him.

Jim pondered on what to do next, not sure if he had the courage to knock at the door or if it would be better to wait and see if anyone called or anyone came out. Trouble was, this posh area made him feel very scruffy and selfconscious. Many people walked past pretending not to notice him, others ignorantly just turning their heads as if he didn't exist. Jim sat on the steps hoping for inspiration on what to do for what seemed like hours, unaware of a pair of brooding dark eyes staring out of a lower window at him. Suddenly the front door opened. Jim shot up and turned to see the massive frame of Judge Durville standing before him, filling the door frame with his bulk.

"What are you doing here, young man. I have been watching you from the window and I would rather you moved on before you get into trouble."

Caught off guard, Jim found himself stuttering, lost for words, finally spluttering out, "Er, I'm looking for a friend of mine called Ruth from the Orphanage. I'd heard she was in trouble and you might know where she is."

The Judge looked left and right, before ushering Jim inside, guiding the youngster into his office.

Jim grabbed his battered old cap from off his head, wringing it hard between his hands nervously as he stood before the big man in silence, not knowing what to expect. The man's eyes never seemed to waver from Jim's face, as if boring into his very soul.

The big man eventually eased his vast bulk into a chair and finally answered Jim's question. "Yes, your information is correct. You must be Jim. Ruth told me about you being a true friend to her, that you helped her enormously through the difficult time spent at the Orphanage. Ruth works here now and has a different life from what she has experienced before. She has settled in nicely and I would rather she has no more contact with people who may drag her back into trouble. She now has a chance to make something of her life from now on and I do not want to see her revert back to the devious ways of her past. Do I make myself clear?"

Jim's mouth had suddenly gone quite dry, like sandpaper, but he knew he must ask the question. "Yes, but why did you take her out of prison and bring her here? She should've come back to the Orphanage where she had friends."

"That is really none of your business but I shall tell you why. It was because of her age, Ruth should never have gone to prison. Not only that, after speaking to her, I thought the girl deserved better than being locked up with common criminals or with the waifs and strays in the Orphanage at such a young age, especially after she explained her circumstances. I had the authority to do something about it and did so. But, let me tell you one thing before you go. Ruth would not say who her accomplice was on her thieving spree, but I believe I now know the answer. You are a very brave man to come here and see me in my own home."

Jim's face paled and he looked down at the floor. He couldn't hold the gaze of those black pearls. What would happen now? He knew he was in trouble.

"I didn't know what else to do." Jim whispered this.

"Before you go, I just want you to know that I understand what many of you children are going through..."

Chapter 27

This proved the final straw for Jim and he suddenly lost control, his fiery temperament letting him down.

"Understand?" Jim butted in, anger flaring, chin jutting stubbornly out, his top lip quivering with emotion. "Understand. No, you don't understand one bit. None of your sort will ever understand what us children go through and what we suffer. It's not our fault we do what we do, or that we have no proper clothes. It's people like you that never understand and never, ever do anything to help." This was typical Jim, going all out, not thinking, just wading in, resentment boiling up at the mistreatment over the years. How all the children like himself were treated.

The Judge let him simmer down until silence reigned in the room. "Have you quite finished, young man?" the Judge asked.

"Yes." Sullen now as he realized he'd overstepped the mark with this man.

"You may not believe me, Jim, but I am beginning to see the faults in the system and what actually goes on. Most of the time it is not your fault, and it has taken a young girl like Ruth to make me realize that sometimes, some of you, are forced into crime by circumstances far beyond your control. But that does not give you the right to take the law into your own hands for whatever purpose and steal. Now, your friend Ruth has a genuine feeling for what is right and wrong and I will send you away with those thoughts if that is any help. Goodbye, Jim"

Jim didn't answer, preferring to stay silent, head bent with nothing to say. Feeling very miserable at this sudden rejection, he shuffled out into the bright sunlight, heart laying heavy as lead in his chest. I should have asked to see her, he thought, and pondered with the idea of waiting outside, out of the big man's sight of course, and waiting to see her. But what if Ruth didn't want to see him, if she turned her head away? That would be unbearable. Despondent, Jim wondered if they would ever meet up again. Suddenly, he couldn't hold back the tears of rage as, with trudging footsteps, he walked forlornly back to the Orphanage.

Deep in thought, Jim realized he must change his ways and leave the life he was leading. But how? He knew, if he wanted to see Ruth again, and he did, with such a longing it hurt, the only way was to somehow find a job.

The Judge's words rang in his ears "she is not to fall back into her old life."

These words haunted him as he dropped to sleep that night, vowing to get a job. Then, by God, someday he would walk back up those steps a different man.

Chapter 28

Bella decided the time had come to confront Henry the next time he called. Keeping a watch for visitors, Bella finally saw him step from the cab and luckily it was Ruth's day off. Scuttling quickly back to the kitchen, she thought it best to appear busy by washing and drying the pans. After a few minutes, footsteps sounded outside the door and in walked Henry.

"So, you have come out of hiding I see, Bella. Has your new-found friend deserted you already? Have you no desire to see me again?" Wandering over, he grabbed her by the hair forcing her head back and crunched his lips roughly onto her soft mouth, waiting until her body responded. But not this time. Cold as ice. He pulled away from her and holding her at arms-length he asked "What has got into you, Bella. All of a sudden, Miss Goody Goody. Don't you like our lovemaking?" he sneered at her.

Finding her voice Bella said, "We must talk Henry. Something serious has happened. I'm with child. Your child and I'm frightened. I don't know what to do."

Henry's face paled. "How do you know?"

"I missed my time. Twice now."

"Good God, you stupid wench. Anyway, what makes you think it's mine? Anybody could have had you." He paced the floor before saying, "Well don't expect me to admit to it. No one will believe you." After a moment's thought, he asked,

"are you going to get rid of it?"

"It is yours, Henry," the hurt showing in her face. "You know you're the only man I've ever had. I was foolish enough to believe what you told me, that you loved me, and at one time we may have had a future together, but I know now that was just to get your way. I see you for what you are, a selfish, dishonest person that treats people like dirt.

Well, you'll be glad to know I do want an abortion, I don't want anything connected with you. Not only that, because if I don't have an abortion I will be out on the street. The only thing I want from you is information on where to go, or what to do, then I hope I never see you again."

Henry could not believe he was getting away so lightly. If this became public knowledge he would be out on his ear and his father would also see that he was cut from his inheritance completely. Henry softened, realizing he needed to talk her through this.

"Listen, Bella, I know this seems a problem but it's not insurmountable. Really it isn't. I'm sorry if I sounded harsh, but it was such a shock, I didn't know what to say. Now, I do happen to know of a woman who does such things, but you must understand, we must keep it quiet and within a couple of days it will all be over with and you keep your position here and no one will be any the wiser. Now, let's get down to business. When is your day off?"

"I have all day tomorrow for myself," she replied, never dreaming it could be over and done with so quickly. No more worrying, no more sleepless nights.

"Right, well that's settled then. Meet me at the entrance to Samuel Street tomorrow morning at nine and by lunchtime it will all be over with. Do you know how to get there?"

"That's a really rough area, isn't it?" Bella's face screwed up with worry.

"No, it's not too bad and after all, what's a couple of hours if it solves the problem. Look, here's the money for a cab. Just ask for Samuel Street, they'll take you straight there."

Chapter 28

"I don't want your stinking money. As I said I don't want anything from the likes of you ever again. I just need you to show me where to go tomorrow and then I never want to see you again." Henry shook his head. "Just as you like. I'll be waiting. Do not be late," and without a backward glance he strode from the room, leaving Bella to worry about whether she had made the right decision.

Chapter 29

Ruth finally managed to find her way to the Orphanage. Strange, now she was dressed in acceptable clothing, everyone she asked proved to be helpful. A cabbie even offered her a free lift but some inner instinct told her not to accept. Thanking him very much, she strode on until reaching the streets she recognized. As Ruth neared the old building, the houses began encroaching as the streets narrowed; the smell from the rotting garbage and rubbish littering the gutters at the side of the roads stung her nostrils and drunks were spilling from nearby pubs, raucous and unruly, even at this time of day. It made her shudder with revulsion and apprehension, as those horrific memories from another life would not let go. Deeper and deeper she went until confronted by the old brick building where she had first met Jim.

Jim, who had watched out for her when she was so far down it didn't seem possible to survive, lifting her spirits so much that it made her feel she could not let him down. Pushing the old iron gate open Ruth knocked at the door. Eventually, footsteps sounded at the other side and the door swung open a few inches and the wizened features of old Jeffers appeared, just managing to poke his head through the small gap.

"Who is it and what do you want?" he croaked, screwing his eyes up against the sun to better see who he was speaking to, not a hint of recognition from

Chapter 29

him, of which Ruth was pleased.

Ruth asked him if it was possible to see Jim.

"Jim. Jim who?"

Ruth suddenly realized she didn't know his surname. "I'm not sure of his second name but he's about this big," she held her hand out to what she thought was about Jim's height, "and he also often got into trouble for fighting."

"Ah, now I know who you mean. A fiery little devil. Aye, always picking fights. Size o' nowt either." Ruth felt like telling the old man it wasn't Jim's fault he was always fighting. Life and the way people treated him made him like that but she held her tongue, thinking it best to just agree with the man.

"Yes, that's the one."

"Oh, he's not here anymore. He left soon after that feisty little girl he befriended disappeared. The police were round asking questions about him as well. Eeh, you aren't a girl he's got into trouble are you, cos he was one for the girls. I think they wanted to mother him." He gave a wheezy laugh that suddenly turned into a coughing fit. When he recovered sufficiently, Ruth answered quite indignantly that how could he think that of her. "Certainly not. It's just that I have a message for him and I need to find him, before he gets into any more trouble."

"Well, I don't think he'll show face here again. I think he burnt his bridges with Miss Wade when he told her she was nothing but a lying old hag after she bad mouthed the young girl he was sweet on.

An inner glow spread rapidly through her. Typical Jim. Still fighting her corner. She must find him somehow. Ruth thought it best not to tell Jeffers she was the girl in question in case he sent for Miss Wade and the last thing she wanted was a confrontation with the evil old woman again.

"Well, did he leave you with any information at all to where he was going?"

"Nope, not that I am aware of but I can ask Miss Wade if you like, if it is very important like. She's about somewhere."

"No, I wouldn't want to bother her," Ruth lied. "Well thank you, Mr Jeffers." Ruth turned to leave, but Jeffers was quick to ask the question.

"Hang on, young lady, just a minute. How did you know my name?"

Ruth, thinking quickly, answered, "Oh, one of the boys told me, Billy I think it was. He told me to ask for you, because you know everything that happens in here."

"Did he now? Well he's right you know, I do know most things," tapping the side of his nose as if this explained everything. Ruth made a quick exit to make the long walk back to Darwin Court no wiser as to the whereabouts of Jim. But she had certainly enjoyed her day of freedom and no one could take that away from her.

Chapter 30

Bella spent a restless night but rose early and left without having to lie to Ruth as to her plans, or her whereabouts. The damp, miserable morning did nothing to lift her spirits as she walked well clear of Darwin court before hailing a passing cab.

"Samuel Street please, driver."

He shot a questioning glance at her. "Are you sure, miss?"

"Yes, quite sure, thank you." But deep inside, she was definitely unsure, her stomach churning at the thought of what lay ahead. It was too far down the line now to change things.

Never having cause to visit Samuel Street before, as they drew closer, the grim truth hit her. Rows of terraced houses, many of them derelict, no longer fit for habitation, windows boarded up, poverty and hardship etched on the faces of every passer-by. What had she let herself in for?

After a long ride, the driver drew to a halt and jumped down, opening the door for Bella. "Here we are, young lady. Now are you quite sure you will be okay?" he said, concern showing on his face. "It is a bit of a rough area you know." He surveyed the narrow, litter strewn street and out of the corner of his eye he spotted Henry Durville duck back into the alley. He knew then what was afoot.

"Do you want me to wait here for you, miss? I gather you shall not be long, here."

"No, thank you, I'll be fine. I have someone to look after me," and she paid the fare, then waited until the cab disappeared from view, before slipping into the obscurity of the street. Henry suddenly appeared from one of the back alleys.

"This is where you need to be," and he tapped on the door. It opened a couple of inches.

"Who is it and what do you want?" It was more of a squawk than a human voice.

"It's me, Henry, you stupid woman. I told you yesterday I was coming. Now open the door and let us in before anyone recognises me."

The door squeaked wider for them both to squeeze into the dark little room. Bella surveyed what she could see of it. A dirty old bed along one wall, the old black fireplace piled high with ash, but no fire burning today and a jug of water next to the bed. Cobwebs, hung as thick as curtains around the only small window, limiting any daylight that threatened to break into the room, creating a claustrophobic atmosphere and Bella, nervous as a kitten, jumped at the sound of the door slamming shut as the old woman shuffled in behind her.

"This is Mrs Jenks, Bella. Tell her what you want and she will take care of you. Right, now if there is nothing else you need, I must be on my way."

"Hey, not so fast, young fella. Mrs Jenks blocked his way out Where's the money you promised?" Henry looked questioningly at Bella.

"Don't worry, Mrs Jenks, I have the money right here," patting her bag. "You better go Henry, get out of our way."

"Very good, young lady, it'll cost you ten pounds." Bella studied the woman more closely. Maybe not as old as she first thought, possibly fifty years old. No more than that. Her clothes were filthy, no better than rags and the ravages of poor living conditions, lack of good food and desperate poverty had left her face and body almost skeletal. She also repeatedly pursed her lips together in a toothless mouth, to make a loud smacking noise which irritated Bella. But Bella knew she had far more to worry about than Mrs Jenks personal habits.

Chapter 30

Turning to Bella, the squawky voice quietened. "You do know this is illegal, don't you? You must never utter a word about it. Not to anyone." She held out her hand for payment. Bella drew the money from her bag and, quick as a flash, the bony fingers snatched it quickly away and stuffed it into her apron pocket.

"I realize that," Bella said. "Now please can we get on with it."

"Impatient little madam aren't you? Right, lay on the bed and take your underclothes off, this won't take long, then I'll give you some medicine to take which will help kill the pain."

"First of all, please tell me what to expect. Will it hurt really badly?" Her insides were contracted with fear at what was about to happen.

"Oh no, just a sharp stabbing pain to start with and then after that, nothing much to bother about," she said in an abrupt, off-handed way. "Now spread your legs and let me do the work."

Bella lay back, skirt waist high and legs apart on the grubby old bed. She felt Mrs Jenks fumbling between her legs, closing her eyes in shame at what was happening. Then a sharp, fiery pain suddenly shot into the pit of her lower stomach, forcing a cry of agony from her lips. Never having suffered such agonising discomfort as this before, she almost passed out. Too stunned to speak, she lay breathing hard, knees crunched to her chest, too frightened to move a muscle, the stabbing painful cramp in her body not releasing its grip.

"Right, cover yourself up girl. All done." Reaching into the cupboard at the side of the fireplace, she poured a foulsmelling medicine into a cup and suddenly nipped Bella's nostrils. When her mouth opened, she quickly and efficiently, poured it down in one fluid movement. It happened so rapidly that the taste hit moments later, which almost made her gag, but with great effort kept it inside her.

"Now, you must take this twice a day for a week. It will help ease the pain and also get the job done sooner. Right, let's see if you can walk," and she helped lift Bella from the bed.

Unsteady on her feet and her insides still on fire, Bella grasped the mantelpiece to save herself from falling, her legs weak. She needed time for the pain to ease, but Mrs Jenks hurriedly shoved the bottle inside Bella's bag and then ushered her to the door.

"Now remember, not a word to anyone and your troubles are over, young girl and let that be a lesson to you." The woman almost shoving Bella outside, as if glad to get rid of the young girl, then slammed the door quickly behind her.

Bella couldn't walk, the agony proving almost too much but, with gritty determination, she somehow managed to stagger to the end of the street, causing a few curious glances along the way, before hailing a cab to take her home, hoping that no one was about to witness her terrible state.

Chapter 31

Henry lay sprawled out on the bed of a room that he rented at the Three Tuns Hostelry whenever his passion needed sedating. With Bella hitting him with the news of her pregnancy, that really was a blow, but he was pretty sure Jenks would take care of that little matter, so, over the next few months he needed to resort to other ways.

The problem was he yearned for young, underage girls. They were his weakness. He knew it was risky, but this risk just heightened his passion, exciting him even more. All had kept their mouths shut when money changed hands, and the landlord was wily enough to know that he would be in bother if ever this reached the public domain, especially with the main culprit the well-to-do Judge Durville's son.

He liked his young girls slim and preferably vulnerable, not the over-age sluts that usually plied their trade around the back streets of the city. Never short of money, the allowance from his father kept him in a manner that proved quite comfortable and that he had become accustomed to. But, just lately, he had spent more time here than he would have liked as Bella had kept out of his way since missing her 'time'. He did wonder if she may have confided in the new girl and could be conspiring against him. If that was the case, then he would have to take Ruth to one side and have a quiet word to make her realize just how vulnerable her position really was. On the other hand, with a little pressure applied, she may come around to his way of thinking. Oh, what a catch that would be.

A gentle knock on the door interrupted this fantasy and Henry shouted, "Enter," and in walked two young, voluptuous girls, both corseted so tight it pushed their pert breasts up high and plump. Giggling and smiling, they swayed across the room as in unison, cheeks ruby red, one carrying a tray with a bottle of wine and glasses. "Your wine, sir, just as you ordered," flashing a smile at Henry as she placed it gently on the bedside table.

"Thank you. Now girls, before we get down to business, tell me your names."

"I'm Emma. This is my sister Nancy and I'm the oldest," answered Emma, giggling as she did so.

"So, siblings are we. I don't think I have had the pleasure of bedding siblings. How old are you?"

"Fifteen, sir," replied Emma, "and Nancy, thirteen."

"Have you had sex before, either of you?"

This brought them into fits of giggles again. "Oh no, we are both virgins. Never known a man, sir. Don't do that sort of thing, sir. We're good girls."

"Then what are you doing coming to my room done up like a couple of whores and acting like grown women?"

"We was asked to come and entertain you and that's what we're about to do."

Henry had risen from the bed when the girls entered and strutted across the room, never taking his eyes from them.

"Now, if sir would like to just settle himself on the bed, we will show you our speciality. Nancy, pour the drinks please, then we can all have a glass of wine, while I make you comfortable."

Henry now became interested and lay back down on the bed. Nancy brought the wine as Emma began to unbutton his shirt and run her fingers through the thick thatch of hair covering his chest.

"Put more coal on the fire, Nancy. We don't want sir catching his death, do we now?" A conspiratorial wink past between the two.

"My, what a fine body you have, sir. It fair ripples under my touch. Here, have some more of this lovely wine," and Nancy filled his glass to the brim again.

"Now let me pull those boots off for you, sir. Done up in all your finery doesn't do you justice. I really want to see what you have to offer under all these lovely clothes." She said this with a wicked giggle and a mischievous gleam in her eye.

Henry couldn't believe his luck. Old Tom had certainly come up trumps with these two fine wenches for him this time. Different from the sluts he usually had to put up with.

"There now, does that feel better. Have another little sip of wine and then lay back and relax. I'll just undo your belt. Not too much eh, don't want you to think I'm that sort of girl, sir." Henry did as he was bid but the trouble was, he was beginning to feel drowsy.

"Come on girls, get on with it, I haven't got all night you know." His speech was beginning to slur as he took another gulp of wine before dropping back on the bed, his eyes closing.

Emma caressed his chest for a few more minutes, then loosened his belt further and pushed her hand down his trousers. There was no response from Henry. His head lolled to one side and his eyes remained closed.

"Well, if anything was going to rouse him that should have done, cos I gave him a good old nip that would have raised old Nick himself," and they both collapsed in a fit of giggles.

"Quickly now, let's see what he's got in his pockets."

Nancy sifted through his jacket and came up with a solid gold pocket watch and some small change, but Emma found his wallet stuffed with five-pound notes. Her mouth dropped open.

"Good God, Nancy, how much do you think we should take." The girls had never seen so much money.

"Well, let's see. Why don't we sit here a while longer, finish the other bottle of wine, then take the lot?" Then they both collapsed in laughter.

Chapter 32

More than a week passed without incident, although Bella appeared more subdued than ever. Ruth asked if she could help, but Bella told her she just felt a little weak and although Ruth found the old lady very hard work, her learning was coming on a treat and Miriam appeared to enjoy passing on her knowledge to such an eager pupil.

Although only one day off a month, she was now becoming accustomed to this living in luxury, so different from anything that had gone before. Her only disappointment was in losing touch with Jim and for the life of her could not fathom out a way on how to make contact. It was these thoughts of Jim that flooded her mind while preparing Miriam for bed after the old lady began complaining of tiredness. By the time Ruth finished, night was closing in but, seeing it was still early evening, once Miriam drifted off to sleep, Ruth returned to the library, drew the curtains for privacy and to make it more cosy and secure, then began reading. Ruth always looked forward to these times as whenever her charge was awake, she was always at her beck and call and sometimes Ruth began to think the old lady had got used to having the company of someone around her, whereas before, a very lonely life beckoned with her husband working such long hours and a son that never actually had time to see her.

Chapter 32

Miriam was very good and Ruth had thanked her lucky stars every day since she arrived at Darwin Court, but moments such as this were precious to her as the old lady could be very demanding. So, making the most of this quiet time, Ruth was well immersed in a book when the door suddenly burst open and in strode her worst nightmare, Henry. Ruth shot up out of her chair, the hairs on her neck bristling with fright.

"How dare you barge in like this, Mr Durville. Did no one teach you to knock before entering?"

"I have the best of manners when needed in the company of my betters but I do not feel I should make you aware of how and when I enter my own home, especially to servants." Ruth bit back on the anger that welled up inside her. She had never known she possessed such rage but she forced herself to keep calm.

Curtly and under control she said, "Should I ring for the master and let him know you are here?"

"No, you know that is not possible, Ruth. The master has not returned from work and my mother is safely tucked up in bed. There are only you two young girls alone in this big rambling house."

"What do you want?" Ruth by now was up out of her chair, standing guardedly with her back to the huge fireside.

"Well, I would have thought that is obvious." His eyes never wavering from her as he spoke. "Bella has been unavailable, for whatever reason, these last few times I have called round and I wonder if you two girls have been talking. Do you know more than you are letting on, Ruth? Has Bella been confiding in you?" The sneer more prominent as he closed upon Ruth.

"I don't know what you are talking about. Now please go before I ring the bell to let Mrs Durville know you are here." He laughed at this, but without mirth. They both knew the old lady hardly had the strength to raise herself from the bed, let alone wander about on her own. Ruth was almost in reach of the bell pull by the fireside, but Henry knew what she was thinking.

A split second and he was onto her without warning, grabbing and twisting her round, putting one hand across her mouth. Ruth kicked and fought with all her strength but she was no match for the young man. Eventually he forced her down to the floor and fell on top of her, knocking the wind from her body, while forcefully pushing his knee between her thighs. Ruth, even in such a terrified state thought quickly. He was easily overpowering her strengthwise, so bravely let her body go limp in his arms. Slowly, he moved his hand from her mouth as Ruth pleaded, "Please don't hurt me, sir. You must realize, I am too young to have experienced a man. I am still a virgin, so please be gentle with me. I promise I will do my best to please you and do exactly what you tell me."

Henry's eyes sparkled with lust at the thought of this young girl succumbing to his love making and was already in such a state of arousal, he released his vice like grip on her arms to undo his breeches.

Now fuelled by lust he hissed from those thin lips, "I am glad you have seen sense." His eyes were wild, sweat pimpled his brow as his passion for this sweet young body rose uncontrollably inside him like the tide. He could not tear his gaze from the pale, bare flesh of her shoulders where he had roughly torn the dress from her in the ensuing struggle.

He never knew what hit him. Ruth grabbed the heavy, brass poker and swung with all her might hitting him square on the side of his face. She heard the dull thud then the sickening crunch of bone as the poker burst through the soft flesh of his cheek as it connected. He slumped on her like a log. Ruth, using all her remaining strength, pushed him off sending him crashing into the small coffee table to lie like a dead thing on the plush red carpet, blood seeping from the gaping wound.

Suddenly, the door swung open and in dashed Bella, only to stand open mouthed, frozen in panic. Ruth, resisting the urge to throw up, tried to think. Body and limbs shaking but still in control of her senses, she spoke to Bella who had not moved a muscle since entering. No response from her. Ruth slapped her face to snap her out of it and said, "Listen, you have to believe me, Bella, he tried to attack me and God, I think I've killed him. Nobody is going to believe what happened, especially a respected family such as this. I have no option but to run away and hope I can get clear before the police come."

Ruth hastily grabbed a pen and scrawled a note for the master begging

Chapter 32

him to believe her and that someday she may be resolved from this horrible deed. She left it on the desk. Bella had not spoken once, she was still in shock. Ruth said, "Look I am going to grab a few things now and go. Please tell them what happened, that I wasn't to blame."

Bella hung onto Ruth as she tried to dash from the room.

"Take me with you, Ruth" she begged.

"I can't, Bella, you are not up to it. You'll be fine here, he will not bother you again. I'm sure he's dead. Now let me go." Ruth feverishly fought to free herself from Bella's clutching grip.

"I'm coming with you. I am not stopping here. I have some money and we'll find somewhere together."

"Bella, you don't understand. I am going to have to sleep rough, beg food, keep out of sight and possibly travelling only at night, because the police will soon be looking for me. I will be wanted for murder. Do you understand? I know I can do this, but I am not sure that you can."

"I can help, Ruth. It will be easier for two of us and I have money to buy food."

Ruth had little time to argue, rushing upstairs and throwing a few things into a small reticule, grabbing the one thing out of the drawer she cherished more than anything else in her possession, the necklace that her mother had given her as a gift before her death. Ruth realized the life she was living was too good to last. It was not meant for the likes of her, but, for a while, she had dared to hope. Now she would be back on the streets. Worse than on the streets. She would be hunted down as a criminal, wanted for the murder of Judge Durville's son.

She shivered as she remembered the tormented dreams she endured after losing her mother, the agony of not knowing if her father mounted the gallows steps, a black hood covering his features with an angry mob baying and shouting for him to be hanged. These thoughts invaded her mind so she couldn't think straight. Was she about to follow in his footsteps? How had she got into this mess? But she would be damned if she would have let that reptile force his dirty paws on her. She would rather have died, or even follow her father to the gallows rather than let that happen and she thought that may be the outcome for both her and Bella if Lady Luck did not shine on them.

Making sure all was quiet in the house and checking the old lady was snoring peacefully, they crept out into the overpowering blackness of the back street.

Chapter 33

The fog crouched low, a swirling murk that reeked of sulphur in the thick, night air that the flickering gas lights struggled to break through. Ruth had hurriedly grabbed her old boots and put them on and her old cap that Jim had given her, thankful she had hung onto them and not thrown them out, plus a full-length coat which almost reached her ankles and she could easily pass for a boy in this light. Bella had also thrown a cape across her shoulders and had the forethought to bring a brolly of all things, but it was as good a disguise as any as they made the journey back toward the area that Ruth knew so well. "We must walk at a steady pace, Bella, so as not to attract attention."

Her brain began to clear. Although frightened, the panic was over. Desire to escape now dominating her thinking. They passed the many butcher's shops, the stench of rotting meat still strong enough to sting their nostrils in the dank night air, even though all was cleared away.

On they walked, steadily, the urge to break into a run strong in both of them, through the Shambles and into the dark, narrow alleys that led down to the river. This is where Ruth reckoned would be there best bet of escape. Hide in tunnels that ran down to the Ouse, grab a boat in the early hours of the morning and head toward the country. But she knew not where.

Keeping their heads down, they walked arm in arm as if returning home.

They were now both feeling pretty confident, having walked a good hour away from the better parts of York and were now only a short distance away from the area that Ruth knew would lead through to the tunnels and sewers, sluicing down to the river, when a hand settled on her shoulder, bringing a cold stab of fear to her already fast beating heart.

"Now then, what are you two skulking about for at this time of night. Up to no good, I bet." Ruth turned and lifted her eyes to confirm what her heart already knew, the uniform saying it all. Quick as a flash, Ruth brought her knee up into the officer's groin, doubling him up with pain. He had no time to shout, just a short, sharp intake of breath as he bent forward and dropped to his knees, gasping for breath.

"Run," hissed Ruth before the policeman had chance to recover his senses and they were well away before he even had the ability to croak the word, "Stop!" such was his agony. The sound of the shrill, piercing blast of a whistle rent the stillness of the night and echoed around them as they dived deeper into the passage ways.

By now Ruth was on home ground, knew these streets like the back of her hand. 'Thank you, Jim,' she muttered to herself, running from alley to alley, the sounds of their pursuers shouting in the distance. The grating came away in her hands at the first pull and they dived through and replaced it just in time as the sound of clattering boots rang out on the stone flags. Breathing heavily, hearts hammering out of their chests, they crouched in the darkness for what seemed like hours not daring to move a muscle, before silence reigned.

Ruth heaved a sigh of relief knowing they were safe for now and glad she'd had the foresight to stuff some candles and matches in her pockets before fleeing.

Now the immediate danger had passed, she thought it safe to light them, and the flickering flame cast an eerie glow on their surroundings, lighting up huge wads of orange fungi forcing its way through the flaking brickwork. Rats scurried away from the light along the shimmering line of trickling water. The walls were slick with a fatty dew that gleamed silver in the light of the candle and a row of yellow, stalactite teeth hung from the

Chapter 33

brickwork above. They made their way steadily into the innards of the tunnel and finally stumbling on a dry patch of earth, they stopped to catch their breath. Finding the blankets that she and Jim had hidden away, they wrapped themselves up in these to keep the chill from seeping into their bones.

"Now, we are safe here but it is going to be a long couple of days. I know there are boats moored outside these gratings. We'll grab one from the riverside and let the tide take us downstream, well away from where anyone will be looking for us. Now, try and settle down and keep warm."

For the first time since they made their dash for safety, Ruth had time to take notice of Bella. Her teeth were chattering, whether with fear or cold Ruth could not be certain, so, wrapping her in an extra blanket she settled by her side with her arms around her. Deep in her heart Ruth knew Bella was not up to what they would have to endure over the next few weeks and worried about her. She could hear the continuous gurgle of water from the many drains and tunnels as it fed its way down to the river. Sometimes it became so loud it muffled the clatter of horses' hooves and iron clad wheels on the cobbles above them.

Eventually, through sheer exhaustion, they both dropped into a fitful sleep. A shaft of light from a grating leading up to the street above brought them both awake in the early hours of a cold, bright morning. Ruth put a finger to her lips as footsteps and voices filtered down to their hiding place as people passed by overhead. Carriages once again clattered past, horses whinnying as over-zealous drivers came across their hindquarters with the whip as they skittered across the wet cobblestones.

Ruth broke the deathly silence. In a whisper she said, "We'll be quite safe here. They will stop looking for us in a few days. We have enough food and water for the time being and then, if we need more, I will sneak out and get some. I know my way around here pretty well. After that we'll set off for the river and the countryside." Ruth noticed that Bella was still shaking and she was complaining of headaches and stomach pains, her face had taken on a lettuce green tinge since the night before.

Worried for the girl, Ruth said, "Bella, please go back. You are ill and need a doctor. Please go back, just don't tell anyone where I am."

"I'll never go back, Ruth. There are too many nightmares there for me. I would rather die here, on the run, than go back." Ruth had never realized just how miserable a life Bella had endured all her young life. Never known a friend, or even family. No one ever showing concern or love. She never stood a chance in life from the beginning. At least I have the memories of my mother, she thought, and also the friendship of Jim. Her heart warmed just thinking of him. But at this point, she began to wonder if she would ever see him again.

Chapter 34

Ruth stayed by Bella's side as her condition steadily worsened. At one point she almost decided to give herself up, but then reasoned against it as nothing could be gained from that. Cuddling together for warmth and trying to comfort her by constantly talking, eventually she felt her stop shaking and thought maybe the fever had passed. Ruth remained calm and spoke of what they would do when reaching the open country as they let the day drag slowly by. By night time Ruth slept soundly, hoping Bella would be fit enough to escape to the boat come morning.

On waking after another cold, damp night she gave Bella a nudge to wake her but the body was stiff. Bella had died during the night. Breaking into tears Ruth sobbed, "I'm so sorry, Bella, so terribly sorry. I was not strong enough to help you when you most needed a friend."

Heartbroken with grief and blaming herself for Bella's death, Ruth knelt by her side holding onto Bella's icy cold hand. And it was a cold hand that clasped itself around Ruth's heart as she tried to figure out a plan. She knew not how long she stayed by Bella's side, but finally said a few words of prayer that she thought suitable. Not really understanding God, or religion, it didn't mean much, but she thought it the right thing to do.

It was while she sat next to the pale, lifeless body of her friend all through the next long day that she knew what she had to do, however hard it proved.

Taking her mother's necklace from around her neck, sobbing steadily, she clumsily began to change into Bella's clothes, then, shutting her mind at what she was about to do, dragged the now stiffening body to the grating that led directly into the river.

A quietly whispered, "Oh God forgive me for what I am about to do," before forcing the body through into the fast- flowing current to be soon swept away into the darkness. If only she could have swept it from her mind as easily, she thought. Although plagued by guilt, her only plan was how to stay clear of the law and survive. She had come too far down this slippery road of sin now, that there was to be no turning back, no chance of repentance.

Ruth fervently hoped that the body may never be found but, if it did wash up, the identity would naturally be thought to be herself, the police assuming that her escape bid had gone horribly wrong when trying to cross the river and drowned in the process.

Chapter 35

Early morning mist hung low over the water and very few people were about as the first shards of daylight began to break through a brightening sky. Ruth reluctantly shrugged the long warm coat from her shoulders and squeezed herself through the grating, quietly wading waist deep into the water, the coldness almost taking her breath away as she made toward the nearest small craft.

With fingers and hands already numbing with cold, she eventually managed to untie the small boat from its mooring and quickly scrambled over the side, as the boat suddenly caught the strong flow and almost snatched it from her grasp. Sliding in Ruth ducked under the tarpaulin sheet, just willing the boat to keep straight and hoping against hope that it wouldn't snag or run aground. Eventually, her courage bolstered by what she believed to be a successful escape, she risked a peek out from under the sheet, and a quick glance had her breathe a sigh of relief as she watched the old factories and mill workings drift by, the boat sliding silently past and onward to she knew not where, and soon the city became a distant silhouette on the ever-brightening skyline.

Cowering into a foetal position in the bottom of the boat, after the initial euphoria of her escape going to plan, Ruth suddenly felt the bitter cold biting into her, the wet clothes clinging to her body like a second skin. When next stealing a glance from under the cover, there was nothing to see but river bank and trees. No buildings or factories in sight, all left behind, along with her past, Ruth hoped, and with the sun beginning to break through the temperature rose, adding warmth to the little craft. Now approaching open country side, the grassy river banks were lined with trees and wild flowers hiding the river from sight, so much so that she plucked up courage to actually straighten up from her cramped position as there did not appear to be anyone in sight.

Ruth forced her brain to try and function logically, to find a solution to the situation she was in. Oh, if only she had someone who could help or advise her. Or even just to talk to.

Suddenly, the boat veered sharply left, the current forcing it toward the banking, jolting her back to reality. Bumping and slipping along the steep river bank, it travelled on for a few more yards before coming to a complete halt. Darting a quick look about her, Ruth thought maybe her lucky star had finally noticed her predicament, the nose of the boat snagging amongst the straggly, gnarled roots from the forest of overhanging trees extruding down into the river. This wooded area would surely afford her some security from any prying eyes that might just be watching her.

Grabbing the opportunity, she flung the small case high up on the grassy bank and swiftly followed it, jumping nimbly ashore and dashed for the covering and security of the wood. Once feeling safe, she sat in the warmth of the now strengthening sunlight, allowing her dress and boots to dry.

Her first thoughts were to make for the coast and the seaside town of Whitby. She had learnt from Mrs Durville's lessons and readings that the town was a busy, prosperous port due to its fishing fleets, so there must be work there, either as a servant or even gutting fish on the harbour side. Her nose crinkled at the thought, but if it kept body and soul together, no one would recognize her, although she realized she must change her name so as not to be connected with the murder in York. Her stomach lurched, suddenly feeling nauseous at the thought of what she had done, but knew she had no option. After a while the feeling of sickness passed and she began to think positively once more now the plan had formed, and with that in

Chapter 35

mind, set out in a more determined fashion and a somewhat lighter step than for some time.

She had no idea what time of day it would be, but what did it matter. The only problem would be food and how to obtain it, but she would worry about that when hunger struck. She was thankful for the money Bella had brought with her. But, along with that thought came the sense of shame, the terrible realization hitting her at how low she had sunk and would stoop, to save her own skin. It appeared she would do anything to survive. Oh, there must be badness bred in you, Ruth Brennan, she scolded herself.

As the sun rose higher in a brilliantly clear blue sky, a pleasurable warmth began to spread through her body, continuing to dry her bedraggled clothes after her early morning wade through water. Penetrating deeper into the wood brought more satisfaction, the chattering birdsong filling the air lifted her spirits even more and the abundance of wild garlic flowers, releasing such a strong, pungent scent in the stillness of the glade stung her nostrils. Somewhere in the distance, the clatter of hooves reached her ears, meaning a road must be close by, but for the time being, Ruth knew the only way to stay undetected for a few miles until well clear of the city, was to stay out of sight, as a young unaccompanied girl would almost certainly be treated with suspicion.

Chapter 36

Judge John Durville arrived back home after another long, stressful day at the office to find the house in darkness. A certain uneasiness gripped him on mounting the front steps and this feeling deepened as the door swung silently open at his first touch. "Ruth, Bella, are you there?" No answer. Heart beating a little faster he first entered the library and there, rising unsteadily from the floor was Henry, a huge disfigurement on the side of his face now congealed with blood.

"Henry, whatever has happened? You are badly hurt. Sit down and I shall get one of the girls to summon a doctor." With that he shouted through into the hallway, "Bella, Ruth, come quickly, there has been an accident. To the library. Hurry." He instantly turned his attention back to the injured Henry who had now found his voice.

Angrily, he shouted, "You will not find Ruth here, father. It was that brazen hussy who inflicted this on me." John considered his son, a look of utter disbelief spreading across his features.

"That cannot be possible, Henry. Ruth would never do such a thing. Why, she has performed marvellously with Miriam this past year or so, making her more like her old self before we lost ... "his voice trailed off as emotion took over, "before we lost Tiffany," he finished.

"Father, are you going to get me a Doctor or not, before I bleed to death. I tell you she was in here pilfering, looking for something to pinch. I came in and surprised her and that is when she hit me with the poker and now, she will be far enough away."

The Judge looked dubious. "Then where is Bella, may I ask? Bella had no need to run away." John stared at Henry, the piercing black eyes searching the young man's face for a sign of guilt. This had become part of Judge John Durville's success, able to read a criminal mind from the eyes alone. Henry's eyes dived to the fireside, "look, there is your proof," as he pointed to the blood-stained poker lying in the hearth.

The older man never let his gaze falter as he quietly said, "I don't believe a word you are saying Henry. Don't think I have not heard the whispers behind my back from the socalled gentry that I have no option but to socialize with. From the stories doing the present rounds, I understand that you are a devious and disgusting specimen of a man who delights in the pleasures of young girls. I forced myself into believing it to be just rumours, as you are my flesh and blood and it was only because you are my son that I have kept quiet, but now if you will not speak the truth, then I am calling the police."

It was only then John spotted the hastily written note left on his desk by Ruth and began to read it out aloud.

"Please believe me when I say your son attacked me. I struck him with the poker to save myself. I am so sorry. Ruth. Henry's face was ashen. The flow of blood had eased, but the side of his face had a huge swelling, like a huge, over ripe bulbous fruit which had split open and was beginning to colour a deep purple. He went to the desk and began to pour himself a whisky. The Judge strode across the room, instantly swiping the glass out of his hand, smashing it into a thousand pieces against the marble of the fireplace, such was his fury. Henry flinched, taking a step back. Never had he seen his father in such a rage. Frightened, he cowered away from him.

John Durville brought his huge frame directly in front of his son. "The truth, Henry. Now," he ordered. There was no way out, but Henry, devious to the last in saving his own skin thought quickly, telling his father Bella had become infatuated with him, wanting them to run away together and marry him. He had scorned her and a woman scorned is dangerous. Her and Ruth had collaborated and began to demand money from him.

"Pah, if you think I believe that concocted story you are a madman as well as a fool. I have no further use for you Henry. Get out of this house and don't come back. My duty now is to find those two girls before anything serious happens to them. Now, get out!" He shouted these words in such anger that the whole street may have heard, but he was past caring. Grabbing Henry by the shoulder, he frogmarched him to the door and forced him out onto the street.

Clutching his head which had started bleeding again, he hissed "You'll be sorry for this father. Wait until Miriam hears the full story. She'll believe me."

"Begone, you are nothing but a whimpering monstrosity," and with a contemptuous wave of the hand, he slammed the door behind him. On returning inside, he ran upstairs to check on Miriam, but she slept soundly. John could see the end before long and with both the girls disappearing, he was not sure how she would take it in her frail state. He poured himself a drink, frantic with worry as to where on earth would those two young girls, alone and late at night, likely to head for. He tried telling himself they may just have panicked and could possibly return in the morning, but the thought had no real conviction and brought no comfort.

Again, through no fault of her own Ruth had been forced back out onto the streets. Somehow, he had failed to give her the love and care that she secretly craved. And deserved.

He poured himself another whisky in an attempt to try and stem the tears. It didn't work. He knew in his heart he had let her down. Hoping to God nothing serious had happened to the pair of them, he vowed to try and find them somehow before anything did happen to them.

Chapter 37

But to no avail. After enduring two long days of anguish hoping for their return, John reported the two girls as missing. Now, more than a week had gone by without a word, as if they had just vanished, but as John prepared to leave for work, having brought temporary staff in to care for Miriam, he answered a sharp knock at the door. It was his regular cab driver who informed him a young girl's body had been fished out of the river this very morning. John's heart missed a beat. He asked the cabbie if the body had been identified.

"Not as yet," replied the driver, "but I did hear that as there is a shortage of information on missing people, they are asking for help from anyone who could possibly go and try to identify the body."

"Cabbie, head for the police station and drop me there."

"Very well, sir." He clicked his horse, urging it forward and within ten minutes they arrived outside the police station.

"Thank you, driver." He tipped the man and striding purposefully over to the huge blue door, he swung it open to find Sergeant Porritt sitting with his feet up on the desk. Like a startled rabbit, he jumped up out of the chair standing to attention as soon as his flustered mind realized who it was.

"Morning, Porritt. I hear there was a body taken out of the river. Has there been any identification yet?"

"Morning, sir. I am not really sure. I haven't been told anything."

"Where is it, man, in the morgue?"

Porritt looked extremely uncomfortable as he could offer no information at all. "I haven't heard a thing, sir. They never tell me much, you know."

Exasperated, the Judge said, "Oh, for God's sake, Porritt, I sometimes wonder why they pay you a wage at all!"

John strode round to the austere looking brick building a further three streets away and asked to see the body. The porter, recognizing him instantly, ushered him down the steep well-worn stone steps that led into the depth of the morgue. John tried not to notice the numerous white sheets that covered many of the horribly mutilated bodies, but others, pallid and white as if just asleep, lay like so many pieces of meat upon the cold slabs of marble. How do people work in places like this all day without it affecting them, John wondered? The deathly silence and the cold temperature chilled him to the bone. The pathologist, Doctor Miller, was about to begin work on the badly damaged body of a man when John arrived.

"Ah, John, good to see you," removing his glove before grabbing John by the hand and shaking it.

"Are you here on business or pleasure?" the doctor asked.

"Now when have you known me enter this cold, depressing building on pleasure, Doctor?"

"Well, there is always a first time, John, but I know what you mean. I must admit this job must seem strange to most people, but someone has to do it," and smiling, replaced his glove and clasped his scalpel to begin the examination of the body before him.

John was not a particularly squeamish man, but if he could delay the Doctor for a few minutes it would help.

"Doctor Miller, I heard the body of a young girl had been dragged from the river. As we had our two maids Bella and Ruth go missing more than a week ago and nothing has been heard since, I have a dreadful feeling that this may be one of them."

"Follow me, John," and he immediately walked across to another slab at the far side of the room, dragging the cover from the lifeless young form,

Chapter 37

grotesque in its nakedness, the bloated face and body, terribly discoloured due to the length of time in the water before being discovered. It bore little resemblance to anything human, but even as John forced himself to try and identify this corpse, he knew in his heart it must be either Bella or Ruth. He guessed she was maybe of a similar age to the girls, and roughly the same height and build, but he had no idea how to go further. Apart from the clothes maybe.

"What clothes was she wearing, Doctor?"

Doctor Miller pointed to a pile in the corner. That is when John thought he would faint. Nausea swept over him, his legs buckling, almost giving way, as if every ounce of strength had been punched from his body. He did have some recollection of the boots and coat, but the telling factor was the small delicate necklace placed neatly on top that caught his eye. While John studied the small heap of belongings, he realized the Doctor was speaking to him, bringing him back to reality, the serious tone of his voice cutting through the dark thoughts racing through his mind as to the possible end of this girl's life.

"I have already carried out an autopsy, John. I'm sorry, but surprisingly, the girl was also with child and, not only that, it appears she had been treated by some butcher or other who failed terribly to abort the child. Now, if you will just take a closer look here, you can see…"

"No, no thank you, Doctor. I don't need to see any more. I will take your word for it." John, leant on the side of the slab, trying to pull himself together as he took this new information in. This couldn't be Ruth, could it?

"Is it one of the girls you are looking for John, do you think? You look a little uncertain. I know it's difficult to tell when they've been in the water for such a long time, but if she is of similar build and height then it stands a good chance of being one of them."

John felt sick. He always did when having to attend this place, but before there was never any association with the figure laid out on the slab. This time it was different, proving more personal, closer to home. He knew Ruth was not just an innocent child. She was street-wise and quite adept at surviving. John was struggling to accept the fact that this could have happened to her. Fighting hard to control his emotions, he tried to think logically. He needed someone to help him, to be absolutely sure if it was either of the girls. And if it was Ruth or Bella, where was the survivor now?

Regaining his composure, he said, "Thank you, Doctor, I may need a second opinion on this. Please could you delay on this one before doing anything with the body until I have seen you again."

"Of course I can, John. As you well know, no one is going to get up and run out of here, are they?"

At times like this, John really struggled to appreciate the Doctor's dark humour and was glad to make a hasty retreat from the dank, cold building into the fresh air.

On surfacing he tried to gather his thoughts. They were definitely Ruth's clothes, he knew that, the most telling of all, the necklace, but there was something nagging at the back of his mind. If that is Ruth laid out in the morgue, then where the hell is Bella? John knew there was no way Bella could survive on her own and would surely have come home as soon as Ruth was not by her side.

But where do I go from here? Or, more importantly, who do I go to that would know her well enough?

Suddenly an idea flashed into his head. Hailing a cab, one pulled up instantly. "The Orphanage please, driver."

"Yes, sir, without delay," and with a quick flick of the whip the horse lunged forward, scattering a few passers-by in the process.

Chapter 38

Never having had reason to visit this area of York, John had never given a thought to how poverty stricken it was and it set his mind racing. He always knew and understood how lucky he was, coming as he did from a wealthy background, enabling him to gain a good education which set him on the road to running a successful business. It had not always been easy, working hard to support his lifestyle, and made many sacrifices for it along the way. But for what, he now asked himself? Living the good life had softened him. Until taking the young orphan girl Ruth off the streets, he never once spared a thought for the people with never enough money to make ends meet, struggling to buy enough food just to stay alive, never mind keep a roof over their heads.

Broken bottles and rubbish littered the sides of the road, and the stench from the sewers, acrid in the warm, summer air, which clung to his throat and nostrils, brought him back to the real world. Finally, they pulled up at the grim, red brick building. Paying the cabbie, he said, "I'll make my own way back, driver. Thank you."

"Are you sure, sir. It's not the sort of spot you want to be hanging around in. Make sure you hang onto your wallet."

"Thank you for your concern but I will be fine. I shall hopefully have a companion who knows the area well." And with that he strode toward the building. Rapping on the huge oak door with his cane, he waited and waited. He knocked again and eventually the door creaked open and Miss Wade stood there.

"Well?" she said, surveying him up and down with her steely eyes.

"I am sorry to bother you, madam, but I am enquiring about a young boy by the name of Jim. I do not know his surname or even if he has one but he is a small boy with a crop of unruly black hair. A pretty confident chap, I would say."

"That could be anybody," the old lady said contemptuously, "And, by the way, who is it asking?"

"Judge John Durville from Darwin Court, Madam and I am enquiring about the young boy because I need his help in a certain matter."

"Hmmph, you'll not find him much help. He's a wrong 'un is that if ever there was one."

"Ah, so you do know of him?"

"Ah 'appen I do, but what's it worth?"

The Judge leaned forward, his face furious, only a few inches from the old woman's. "You will tell me what you know or I will have the authorities call round to this establishment, and I have no doubt they will have you closed down in a matter of weeks." The old lady backed away from the big man who had struck terror into her heart with just a few well-chosen words.

"He upped and left here a while since. I did hear he works at the market now for some basket trader or something. But that's all I know."

"If he returns here, I want a message sent to this address," he handed out a card, "without delay. Do I make myself clear?"

"Yes, sir, you do." The old lady was visibly shaking and had to hold onto the door to stop herself from falling.

"Good day to you, Madam."

"Good day, sir," she finally got spluttered out, relieved to be able to slam the door and retire to her room, leaving old Jeffers in charge.

John strode from the building, his rage now subsiding. His mind now on the horrendous conditions that the children were forced into enduring and he made his mind up to do something about changing this as soon as

Chapter 38

he possibly could. It had taken just a short time for a confident young girl to make him realize just how pompous and selfrighteous a person he had become.

Mopping his brow, he immediately made for the market. From streets away, he could hear the noise from the bustling crowd and the raucous shouts from traders all trying to coax the passers-by into parting with their hardearned cash for their wares of vegetables, oatcakes and fish and other such produce.

John was flummoxed, he didn't know which way to turn. He felt very conspicuous. He should have thought to change before coming here. Eyes were on him. A young boy suddenly appeared from nowhere and tapped him on the arm.

"Want any help, sir? Are yer lost? I'll help yer!" John studied the boy. He was dressed in cast offs, patched and filthy, his face, never having seen water for a matter of weeks, John guessed.

Bending down to the level of the young boy, he said, "Yes, I do need your help. I am looking for a boy called Jim who used to be at the Orphanage but is now working for someone in the market."

"Well, that's different. I can't help you wi' that, cos I don't know him yer see." He made to scamper off but John grabbed him by the arm. "No, you don't understand. He isn't in trouble. I need his help." The boy eyed him suspiciously.

"You sure you're not having me on, guv'nor. How much is it worth?" John pulled a shilling out of his pocket.

"Wait here, I won't be long." And with that he dashed off, his hobnail boots clattering over the cobbles.

Jim had begun work for Harry Styles at the other end of the market and the boy spotted Jim as he brought another batch of baskets out onto the tables to sell.

"Jim, are yer in trouble wi' police at all?"

"No, course not. I packed that in when Ruth got caught. Why, what is it?" Jim was grinning at the wide-eyed youth as he told him his tale. "If yer not in trouble yer have to come wi' me then, Jim, and I'll share the shilling with yer."

"Back in a minute, Harry," Jim shouted this over his shoulder as the two ragamuffins ran back to where the Judge waited, sitting on an upturned crate, wiping the sweat from his face when they ran to meet him.

"Well, Jim, we meet again," John said, "but this time in your territory." The Judge could see the boy was cautious, eyeing him suspiciously.

"What do you want me for? I'm doing me best now. I'm working at the market and keeping out o' trouble."

"I'm glad to hear it, Jim, but that is not why I want to see you. I need your help, if you are up to it because I think you are the only one who can help me." John was stared at now by two pair of eyes as the boys couldn't believe what they heard. Jack was the first to speak.

"What about me money yer promised, mister. I brought him for yer, didn't I?"

"You did that," and John handed over the shilling and Jack dashed away.

"Tell me what it is, 'cos I can't stay long. Harry is on his own at the stall and won't be able to manage wi'out me."

"Can I come to see your boss and explain. That may help? It is important, Jim, I promise you."

"Okay, but he might not let me go if he's in a bad mood." Jim's eyes were serious as they gazed up at the big man.

"Well, let's hope he is in a good mood." John replied.

On arriving at Harry's stall, things had quietened down as lunch time neared and Harry, spotting Jim with the welldressed man, was sure he had caught him for lifting his wallet, or his watch or something like that.

"Jim, you've not been nicking agen have yer. If yer have I'll give yer a good hiding and yer'll be on yer way."

"Now't like that, Harry. I'll let the big man tell yer."

John held out his hand and the men shook hands. Once introductions were made, John tried to explain, without going into too much detail, that he would really appreciate Jim's help for about one hour and that he would gladly pay for the boy's time.

Harry looked around him, noting the customers had dwindled. "Well,

Chapter 38

seeing as we've slacked off, you go wi' this feller and get back when you can." John thanked him and off they went, Jim almost running to keep up.

Chapter 39

Once out of the market, John hailed a cab and they jumped in to head for the police station. Jim's heart missed a beat when he realized where they were going.

"I'm not going to the police, they'll lock me up. Let me out. I can't help yer, sir." He made a grab for the door, but John caught him by the flap of his jacket.

"It's okay, Jim. You are with me. They will not lock you up. I think it is time I explained." John became sombre. "Jim, you remember your friend, Ruth, who was working for me."

"Course I remember her. I always will, we were good friends. I would do anything for Ruth."

"I can see you would. Now this is difficult Jim, because Ruth ran away from my home more than a week ago and has not been heard of since. Until this morning that is, and the body of a young girl was found in the river Ouse and I believe you are the only person who can identify the body."

Jim turned white. He felt sick. Again, he made to jump out of the carriage. Again, John was quicker and held him with both hands. In tears and almost screaming with despair, Jim shouted, "I can't do that, sir. Don't make me do that. It's cruel."

John took the young boy in his arms and held him tight until his sobbing

Chapter 39

subsided.

"Please, Jim, do this for me and I will be forever grateful. Ruth was left with no one through no fault of her own. If we walk away from her now, even in death, her life will have been as nothing. So, please do this for her so at least she will have a decent burial."

John took a handkerchief out of his pocket and handed it to Jim, who dried his eyes and handed it back to the big man.

"No, you keep it, there may be more tears ahead, Jim. You now need to be brave. Think you can do it?"

Jim looked up, his eyes searching for some kind of help, some kind of trust from this man and said, "If you stay by me side, I can do it, mister."

John fought hard to retain his composure as a sudden surge of emotion tightened his throat as he realized just how hard this was going to be for Jim. It had been a long time since anyone had needed him as a father figure.

"Yes, we'll do it together, Jim," he said, relief flooding through him, and at that precise moment John knew that if they could face this together, a special friendship would form between the two of them. A bond that he had once felt for his son Henry, until broken due to his law breaking, selfish and abusive lifestyle.

Striding into the morgue with Jim by his side, John nodded across to the Doctor as if asking permission to see the body. The Doctor nodded back, not a word spoken. The pair looked neither left nor right, until stopping at the covered body on a marble slab.

"Are you ready, Jim?"

"Yes, sir." And John pulled back the sheet. Jim's knees buckled and the colour drained from his cheeks as he studied the distorted body and face of the corpse for any sign of recognition. He didn't speak, couldn't speak but bent closer to the body to peer closely at the rise of the left shoulder. Stepping back abruptly, he said, "Can we go now, sir?"

Once outside John asked him, in a concerned voice if he was all right.

"Yes, I'm okay now." Then with a definite shake of the head, he added, "but that wasn't Ruth, mister."

"Good God, Jim, how can you be sure? The body is almost unrecognisable,"

"Ruth had a birth mark, just here," and he pointed high up on his shoulder. "It was usually covered, but I knew it was there."

The pathologist had confirmed that cause of death was not drowning, but due to the butchered abortion, with the body not strong enough to fight the inevitable fever and exposure that followed. John now knew it must be Bella and could it possibly have been Henry's child she was carrying. What a mess. Helplessness and guilt crowded his thinking, knowing he should have spent more time to see things were right at home instead of being so obsessed with his blasted work.

Too late for regrets now though. All he could do was try to make amends for his own selfish lifestyle and that of his son.

On parting company with Jim, John said, "I remember what I said at our first meeting Jim and I would like to amend that and ask if you would please let me keep in touch with you," and with that drew a card out of his pocket with the firm's name and address on it, along with a telephone number, "and if you hear anything of Ruth, please let me know. Now, if I give you this money, will you see that Harry is paid for your loss of time and if you do know where to find the boy who knew where you worked, thank him again from me?" He handed the money to Jim who hurriedly stuffed it into his trouser pocket.

"I will, mister. Honestly, I will. But as for Jack, I don't know where he lives, but I know where he hangs out if that's any good." Already the irrepressible, cheeky grin was back on his grubby face and on waving goodbye he was soon lost among the narrow alleyways once more.

Chapter 40

Jim arrived back at the market stall out of breath to find Harry rushed off his feet. It was almost time to load up and customers were buying baskets to transport their goods home. When things quietened down and they were taking the stall down Jim handed the money to Harry and after a little while he asked, "Harry, would you miss me if I got a job in the country somewhere?"

"Course, I would. You can miss toothache if you've had it long enough," replied Harry with a grin. "And where do yer think o' getting a job?"

"Oh, I don't know for sure, but I bet there's plenty o' fishermen, or mebbe farmers who could do with help and seeing as I'm going on thirteen, I could hold me own among men now."

Harry smiled at this spirited young boy. Never an ounce of love, or respect, shown to him in his short life. No parents to guide or show or tell. Yet here he was, willing to go tackle jobs that some men would find daunting.

"Well, joking aside, I would miss yer constant chatter and I must admit yer a good little worker, but on the other hand, I may just be able to help out. "Me brother owns a small farm out on the moors at Roston. Most o' the land out there is Lord Darley's Estate, but Albert does own the farm and he was telling me only last winter he could do with a reliable, honest lad to help out wi' work on the farm." Then Harry stopped abruptly, scratching his head, as if deep in thought. After a pause, he went on, "but on second thoughts, ah'm not sure you'd be able to do that, would you Jim, what with the animals an' all that, you been a city boy like."

Jim also looked doubtful, his face clouding over. His initial thoughts were of a seafaring life on the coast. But any job would be a start and he could always move on if it didn't suit. He wasn't at all sure he could look after pigs and cows all day. It sounded like a bit of a lonely life.

"Harry, stop joking about it. I'm serious. D'yer think you could put a good word in for me and get me a start?"

"Course I will. Albert and his wife will be through at market next week. If you haven't run off or the big fella hasn't locked yer up, yer can meet 'em then."

Jim threw his arms around Harry's waist and looked up, earnest in his reply. "I'll not let you down, Harry. You'll see, in a few years' time, you'll be proud o' me." Harry looked away, because he knew he would miss this little fella' who never seemed down in the dumps for long and, by God, he had more reasons than most to be miserable.

Chapter 41

Ruth made good progress through the wood as she tried to push the past few days to the back of her mind. The sun beamed warmly down and, although unsure, frightened and alone, Ruth kept her spirits high by thinking of Jim, wondering if he was searching for her. She had no way of getting in touch or even finding out where he was, but now thinking clearly and being more positive in her bid to survive, she felt a little brighter and knew she needed some sort of plan if her journey was to work. Obviously, she would have to keep away from the busy roads and stick to well covered areas wherever possible, such as the many footpaths weaving their way through the forest, but always heading for the coast, as this is what her and Jim had planned for in the cold, bleak days at the Orphanage.

Heavy hearted but much more settled, she suddenly realized that some kind of shelter must be found before nightfall. Ruth had enough food to last for the day, but would need to find more. Sticking to the narrow woodland path that luckily appeared to follow the contour of the road, but set deeper in amongst the trees, Ruth noted fewer and fewer travellers as she made her way further into the countryside with just the occasional motorcar puttering steadily past.

As the orange glow of the sun dipped low toward the horizon and the best of the day had passed, her aching limbs cried out for rest. She knew not how many miles she had walked, but in the distance, with the light beginning to fade, she spied an old timber shed in the corner of a field at the edge of the forest. Maybe an old stable, or even a barn. At least it will provide me with shelter for the night, thought Ruth.

Easing out from the cover of the trees, Ruth looked furtively about her. Satisfied there was no one around, she ran across the short open space, heart racing, and reached the safety of the shed. She allowed herself a smile. Here she was, used to the hustle and bustle of city life with people always milling around, where out here there appeared to be no one in the vicinity. It seemed odd that she was creeping about, afraid that someone might recognize her.

At first glance the shelter for the night did not look very promising. Cautiously peeping in to make sure it was empty, she quickly slipped between the half open doors. All safe, all quiet. Not a sound. Ruth tried pulling the doors together for extra warmth through the night, but the screech of rusty hinges echoed loudly in the stillness of the dusk evening. Suddenly a flurry of flapping wings high in the rafters caused Ruth's heart to almost leap out of her chest in fright, before realizing a flock of pigeons, already roosting for the night, were more startled than her, flying out through the ragged old sacking hanging limply across the shattered glass of the window.

Once her pulse settled back to normal, she took stock. Dark and musty though it was, she had faced worse. It was better than having to trust to the elements outside and would give refuge for one night at least.

Pulling the old blanket tight around her, she settled in the corner of the wooden shack, amongst a pile of straw to await the dark tentacles of night to encroach. Although there was warmth from the sun during the day, it turned cold on a night. But warmth was not a problem. It was the many strange sounds echoing eerily around the old building that kept her awake.

Through these solitary hours that dragged slowly by, the silence, the isolation became almost intolerable. She could not recall ever feeling so lost and alone. Closing her eyes and lying back amidst the prickly bed of straw for the night, the vision of Jim casting a cheeky glance at her, or the sudden sparkle of optimism in his eyes as he spoke of the future, and, yes,

Chapter 41

the ever-ready smile came to her.

Oh, how she missed him, longed for him. If not for this image, and also the frightening thought of being held responsible for murder, she could so easily have weakened and returned to the safety of the city. Somehow though, her resolve remained strong, even though her feet and limbs were sore and aching from the long journey. Huddling deeper and deeper into the makeshift bed of straw she finally, through sheer exhaustion, dropped into a deep sleep.

Chapter 42

On waking, the heaviness of sleep clouded her thinking, her brain unable to break free from the wispy binding cobwebs muddling her thoughts. Where am I? Whatever has happened for me to be covered with straw in a draughty old shed? Then, as her fuddled mind cleared, she remembered and reality kicked in. Fighting the rising panic that threatened to have her losing all control, she took several deep breaths and began talking quietly to herself, bravely conquering her fears and tumult of emotions, to finally remain calm once more and think rationally.

Reluctantly, leaving the straw bed, which, although spiky and causing her skin to itch, had proved surprisingly warm through the long night. Peering out into the early dawn, the sky was already changing to a stunning, deep crimson. Gathering her small case of meagre possessions together, Ruth faced the sharp cold of the morning and cautiously, to start with, set out once again on her long journey to the coast.

Walking briskly along a well-trodden path skirting the timberline at the edge of the fields, she kept sight of the fiercely ascending road to her right as it wound its way ever upward and over the distant moors, the rising sun already beginning to glisten the dewy grass, turning every small droplet into sparkling jewels and the fields into carpets of shimmering silver as it burnt the early morning mist away. Ruth made good distance as everywhere

Chapter 42

appeared desolate, only one or two farm workers out and about, but they were more interested in their work than her. All the same, Ruth thought it best to keep well out of sight of the stout stone houses hugging the roadside of the villages she passed on her journey.

At this time of morning, she could so easily have believed that there was no other living person left in the entire world, such was the silence, only the contented, grazing cattle out in in the open fields lifting their heads occasionally, before returning to more important things. Not a breath of wind rustling the leaves in the trees, the serenity and silence broken only by the gentle pad of her feet and the soft burble of water from the stream trickling alongside. Ruth began to wonder if she would ever see anyone ever again, but realized, in her situation, this was all for the best as there was less likelihood of being seen.

Sticking doggedly to the path, it suddenly veered away to the left, following the route of the twisting, snakelike stream, the main road sweeping ever upward continuing on its tortuous potholed route over the fiercely rising moor to her right. The footpath, roughly cobbled and uneven underfoot, chafed her sore feet even more as it plunged sharply down to enter a dark, wooded area again where the surface of the forest transformed to a spongy, springing softness underfoot, a relief for Ruth, easing the extreme pain from her raw blistered feet. Here, only slim shafts of light speared toward the springy carpet of green through the dense canopy of leaves, like many vivid spotlights, illuminating occasional patches of moss and wild flowers into a brilliance of differing colours, creating such a captivating sight that Ruth knelt to finger the delicate heads, the scent so strong it almost made her dizzy.

Resuming her walk, the sound of tumbling water in the distance reached her ears even through the denseness of the forest, as the stream continued on its sharp descent. As she neared, the louder it became and finally the steepness of the path eased, dropping steadily down to run alongside the banks of the fast-flowing river, where Ruth came upon a sight that almost took her breath away. Looking up to her left, the stream rippled over a jumbled pile of rocks, before breaking steadily into a vast, circular pool, spreading a series of ever-increasing ripples toward the river bank.

A small, open clearing with a grassy bank of emerald green unfolded ahead of her, catching the full glare of the sun through the opening in the trees, casting a silvery, shimmering reflection over the surface of the water. While gazing in wonderment at this gem of nature, seemingly secreted away in the wild countryside, Ruth realized, for the first time since running away, that she actually felt a sense of safety. In fact, safe enough to admire and enjoy the beauty of her surroundings.

With this feeling uppermost in her mind, Ruth decided this a good a place as any to rest awhile and possibly bathe her blistered feet and wash her clothes but first, she thought, she must go in search of shelter for the coming night. Luckily, only a few yards away from the stream, hidden deep in the undergrowth, she stumbled upon a jagged outcrop of overhanging rock jutting out from the steep hillside that would provide, at least, some security if staying here. Surprisingly, she felt quite secure now, having found a place of protection for the night and also a pretty safe haven tucked neatly away from the rest of the world.

Although still facing the predicament of not knowing how far away the coast actually was, the beauty of her surroundings and the seclusion, gave her respite from her journey and the occasional twitter of birdsong added the small comfort in the sense of not actually being totally alone, providing her with a pleasant company of sorts. Food could prove to be a problem, but time enough to worry about that later when hungry.

Nervously, but telling herself to be brave for there was no one about, Ruth stripped off her clothes, all the time her eyes darting toward the undergrowth as if expecting someone to burst through into this clearing. Clutching her bundle of clothes tightly to her chest, she tiptoed cautiously up to the water's edge and dipped a toe in, a sharp gasp of delight escaping her lips as the shock of the ice-cold water hit her, then settled down on the soft grass to bathe her aching, blistered feet. As the pain receded Ruth waded in knee high and began to wash her clothes in the deep pool, the strong sunlight beaming down, spreading its warmth across the surface of the water.

Chapter 42

Once finished washing Ruth hung her clothes out to dry on a thicket of bushes on the hill side and noticed an abundance of juicy blackberries which she ate greedily for a few minutes, thus helping placate the pangs of hunger for now. Returning to the water's edge, she plunged into the beckoning clear water. Unable to swim properly, she doggy paddled over to where the stream tumbled its way down over the rocks. After a few moments building up courage, she ducked under the small waterfall, the force of the water instantly plunging her deep below the surface. Resurfacing and gasping for air, she quickly splashed her way back to the river bank and lay out of breath. But this brief interlude of an adventure into the ice-cold water, had nonetheless brightened her spirits.

Enjoying the sense of freedom and refreshed, Ruth lay basking in the warmth of the sun as it rose high in the sky, making the excuse in her own mind it would allow her clothes time to dry, but in reality, she was loath to leave this peaceful haven of solitude she had stumbled upon. With the knowledge that she appeared totally alone and safe here, Ruth lay on the grassy bank and may just have relaxed enough to doze for a while.

Chapter 43

Awaking with a start, uncertainty clouded her mind, unsure of how long she had slept; unsure if the dreams she suffered had brought her back to the brutal reality of her situation, or was it from the sharp stab of fear in her chest, a feeling of dread, a feeling of eyes watching her every move from afar? Trying to control this gut-wrenching panic rising in her throat like bile, which was threatening to make her flee and hide in the thickness of the trees due to her nakedness.

She forced herself to slowly open her eyes and lie motionless, not moving a muscle but listening intently, her every sense sharp and alert. Suddenly, a slight, soft rustling of undergrowth on her right reached her ears. Turning her head ever so slowly, a black and white mongrel dog sat in the distance watching her, tail wagging in expectation. Ruth let out an audible sigh of relief, the tension leaving her body, but then immediately realized that the dog would not be on its own. It must have an owner. Quickly, she dashed to the bushes, grabbed her clothes and hastily dressed, her clothes feeling fresh and dry.

Glancing nervously around, she studied the density of the forest. The dog must belong to someone, but where were they? Were they watching, and if so for how long? It was not so much the thought that she might be caught, although that was always a fear, it was much more the embarrassment of

Chapter 43

being naked in front of a prowler. With no idea of time, she tried to tell from the position of the sun but she could not be really sure, only her stomach telling her it wanted something inside it, the meal of blackberries not sufficient.

The dog sat quite still, never taking its sad eyes away from Ruth, its head cocked to one side as if ready to go for a run. As hungry as she was, she broke her last piece of bread in half, offering it to her new-found friend, but the dog ignored it, ran away a few yards then sat down. Ruth quickly grabbed her small case, continuing to follow the dog as it kept repeating the procedure, leading her into the very heart of the wood, the footpath becoming almost unpassable, the long, spindly briars snatching at her shawl and scratching painfully at her bare legs bringing trickles of blood to the surface. Thistles, taller than herself prickled her bare arms, but all the while she kept a watchful eye out for strangers.

After almost a mile of rummaging through the heavy undergrowth the dog eventually ran and sat on top of a steep rock outcrop. Peering over the edge of what used to be an old quarry working, Ruth saw the spread-eagled body of a man lying motionless at the base of the rock face, one leg at a grotesque angle. Whimpering and shaking, the dog seemed to be pleading with Ruth to help.

"Oh, you clever thing," she said, stroking its smooth head. The dog only whined again like a small child, all the time turning to stare at the motionless figure at the bottom of the ravine. "What have you got me into, little dog?" Ruth remarked, but it was said with kindness, her own problems forgotten for the moment. Eventually, after a good search, Ruth found a way round to the far edge of the quarry face, but her boots were no good for scrabbling down the rock, then spying a steep, grassy bank on the far side, she ran towards it. Half way down, her footing went, the boots sliding away from underneath her, ending in an untidy heap at the bottom. The dog, more sure-footed was soon by her side, making certain she was uninjured, then licking her face, before running over to the man to do the same.

He was unconscious but still alive, Ruth detecting a faint pulse on holding his wrist. The biggest problem she could see was the badly broken limb and tried to think of a way to splint it somehow as she knew there was no chance of a Doctor. She began to search for pieces of timber and found two branches and while the man still lay unconscious, she tied them tightly to his leg with strips torn from her blanket come shawl.

Hunting further afield, a stout Y shaped branch appeared to be about the right height for use as a crutch when he regained consciousness, for he was a tall man and no way could she possibly carry him. She also noticed his gun and a handsaw at the base of the rock face among the rubble, Ruth assuming the accident must have happened when cutting timber down. The dog was now scurrying about excitedly but never venturing far from his master's side.

Eventually, the man's eyes flickered open. "Where am I? What happened? Oh, my leg. It's hurting like hell?" he grimaced, almost passing out with the pain.

"Lie still," Ruth commanded, her voice stern. "Your leg must be broken. I've tried to splint it but I am not sure how good it is. Where do you live?"

"A little cottage not far from here." Sweat poured from his brow, his face a deathly pallor from the shock of the fall and also the intense pain from the injured leg.

Ruth, trying to stay calm, said, "Well, first off, we must get you back home somehow. Do you think you will be able to manage if I support you?"

"You'll never manage me young lady, you're only a slip of a girl," as pain continued to distort his features. Then, after a moment's pause, he said, "I haven't got much option though, have I?"

Defiantly, Ruth told him, "well, I'm stronger than I look. We must try," and turning him onto his good leg, lifted him to his feet. "Now, that's the easy part done," said Ruth optimistically, "let's see if we can walk."

She was right about the easy part as once they started to walk the rough ground had them stumbling and falling every few yards and each time, he cried out in pain but, every time, he raised himself up, refusing to be beaten.

"Not far now, girl, there it is."

As they stumbled out of the dull light of the wood, Ruth rubbed the sweat from her eyes and saw, with relief, a small cottage in the distance. As they

Chapter 43

edged nearer, it appeared almost derelict. Built from a roughly hewn stone, a thick, rough thatch covered the roof, with a small wooden porch giving shelter over the doorway. Windows either side of the door were split by stone mullions dissecting each one, the timber in much need of repair and a coat of paint. Set as it was at the very edge of a grassy bowl of a field, the surrounding trees growing from the steep bank behind dwarfed it, their huge branches reaching out like loving arms, as if trying to protect the small dwelling from any further damage.

Ruth, her breath ragged and almost on her last legs just needed this ordeal over, praying she would be strong enough to last out. He was leaning so heavily on her now that her own body and knees were weak with fatigue. Her feet hurt so bad, sweat stung her eyes from the effort and her muscles were screaming stop, but his statement of 'you're only a girl,' forced her onward with a stubborn defiance, refusing to give in.

Leading the way, the little dog ran up to the front gate, jumped up and opened it with his paws, then did the same with the house door.

"You are a clever dog," Ruth gasped, never believing an animal could be so intelligent. Somehow, she managed to half drag and half carry him inside the house as he began to lapse in and out of consciousness, finally dragging him over to the settle in the corner. Ruth dropped to her knees with the effort and lay gasping for breath for a full ten minutes before she had the strength to see to her patient.

Chapter 44

The man still lay unconscious, the pain and effort in getting him home far too much for him to bear. Ruth, now her breath had eased, began to take note of her surroundings. The pine table crushed tightly against the far wall of the cottage had two cushioned chairs positioned either side with plate and cup still remaining from that morning's breakfast, she supposed. Ruth then drew in a quick breath as her gaze fell on the long-barrelled gun displayed in plain sight on the rough stone wall above the inglenook fireplace, so highly polished it glinted brightly, even in the dull light of the room. She knew from information gleaned from Miriam that the gentry, such as Lords and Ladies, in some parts of the country employed men to actually rear birds for shooting. Although the thought horrified her, she wondered, is it too much different to gutting fish on the quayside. She was prepared to do that. Shuddering, she shut her mind to such thoughts and even if he was a man who earned his living from shooting, it was no business of hers.

Ruth decided to wait until he became conscious, get help to him somehow and then be on her way. But, at present, it was more important to see that he was looked after, instead of worrying about guns. She suddenly remembered the fallen gun out in the woods, but she had no intention of retrieving it as guns frightened her. Best left to him when fit enough. It was highly unlikely

Chapter 44

anyone would be passing by to pinch it.

On the hearth stood a bucket of coal and a pile of logs ready for use in the colder weather, the blackened sandstone front showing its continuous use over the years. A drab net curtain stretched limply across one of the windows, before which a sink full of pots lay waiting to be washed. The only lighting for the room came from a lantern swinging from the bowed oak beam in the centre of the room as far as she could see, and a staircase, no better than a ladder really, must lead to a little loft above.

Searching through one of the cupboards, Ruth found matches to light the fire, knowing full well boiling water would be needed to wash the wound. Once it crackled into life, she swung the iron crane holding the kettle over the flames to boil. In the meantime, she again rummaged through cupboards and drawers to find clean cloths and bandages, making the most of the time she had while he still lay unconscious.

Ruth, not sure she was doing the right thing but better than doing nothing at all, slit the leg of his trousers and bathed the wound clean. The bleeding had stopped and the limb appeared quite straight so she replaced the splints with some straight slats found in the tiny shed outside. She also cleaned the graze to his forehead which she supposed had knocked him unconscious, unless he just fainted with the pain.

Now with her patient taken care of, Ruth had time to acquaint herself with these new surroundings while leaving the dog loyally sitting by his master's side. Taking a walk out into the garden, neat rows of vegetables all ready for picking, grew in abundance, and following the stone flagged path leading toward the river, she entered a small orchard of apple and plum trees, laden to breaking point with ripe, unpicked fruit. For Ruth, whose sole knowledge of the countryside, up to this point in her life, had all been gleaned from books, never having ventured out of the confines of the city walls of York. This was a whole new experience opening up in front of her.

As she wandered along the river side, the chatter of birds and the slight rustling of leaves from the trees was like music to her ears. Caught up in the complexity of her situation and the undeniable beauty of her surroundings, by the time her short exploration was over, the sun began its slow descent toward the distant horizon and night would soon be encroaching. Ruth, not realizing how far she had walked along the river bank, quickly retraced her steps, to return to the cottage, before dark if possible. On entering the house, the young man had roused and was sitting upright on the makeshift bed Ruth had made on the old settle and greeted her warmly.

"Now, who am I to thank for saving my life?" His voice sounded weak, but he appeared to be coherent in his speech.

"I only did what anybody would have done, sir," Ruth replied.

"It was fortunate for me you were passing by when you did."

"Well, I wasn't really passing by and it was your dog who found me and led me to you. He's very clever," she said, "and also very loyal." The dog bounded over to Ruth as if realizing she had saved her master. Ruth held the dog's head in her hands and stroked it affectionately. It responded with a rapid wagging of its tail in appreciation.

"What do you call him?"

"It's a her and I call her Nip. She was the only one o' the litter to survive and when I reared her from a pup her teeth were as sharp as needles, and would nibble and chew at anything, even your fingers if you were daft enough to let her. Nothing was safe and that's how she got her name." Ruth laughed out loud as she pictured the little pup nipping and biting the young man's hand. He carried on, "and yes, she is very intelligent. But, you know, the best thing is we never argue, do we Nip," and the dog immediately ran back to him.

"By the way my name is Dan. Dan Parkes, gamekeeper for the Lord Darley Estate." He held out a calloused hand and Ruth took it in hers.

"And your name, miss?"

"Ruth."

"And where might you be heading, Ruth? We don't get many walkers through these woods. They usually stick to the road where the stage runs."

"I'm hoping to head to the coast to look for work. I cannot afford fares so I thought I would follow the river. It must head to the coast at some point."

Dan stared hard at her. Could not believe what he was hearing. "You must be mad – or in trouble - a young slip of a girl all alone wandering the

Chapter 44

countryside. You could get yourself killed, Ruth. Don't you realize there are vagabonds and ruffians out there that would think nothing of robbing you. Or worse!" He stressed the last words so Ruth had no difficulty in understanding what he meant. She had heard stories of girls being raped and left for dead.

"I only have a small amount of money," she said, which was true. Even with Bella's savings it didn't amount to much, but she knew it may just help her buy food in the future. "But I do get frightened sometimes."

"Where did you set out from, Ruth?"

"York."

Dan gave a shake of the head in disbelief at what he was hearing, "and you walked every bit of the way?" he asked.

"Yes, I had no choice." She did not mention the fight with Henry and why she fled, and she hoped he wouldn't ask.

"Have you any family in York or anyone that knows where you are?"

"No, I haven't anyone. I did have a friend in York called Jim," she said wistfully. "But I seem to have lost him now as well."

When Dan cast her an enquiring look, she decided to explain a little further. "He's a friend who looked after me and helped me through the first awful months when I was taken to the Orphanage."

"Ah, so you have no mother or father then?"

"No, not anymore." Ruth lowered her head, feeling the familiar prickle of tears.

"I'm sorry, Ruth I didn't mean to upset you but I need to know. I might be able to help you."

"It looks as if you will be needing my help more at present."

"I am in a bit of a fix. Even though you have done a good job with the splints it could be a while before I can walk any distance and the nearest Doctor is miles away at Pickering, but I have a friend in the next village who would help me."

"Does he live close by?"

"Too far off to walk."

"How far off the road are we?"

"Only about two miles, but a rough walk."

"Well, if you write him a message, I'll run to the road and stop the next carriage that passes. That is, if you have any money."

"Yes, the money isn't a problem. It's writing." He bent his head in shame. "I can't write a word, Ruth. As true as I sit here I'm just an ignoramus. I feel so ashamed to tell you this."

"Don't be," Ruth said smiling at him. "I know plenty of people who can't write. I can write though," she said brightly. "Tell me what you want to put and I will write it for you. Where are your writing materials?"

"In the cupboard by the fire" He pointed over to the wall cupboard. "There's paper in there as well." Ruth opened the boxes and finally found pen and paper.

"Right what is your friends name?" Dan gave her the details, then his face screwed up in thought.

"I have a better idea, Ruth. You can ride old Dulcie. She's still stabled up as I never got her let out this morning. She knows her way and it will be a lot quicker. And safer," he added as an afterthought.

"Safer you say. Me, riding a horse. I've never been on horseback before. It might be me returning with a broken leg. Or worse," she said with a look of horror on her face but, deep down, the prospect quite excited her.

Dan began to laugh. He could not believe how this young girl's mind worked. She had at some time lost both her parents, placed in a house for waifs and strays, walked forty odd miles from York through unknown countryside, no doubt fleeing from some kind of trouble, and she was nervous about riding a horse. He shook his head in bewilderment before answering. "No, she is really good and very quiet. She'll have you there in no time, but it's too late now, we must leave it until morning."

When Dan assured Ruth that it would be okay to spend the night at the cottage, he said it with a smile. "Well, I can hardly attack you in my state, can I?" Ruth had to admit it was a better option than trying to find her way back to the overhanging rock near the stream, so she trusted him. He would sleep on the settle and Ruth could use the big chair by the fire, or sleep in his bed upstairs, finally deciding it best to sleep downstairs where she could

Chapter 44

keep an eye on him.

After seeing Dan drop into uncomfortable slumber following the dressing of his wound last thing, Ruth flopped into the easy chair and, totally worn out, after such a hard day slept soundly for the first time in ages.

Chapter 45

Next morning after making breakfast for them both and attending to Dan, he explained to her how to feed his menagerie of animals that he kept dotted about in little wood sheds. By the time she was finished, it was almost noon. Although quite apprehensive at the prospect of the horse ride, at the same time excitement gripped her at what lay ahead. Quickly gathering a few things together that she thought might be needed, she was soon ready for the journey.

Dan said, "I'll watch from the window until you are mounted. You'll not need a saddle or bridle, just fling the blanket over her that's hung in the stable and you'll be fine."

Ruth entered the small building, the smell of the stable strong, the warmth from the animal comforting in a way that surprised her. She had seen plenty of horses pulling carriages in the streets of York but none compared to the size of Dulcie. Ruth's head came up just short of the front shoulders of the horse, dwarfing her in comparison. The animals shimmering black coat, shining like polished jet, even in the dim light of the stable, was broken only by the purest of white stars on its forehead as the horse waited patiently for its daily exercise.

Ruth reached out a hand, tentatively touching the skin on her back. Dulcie whickered, turning her head as if to enquire 'Who are you? Where is my

Chapter 45

master?'

Trembling with apprehension and more than a little fear, Ruth whispered soothingly, "It's okay, Dulcie. You and me are going on a ride. Your master is ill and we are needed to go and fetch help." Taking a firm grip on the halter, she led her outside, the thud of the huge black hooves sounding hollow in the quietness of the stable.

Once outside Dulcie wandered obediently over to the stone mounting steps at the side of the garden and Ruth glanced across at Dan watching from the window who gave her a thumbs-up sign. Ruth mounted the steps and threw her leg over the broad back of the horse to begin a journey to she knew not where and was already willing to believe totally in this massive, intelligent animal. But for extra safety and just in case things went wrong, she grasped two huge chunks of the long rough mane at the base of Dulcie's neck and hung on, a worried smile breaking across her features.

The rough cobbled road rose steeply up from the little cottage, pushing higher and higher, before finally reaching the bleak, forbidding moorland. It proved effortless for Dulcie, and Ruth, never encountering such open spaces as this in her short life, only now beginning to realize how beautiful it could be and she loved it. Loved it for what it meant to her. The freshness, the colours, the simple pleasures that were somehow filtering into her very being, a new-found freedom never experienced before in all her life.

Ruth raised her head to the heavens to see slivers of white cloud slide past in the clear blue sky and the sun, beaming down, keeping the sharp northerly wind at bay, swaying the long-stemmed grass in the small garths rhythmically as if the whole landscape was on the move. Climbing higher, up onto the vast expanse of moorland, imperceptibly, the colours changing, becoming tinged with a soft autumnal hue, the tall stemmed bracken now beginning to fall and the once purple heather taking on a softer shade, before dying back to the blackish, brown colour ready for winter.

The long, laborious climb proved easy for Dulcie and, as Dan said, knew her way so well. Ruth's confidence grew stronger, feeling the surge of powerful muscle beneath her from this animal every step it took. She stroked the sleek black hair, the skin rippling beneath her touch.

"Oh Dulcie, I think I have fallen in love with you, dear girl." Even though she had no home or roof over her head, Ruth's spirits were high. Exhilarated on emerging from the long rough track she viewed the vast expanse of rolling hills before her not with trepidation and fear but with a precious hope toward a new beginning. In fact, so engrossed with her surroundings, she almost forgot her mission, such was the vista unfolding before her gaze.

An occasional raucous call from the moor birds as they took flight made her jump with delight and the wild life that scurried clear of Dulcie's plodding hooves took her breath away. The few sheep scattered about hardly gave them a second look, just staring up disinterestedly before returning to nibbling what they could from the moor.

Reaching the highest point which Dan had told her she would recognize by the many hill top cairns and burial mounds of the ancients who walked these moors centuries ago and also a conical shape of small stones heaped together called Stony Rook. From here they began their final descent into the valley. But not before Dulcie decided that it was time to take a drink at the old stone watering trough positioned at the roadside. On lowering her head, Ruth let out a shriek of fright, almost toppling over Dulcie's head, as her white knuckled hands still clutched tightly to the hunks of mane first grasped when setting out on her journey. Finally, having no choice but to let go of the mane her confidence grew and Ruth let Dulcie drink her fill while she took in the beauty of the countryside around her, before Dulcie decided it was time to move on, once more easing into her slow methodical plod.

Ruth, now beginning to relax, lay the full length of this magnificent animal's neck, stroking and talking all the time as the landscape of the dale took on a stunning beauty all of its own. The lush green fields in the distance were parted by the distinct darker lines of hedges and trees, stretching high up the valley side before ending at the intrusion of the bracken, held back by the rugged, dry stone walls built when agriculture first came to these valley's centuries ago.

Off in the far distance, a small hamlet came into view. As she approached, she noticed workers out in the fields and a small cluster of houses with what

Chapter 45

appeared to be an old tin church set way across the moor, separate from the main village, a long winding path snaking through the heather toward it. So, she thought, religion has somehow found its way out into these forsaken parts, but she gained no real comfort from the thought.

Suddenly a cold hand of fear clasped around her heart as she spotted the sombre shape of the Gallows looming into view in the distance just to the right of the church. Also built well clear of the village, but in a prominent position, it stood on a raised plinth of sandstone and solid stone steps leading up to the platform. The tall, oak structure of the gibbet jutted skyward, the rope loosely swinging in the light breeze.

Ruth rode steadily past, trying to tear her gaze away from the hangman's noose, her heart racing as it brought back the reality of her recent escape. If I am caught this could be my ending.

Chapter 46

Pushing these morbid thoughts from her mind, she approached the village and a square shouldered, fair haired boy approached to greet her from of one of the larger houses at the centre of this community. "I've come for help as someone needs a doctor. I was told I would get help here." The boy stroked Dulcie on the nose with a closeness that the horse seemed to acknowledge and he led it nearer to one of the buildings with a water trough by the side of it. As Dulcie took on more water, the boy held his hand out for Ruth to dismount, but she said to him. "I'm sorry, I have no time to waste, I need a Doctor urgently."

The boy made a gesture that she should follow him. Ruth could only assume he was mute for some reason, as he led the way to the nearest house, Ruth finally sliding down off the horses back, only to find her legs quite unsteady after such a long ride.

On entering, an older man sat at a writing desk, long white hair touching his shoulders. On hearing them enter, he raised his head and studied Ruth.

"Welcome, dear girl. Would you care to join me and sit for a while," but Ruth was unwilling to lose any time at all.

In earnest she said, "I need a Doctor for a man with a broken leg. Could you please help."

"Of course I can. It must be Dan at Folly Cottage needing the help is it? I

Chapter 46

recognise Dulcie. Josh get the girl a drink while I gather my bag. I know it well. You have had a long journey."

"I'm sorry, sir, but you're a man of the cloth. What good can you do?" Ruth was wringing her hands together, trying to tell them how urgent this was. "I want a Doctor. Please, I need someone who can help or I am sure he will die. I must find someone else who can help," and she turned to go. "Please, have faith. I will help you. Now, if you will just allow me time to gather my things together, you can follow me back. But first you must rest before we begin the journey back.

"No, I'm sorry, we have no time to rest. We must go now, this very instance. Dulcie knows every step. I have complete faith in her, so we must set off right away."

The old man's pale blue eyes stared kindly at her.

"You are a determined young girl. Very well, mount up and we will be on our way. Joshua, would you be kind enough to harness the trap for me and look after things while I am gone." The boy nodded, all the while watching Ruth, which made her a little uncomfortable. The sky had dulled as if a storm was brewing, or maybe it was just the darkness of evening creeping in around them as Dulcie retraced her steps, sure footed as ever.

Crossing the vast expanse of moor once more, before dropping into the shelter of the lane, the chill night air cut to the bone through Ruth's flimsy clothing and she was glad to see a steady ribbon of smoke spiralling up from the chimney into the trees and a glimmer of light from one of the little cottage windows as they approached the clearing. Ruth was first to dismount and Dulcie nudged the half open door with her nose before plodding into the stable of her own accord.

Ruth's mouth dropped open, amazed at how such animals could be so clever. Rushing in she found Dan still awake, but in a lot of pain.

"I've brought the Vicar, Dan. He says he can help and I wasn't sure what else to do. I hope I've done right," she said, immediately swinging the kettle over the still slumbering fire and also turning the lantern up brighter so the Doctor would be able to see.

"'Course you've done right, Ruth, I can't tell you how grateful I am. This man can sort me out. He knows what he's doing. Don't look so worried," he added, trying to smile across at her but it was more of a grimace.

The Vicar began to work urgently but carefully on Dan's injured leg.

"Thanks for coming so quick, Jacob."

"It appears to be a clean break, Dan, so it shouldn't be a problem but I'm afraid you will be out of action for a while. Have you some boiling water there, Ruth? I will have to disinfect it then bandage and splint it again before administering some laudanum for the pain."

Eventually Jacob finished the task and Dan dropped into a deep sleep, the laudanum doing the trick.

"He needs someone to care for him for quite a while. Do you live here, Ruth"?

Ruth thought quickly. "Err, yes, I'm his niece and have come to stay for a while." The man looked her up and down. "Strange, Dan never mentioned to me he had family living close by."

"Oh, I'm not close by and I don't think Uncle Dan and his brother get on too well."

He eyed her for a second or two, but let the matter ride, nodding as if the explanation was plausible. "Yes, families can be difficult at times. Now I will leave you with the medicine and see that he takes it when the pain is too bad. I will come back in a couple of days to see how you are managing." He smiled and Ruth bobbed a curtsy.

"Thank you so much for helping him."

"That was the least I could do and we will meet again in a few days," and with that, pulling his black hat tightly over his flowing locks and long black coat swishing behind him, he was in the trap and away, the only sound in the still, evening air, the crunch of the wheels as Jacob made his way back to the village.

Then, once again the silence of the night closed in, until somewhere deep in the trees, the mournful screech of an owl reached her ears causing Ruth to stay outside a moment longer and drink in the jewelled beauty of the star-spangled sky, trying vainly to take stock of what had happened.

Again, her life had taken on a dramatic change due to this accident, and

Chapter 46

luckily, Ruth, for now at least, had a roof over her head. For some strange reason, for the first time in her short life, an overwhelming feeling of security settled upon her. A pleasant, comforting sensation of, while not actually belonging in this remote part of the world yet, something was beginning to take hold. Something she couldn't readily explain but, felt, given time it may just happen. Sighing, she realized it may only be wishful thinking and only short term before having to move on again, once Dan was up and about.

Oh, she was not so naïve as to think it would last, nothing good in her life lasted, but for now she could remain well hidden and that meant safety at least. As the chill of the evening closed around her, an involuntary shiver passed through her and, clutching her shawl tightly about her, she wandered in to check that Dulcie had enough to drink until morning.

Chapter 47

Once back inside she plied the fire with more logs, the heat soon spreading to all corners of the small room, making it comfortable and warm. Dan lay sleeping fitfully, an occasional groan of pain escaping his lips, but Ruth would rush to settle him, gently stroking his brow with a damp cloth and reassuring him that she was there. It proved a long night but in the morning after a restless night dozing in the chair, she awakened to find Dan studying her.

Shocked and feeling slightly guilty at not being awake for him, she asked, "How are you this morning?"

"A lot better, thanks to you, young girl." Smiling at her, the serious grey eyes locked onto hers. She looked away embarrassed, although she felt a slight quickening of the heart.

Lightening the mood, Dan asked, "how did you manage, Dulcie, did she take you to the village without any bother?"

"Oh Dan, she was brilliant. I think I've fallen in love with her. We are the best of friends now."

Ruth went on to relate every step of the journey and by the time she had finished she was completely out of breath.

"I don't think I shall do anything as exciting as that in my life again. To think, me riding a horse across the moors, and as big as Dulcie." She spread

Chapter 47

her arms to try and explain the enormity of the adventure, her eyes widening again just at the mere thought of what she had achieved. Dan listened in amusement.

"Well I must say she is a very lucky horse then to have you as a friend," and Ruth once again felt the gaze of this young man hold hers for a second longer than necessary and hoped he didn't notice the sudden rush of colour rise to her cheeks.

Ruth tried to ease her embarrassment by changing the subject. "Oh, that reminds me, I must go feed her after I get your breakfast." Glad of the excuse she hurried to the table, cut the bread to make Dan a sandwich and then brought it to him.

Dan lay back on the bed "You make me feel like a Lord, Ruth. You mustn't spoil me or I will never want you to leave."

"Someone must look after you, or you would starve. Any way as soon as you can walk, I will be on my way. But that may take a while. In the meantime, I will see that you and Dulcie and all the animals are well fed and cared for. In fact, after breakfast would you mind if Dulcie and I went for another ride up onto the moor top?"

"No, that would be good for both of you. It'll give Dulcie the exercise and give you chance to explore. By the way, you did say you were on your way to the coast to find work, didn't you?"

"Yes, that's what I intend doing as soon as you are better. I will have to earn money to survive."

"Well, this is just a thought, Ruth, but next time you see Jacob, why not ask if he needs extra help. I know for a fact there is only Joshua to help out and they are beginning to do more trade on the hiring of horses for travellers and farmers hitting the road to Whitby. Also, there are many people moving into the village of nearby Roston just a few miles away, the iron ore mining industry still going strong and creating such a lot of work. He may appreciate an extra pair of hands."

This was good news to Ruth's ears, but she would not, dare not, let her hopes get too high in case they were dashed.

"Do you think that might be possible? I would feel much safer here, than taking my chance on the road to Whitby."

"I think there is every chance and I being the selfish person I am, would like you to stay." Once again, a momentary glance passed between them that told more than words could say, Ruth decided silence the better option as she would, at this moment, have floundered for the right ones to utter.

Chapter 48

The week dragged endlessly by for Jim. It seemed more like a month. During that time the big man had made a point of calling round to see him, explaining Bella's funeral had taken place, but his main reason was to ask if he had any further news on Ruth. Jim shook his head but, then excitedly, told the Judge about his possible new job out in the country, nearer the coast.

"I'm sure that's where Ruth will have headed and I'll find her eventually." Jim spoke with such conviction that it brought a lump to the older man's throat and he realized the boy did mean what he said. He would search for ever, given the chance, and his devotion for this girl had to be admired. But Jim had to be told the truth.

"I understand how much it means for you to find her, Jim, but I believe Ruth could well think she is still in trouble over the fight with Henry, believing she may have killed him and that's why she ran away. She will be hiding away, fearful of being found."

Jim's eyes blazed. "She can't be blamed for that, he attacked her, or she wouldn't of done it."

"I know, Jim, but Ruth doesn't know that. That's why we both must try and find her. And sooner rather than later."

Jim's shoulders sagged. "I want to find her, more than anything in the world, but I feel so helpless. Maybe this job will take me nearer, 'cos she won't come back here."

"No, I'm afraid she won't, but if it is any help, I will try making a few enquiries and see what happens."

A look of hope appeared in the young boy's eyes. "You really mean that, sir?"

"I really do, Jim. I have decided to cut down on my workload and delve more into the running of the Orphanage as that place is breaking all the rules of the land. But along with that I shall make it my business to spend time trying to find the whereabouts of Ruth."

Genuinely pleased with their talk which seemed to lift a load from Jim's shoulders, they shook hands and the Judge wished him all the best and both hoped for better news the next time they met.

But before they parted company, Jim was so confident he would get the job he asked John if he would write the address of the farm where he was going so that he could keep in touch.

"You'll have to write to me though, 'cos I'm not very good at writing, but when I get to see Ruth again, she'll teach me, 'cos she promised when we were in the Orphanage together. But we never actually got started…" his voice trailed off as he lifted his gaze to John. "She's very clever you know," he added as an afterthought.

John left them to their work, hoping against hope that Harry's brother would give the lad a chance. He seemed to have turned over a new leaf, earning good honest money and working hard.

As John left, he spied a horse and cart laden with bags of vegetables and sides of meat pull up at Harry's stall and the driver alighted and went up to Harry and shook his hand. After a few minutes Harry called Jim over and they stood chatting. John had seen enough. If the farmer had any sense, he would take the young lad on.

Chapter 49

John returned home. A sad, lonely place now Miriam had passed on. It was a blessing really. Once Ruth had disappeared in such circumstances it seemed to tear the heart out of her. She really had taken to the small, gutsy little girl that he had brought into the family home, so very much like the child they had lost all those years ago.

Wandering into the lounge he poured a large whisky and collapsed into the easy chair. He didn't bother with servants now there was just him in this big, rambling house. An empty shell. His mind drifted back to the day when he was called from the office to say there had been an accident. Their daughter Tiffany, just ten years old, had been running home from school when a horse, suddenly startled by one of the rare motor vehicles in the city, bolted and Tiffany was directly in its path. There was nothing the driver could do as it hit the young girl, killing her outright.

Tears coursed down John's face as he tried hard to blot the memory from his mind. And now Ruth and Bella. Oh, he knew he could never replace his daughter, wouldn't want to, but he still could not get over the striking resemblance between the pair of them. It was quite uncanny. Where will Ruth be and what will happen to her now, he began to wonder? These thoughts plagued his troubled mind as he fought to keep the ever-encompassing depression at bay which hung like a heavy, dark cloud around him. All due to the realization just how hard the young girl had fought to make a life for herself, then for it to be cruelly wrenched from her grasp by his own kith and kin, his own son who had destroyed maybe her only chance of happiness.

Now, he knew what it felt like to have no one in his life for comfort or backing, the remorse and grief of losing all who were close to him that his thoughts turned to Ruth, Bella and Jim. They had no one. Not a soul to care whether they were alive or dead.

But, he realized, he cared about them and he could try to do something about it. Surely a grown man of his stature should be able to conquer these bouts of depression and not give in to self-loathing. And it was while sitting morosely contemplating on everything that had gone wrong that he realized he should be concentrating his efforts more on putting things right. After a few minutes, he raised his bulk from the chair, a new determination gripping him, deciding to look to the future, not the past. With a mighty swing of his arm, he hurled the whisky glass against the wall and made the decision that first thing in the morning he would call in at work and prepare young Solomon to look after things. After all, he was twenty-six years old, knew the property law inside out and had a very good head on him. He was also especially good with the customers and their problems.

As his spirits brightened, he made the decision not only to try and find some information on the whereabouts of Ruth, but also to see if it was possible to change how things were run at that blasted Orphanage.

Also, since their fall out, he had never sought contact with Henry, but through other sources, he had recently heard that he had not improved his ways and was treading the path toward destruction with his heavy drinking and gambling.

Too late, John realized he had spoilt him. Made it far too easy for him over the years. Instead of spending time with his son, he had smothered him with a ready supply of cash in his pocket to fritter away, Henry never having to fight for anything in his life. John realized now that this was only done to ease his own feelings of guilt as a poor father who let his son down.

Where was it going to end, a good-looking young man who had everything

Chapter 49

life had to offer and would end up with nothing. Not even his reputation intact. John undressed and got into bed with only his thoughts for company. But a plan was already forming in his head.

Chapter 50

Jim jumped nimbly up onto the back of the now empty wagon and sat down on the sacks, a smile on his face, a new life beckoning. Albert Styles and his wife Martha sat up front, Albert expertly handling the pair of horses, soon leaving the open roads to begin the steep climb up onto the crest of the high moor. Albert had mentioned to the youngster it was going to be a long ride and he better settle down in the back of the cart and the soft, rhythmic clop of the horses' hooves soon had Jim, for all his apprehension of what lay ahead, fast asleep.

Sometime later, the sun easing ever closer to the far horizon, they topped the rise from the last village and Jim opened his eyes to find himself in a totally different world. No messy streets here, no smell of garbage, no horses and carriages, or people milling to and fro.' No houses much either, just rolling hills and wild, seemingly endless expanses of moorland, before suddenly dipping down between steep, craggy hillsides and eventually, just before dusk, descending through an avenue of overhanging trees, Jim saw the small farmhouse in the distance.

Wide awake now, he was keen to take everything in. A couple of stone buildings ran alongside the main dwelling, a few sheep and cows grazing contentedly in the nearby fields, and a few hens squawked noisily as they quickly flapped out of the way of the cart wheels as they clattered loudly

Chapter 50

over the blue, black cobbles of the yard before pulling to a halt outside the stable door.

"Right, here we are, Jim. If you will help me stable the horses up for the night, Martha will go and make sure there is a bed ready for you."

"Thank you, Mister Styles." Then after a short silence, he added, "I hope I can do right by you and do the job. I'm a bit nervous, you know?"

"You will be, Jim, but don't worry. It'll take a few days to settle in then you'll be fine," smiling reassuringly at this young boy who he'd taken on, straight from the slums of the city. Deep inside, Albert was also a little bit worried, though he didn't show it. It was a gamble taking a complete stranger on and a youngster at that, away from the only life he knew and out into the wilds of the country. How would he cope? Albert shook his head. He must be mad. Any number of things could go wrong. But it was too late to worry about that now.

He knew the boy would have to adapt pretty quickly, but he and Martha had talked it over and he couldn't put his finger on it, but they had both spotted something in this slip of a lad that made them think he may just come through and it wasn't just the ever-ready cheeky smile and optimism.

When Jim and Albert had 'stabled up' as Albert called it, Martha had a log fire roaring in the comfortable kitchen as nights were turning chilly and a steaming dinner ready for the pair of them. Jim couldn't believe such comfort, totally different to anything he'd ever known in his short life and Albert cast a quick glance to his wife as the boy stood quietly just inside the door.

"Come in, Jim. You must be hungry?" Martha held her hand out for him to come up to the table. "And while we eat you can tell us all about your life in York," ushering him to a chair and sitting him down. Once seated, Albert bowed his head and recited grace.

"Now then, what would you like, Jim? There's plenty of everything. Meat, potato, vegetables. Whatever you want."

"I am hungry, but I'm not sure what I like. I've never tried any of this. I've never ever seen so much food as this in me life. In the Orphanage they feed us gruel and bread and it's sometimes stale you know, but we have to eat it or else go hungry. That's not right, Mrs Styles is it? It's not our fault we have no mothers and fathers. We didn't ask to be put there, but, nowhere else to go see, but they don't care. Nobody cares." He said this with a sigh of weariness.

Suddenly Martha found tears springing to her eyes and she quickly brushed them away, but Jim noticed.

"Some dust got in your eye, Mrs Styles. No wonder, it were windy coming back in that cart, weren't it?"

She smiled back at him. "Yes it was. Now eat your dinner up and then I will show you where you are sleeping as it is getting late." Martha knew then, as she watched him wolf the food down, this boy, given a chance, may just grow up to be a fine man and make something of his life, even though he'd had a rough start. After eating, Albert pulled his rocking chair nearer to the fire, lit his pipe, giving Jim a moment to take stock of his surroundings.

The big pine table where they had just eaten took pride of place in the centre of the kitchen covered by a green coloured oil cloth, with an old black paraffin lamp hanging from the beams above. The six chairs, placed around the table, each had their own neatly embroidered cushion on the seat and a tall wooden dresser with brass handles stood to one side of the window. The black cast iron range with its large oven doors where Martha did most of her cooking and baking, dominated one wall of the kitchen and a brightly coloured clip mat lay on the floor, where a couple of cats laid smugly in front of the fire, with a rocking chair just to the side. Old fashioned sepia tinted photos adorned the walls, of past family members, Jim assumed. He would have to ask later when settled in more, but for now, he would have to learn how to cope with this new way of life.

A shiver swept through him as he returned to reality, realizing just what a step he'd taken. Although nervous about what the future held, he must try not to show it and hopefully he might just be able to manage the work and be able to make a go of it.

Martha studied him quietly, knowing the lad would need time to settle in. She would not rush him though. Giving him a few more minutes, she gently asked, "are you ready to go up to your room, Jim? It's all ready for

Chapter 50

you." Leading the way upstairs, Martha ushered him into the bedroom. He somehow thought he must be dreaming, this couldn't be happening. A whole room, with proper furniture, all to himself.

"Right," Martha said, "make yourself comfortable Jim and breakfast will be at 7 30. You have a clock on the table there, alongside the jug and basin for washing and tomorrow we'll have to see about getting you some different clothes."

"Thank you, Mrs Styles. I really will keep out of trouble you know," he said earnestly. "I won't steal anything from you and I'll try my best for you and Mr Styles."

"I know you will and that is all we ask. If we are all honest with each other, do our best and tell the truth, there is nothing in this whole world that we cannot overcome as a family."

At the mention of the word 'family,' a solid lump suddenly lodged itself in Jim's throat that somehow seemed to stop him speaking properly and all he could manage to say was,

"Do you think that might happen, Mrs Styles?"

"I'm sure of it, Jim," and with that he flung his arms around her waist, hugging her close, before turning away, just managing to mutter a quick "G'night" hoping that Mrs Styles hadn't noticed the moistening of his eyes before the door closed and she returned to the comfort of her kitchen.

Chapter 51

Jim's room was small but cosy, the bed pushed tight up to one wall and a couple of pictures of rose covered cottages hanging either side of the small window which looked out onto open fields. He quickly washed, poured himself a glass of water before undressing then felt the softness of the feather bed before jumping in. Jim had never once thought that there might be a different life for anyone like him. Now, hardly daring to hope too soon, he could see that things may change, as long as he was up to managing the jobs that Albert gave him. And with that thought uppermost in his mind he tried to sleep, as he had an early morning looming.

Jim was up by seven, washed and dressed in a few minutes, drawing the curtains back to let the light flood in. Peering out of the window, he lost track of time as he sat and watched the steep and rugged purple clad moors appear to rise up through the early morning mist as the sun lifted above the horizon into the clear blue sky. Glancing at the clock, he realized he'd sat too long and was now late.

Rushing downstairs, he found Martha already up and about and a fire in the hearth taking the chill off the early morning air.

"Sorry I'm late, Mrs Styles," he gasped. "It wasn't that I was asleep, I was up at seven, but I must have sat and watched the sun come up. I'd never seen that before. I really am sorry."

Chapter 51

"Don't worry, Jim. I must admit it was stunning this morning. I even sat and had a cup of tea and watched it myself. Did you sleep well?"

"Oh, Mrs Styles, that's the bestest bed I've ever slept in. Mind you," he said with a smile, "I've only ever slept in the Orphanage and that was like sleeping on old boards and sacking for covers. Jim looked around before asking the question, "where's Mr Styles?"

"He's outside feeding up. Are you going to give him a hand?"

"Course I will," and with that he ran outside into the cow byre where Albert sat on a three-legged stool snuggled in between the cows with a half full bucket of milk clutched between his knees.

"Can I do something, Mr Styles?"

"Yes, Jim. If you would grab that fork, stick it into that pile of hay and walk down the front of them and fodder each cow with a fork full."

Jim was slightly nervous, but did not intend showing it, so keeping a wary eye on the cows, he did as asked and the cows were soon feeding away while Albert kept on milking.

"Now if you can do the same for the horses, take 'em a bucket of water from the trough as well, then we'll both go and see to the hens and pigs."

By the time they had all the animals fed it was time for breakfast. Jim could smell the eggs and bacon frying and suddenly he was so hungry, he dashed into the house before Albert and pulled a chair up to the table. Suddenly, he remembered where he was, got up and hung his head.

"Sorry, Mrs Styles, I didn't mean to rush in like that, but it smelt so good I forgot me manners."

"That's okay. Albert's here now so we can start."

Over the next few months Jim settled into the farm work, proving especially good with Tanner and Farmer, proving quick to learn and listening to everything Albert told him, his brain like a sponge, taking everything in.

After a few days out ploughing together in the lower fields, Albert surprised Jim by asking, "d'you think you could handle a day on the plough, Jim? If you just take Tanner on his own, I suggest you have a go at ploughing the small, bottom field below the house. I'll keep an eye on you up at the buildings."

"Yeah, I'm pretty sure I can. I've watched you these last few days and I really did fancy a go at it." He smiled up at Albert, as he said, "you won't sack me if I get it wrong, Mr Styles, will you?"

Albert laughed. "No, you'll get more than one chance here, Jim," and Albert watched as the young man, because that was what he was growing into, harness Tanner and set off to the lower field. Albert took note from a distance as Jim measured the headlands out around the outside before marking the patch to plough. His early efforts proved hard work as the old single furrow plough threw him about like a cork, but with sweat dripping from his brow, after half a day, he felt he had mastered it.

At the end of the day Albert gazed down into the field and sited the furrows through. He could not have bettered it himself, the lad had them as straight as an arrow. Albert shook his head in disbelief. First day out on his own and the boy had ploughed like a veteran. When he himself had started it had taken him weeks before he could hang on to the plough and months before he got anything like straight. This boy did it from the word go.

With the passing of time, Jim's confidence grew, going from strength to strength, settling into the farming community's little oddities and its way of life. The hard work and long hours were tiring but he loved it. Just one thing bothered him. He was still no nearer to finding Ruth than the day he arrived here.

Chapter 52

After a hearty breakfast one morning, Albert told Jim the fencing needed repairing across at the moor wall and once that was finished, he intended making a trip with the beast that were ready for the market by the end of the week. "How would you like that, Jim?"

"That would be good. Where's the market, Mr Styles?" Jim asked mystified, never having heard of the place.

"Well, Jim, it happens to be just a mile or two out of Whitby, so mebbe if we get unloaded in good time you might be able to grab a lift into town and have the day to yourself."

Jim's face lit up. "D'you think that's possible. I'd love that 'cos I've never been to Whitby. And you know what Mr Styles, that's where Ruth and I used to talk about heading for when leaving the Orphanage. I'm sure that's where she'll be. Hey, this is great news. I'm so excited I won't be able to stop thinking about it. This week's gonna seem a long, long time."

"Ah, now, Harry did tell me you were sweet on a little young thing at the Orphanage. Told me you hadn't seen her since she got into trouble for picking pockets. Is that right?"

Jim's head dropped onto his chest, disconsolate as he remembered their parting, him running away, leaving Ruth on her own once again to face the consequences. How could he have been so heartless.

"Ruth would never have done anything like that, but it was me who talked her into doing it. She kept telling me it weren't right and it was her that got caught and I ran away. Not much of a man, am I? Mebbe she won't want to see me now." His face clouded with sadness before looking beseechingly at them both and said quietly, "but I need to know. I need to find her, then she can tell me herself that she doesn't want anything to do wi' me."

Albert glanced across at Martha and saw her studying this growing figure of a boy as she said, "Now, don't get too despondent Jim, but also, don't get your hopes up too high either. It's a long while now since you've seen her and a lot has changed since then. Just look at how your life has changed? And even in the unlikely chance of you finding her, or meeting her, things could be different now because her life will most likely have moved on the same as yours has."

"Are you trying to tell me she might have forgotten me, Mrs Styles. Nah, she'll not have forgotten me. She might not want out to do wi' me, but she'll not have forgotten me." He said this in an effort to bolster his confidence up in front of Albert and Martha, the self-same confidence which had seen him through this far, and he flashed a grin at the ageing couple as if he really did believe Ruth would still not be able to resist him.

"Nah, I bet after a few minutes it'll be like old times when we meet up." Then, he looked in earnest at them both before saying, "but that doesn't mean we would go back to being in trouble with the law."

"Well, I'm glad to hear that," said Martha, smiling at such optimism. "Now out you go and get that fencing done. The sooner it's done, the sooner you can be on your way."

But the week didn't drag. It was such hard work through the day, Jim was pleased to flop into bed every evening and each night, in his thoughts, Ruth drew a little closer. While working together, Albert had tried to tell Jim that it could be a hopeless task, like looking for a needle in a haystack. Whitby was a big place and a thriving port with many people living there. Ruth could be anywhere by now. With nothing solid to go on, they had no way of knowing.

But it was no use. His enthusiasm knew no bounds. "No, I'm pretty sure

Chapter 52

that's where she'll be, Mr Styles. Oh, it might take a few weeks, even months and a few trips, but we'll find her. I know we will."

A sorrowful look came into Albert's eyes. He could see Jim being left with a broken heart if things didn't work out. In some ways he was hoping he didn't find her in case the girl had moved on or was with someone else. She would be going on thirteen now and growing up, not the same innocent child that he remembered.

Repairing the moorland fence went well, using the many posts cut by themselves on the old saw bench and they returned from the moor just before darkness fell. Although Albert was not an old man, he was beginning to feel his age and definitely glad of the extra pair of hands from Jim and with a settled spell of weather lasting all week, it left the two of them a free day to get the beasts ready and be loaded and away first thing Friday morning.

Jim jumped out of bed at the crack of dawn, hardly able to contain his excitement, and while he backed Tanner and Farmer, his two horses for the day, into the shafts, Albert had the four young beasts loaded into the cart and they were soon on their way.

A long pull up out of the valley base had the horses breathing hard, but once hitting the level going made good time and Jim and Albert were quite happy in their own thoughts, enjoying the peace and solitude of the countryside they were crossing. Albert passed on his knowledge of the ancient stone monuments on the roadside and pointed out the old coaching Inn perched high on the bleak moor of Blakey Ridge, now silhouetted on the skyline away to their left. Once past this point, it was a downward sweep all the way to the small village of Gallows Howe where they would grab a change of horses, before the final stage to Whitby.

On arrival at the clustered little hamlet of roughly built stone houses, both Albert and Jim were ready for a drink. Jim noted some of the buildings were in disrepair, but the larger ones lining the side of the pot holed street appeared to be in a state of renovation. Shielding his eyes against the sunlight, he spotted the old tin church in the distance and only a few yards away stood the sinister form of the gallows, no longer in use but left as a stark reminder to anyone who thought of turning to criminal ways to earn money. Not difficult to see how the village earned its name, thought Jim.

After taking in the surroundings of this village, Jim unhitched the sweating horses, leading the pair over to the drinking trough, talking gently to them all the time and understanding they would be glad of the rest. A few people were going about their daily chores and nodded in his direction; or wished him good day.

Albert had already gone to the house at the end of the street to pay for another pair that would see them through to the coast without another stop. On entering Joshua came across to help him. Joshua had an honest, open face with piercing blue eyes, and even though it was quite a warm day, Josh still wore the loose top coat that flapped around his knees.

"Morning, Josh, you look in fine fettle today. Can you fix me up with a couple of horses for today? These two are almost done in."

Joshua smiled and nodded while opening a tattered book on the table where Albert signed his name and handed over the money. Albert well knew that Joshua was mute, had known him since he was a child and heard the story of how he lost his voice. His family were hopeful his speech would return, but it had been many years now since the boy had uttered any sound at all and Albert held doubts this would ever happen.

"Thank you, Josh, and good day to you." Josh raised his hand to show his acknowledgement, but just as Joshua closed the book, a young girl entered from the back room. He caught her eye but she quickly turned away and hurried out. This was someone that Albert didn't recognize, hadn't seen about before. Not that he travelled this way much, but he knew most people around here and this one was a stranger.

Once the girl had disappeared, Albert asked casually,

"Now who was that girl, Joshua? Someone you've been hiding away all these years?" Joshua just shrugged his shoulders and dropped his gaze, but Albert noticed a flush came to the young man's features. Not wanting to embarrass him further, Albert wandered outside into the bright sunlight and sat awhile smoking his pipe while Jim hitched the two new horses between the shafts and harnessed up.

Chapter 52

Puzzled over the young girl, Albert mulled it over in his mind, thinking he must try and find out more on the way back. He would have a word with the boy's father Jacob on his return. He decided not to mention any of this to Jim just yet until he found out more, but there was a slim chance that… no, don't be silly, gather your thoughts, Albert, you sentimental old fool, it's young Jim's enthusiasm rubbing off on you now. Pushing it to the back of his mind, he heard Jim shout he was ready for the last leg of the journey. Rushing out, Albert mounted the cart and they were on their way.

Chapter 53

Soon, they began the descent leaving the high moor behind and quickly heading toward the coastal town of Whitby, the sea a picture of blue, shimmering below them, the magnificent old Abbey standing out in stark defiance against the forces of Nature on the very edge of the cliff. Jim rubbed his eyes to make sure he wasn't just seeing things. He'd never been to the coast, in fact, never ventured out of the city of York. Oh, he'd heard stories from other people that had visited the seaside, even heard tales of Pirates on the high seas, but never in his short life did he expect to go there and witness it and could hardly contain his excitement as Albert explained that, once unloaded, Jim could have most of the day to himself.

Caught up in the bustle and excitement of the market, they both set about the task of unloading the young beasts, herding them into one of the rickety wood pens. Now unloaded they sat together in the back of the cart and ate heartily into the sandwiches Martha had packed, as Albert voiced his concern as to what they would bring under the auctioneer's hammer, as there looked to be some good stock here today.

"Don't worry, Mr Styles, they look as good as any of the others that are here."

"Always confident aren't you, Jim. Nothing ever seems to knock you back."

"Nothing in the world can ever be as bad as what I've suffered. When I

Chapter 53

meet up with Ruth again, I can picture a life for me. That's when everything will be perfect, Mr Styles."

Albert caught the young man's eye. "I'm sure it will be Jim," but it was said with a lot less conviction than he felt. "Now, if you fancy going for a wander, Jim, your time is your own. Keep an eye on the Abbey clock. The sale will be over by mid-afternoon and we must be away by three. Now go on and don't get into any mischief or be led astray by these bonny young girls that flutter their eyes at you."

He winked at the lad and the infectious gap-toothed smile surfaced, lighting the young boy's face as he answered, "Hopefully, trouble is behind me now, Mr Styles, thanks to you and Mrs Styles." Albert's heart swelled with pride as he watched Jim run off to find a ride into the nearby town.

Grabbing a lift from a Whitby man who was returning home from a delivery, Jim had almost forgotten what it was like to have time to himself and to be surrounded by so many people. He knew the town of Whitby relied on its fishing fleet as he and Ruth often talked of running away and trying to find work in this very town and this very thought was uppermost in his mind as he made his way to where the fishing boats docked.

Along the quayside a long line of women stood, of all ages, dressed in rough pinafores and bonnets, quickly and expertly gutting the fish, before tossing them into large trays placed at their side. Jim put a hand over his mouth as the overpowering smell of fish almost turned his stomach but the thought that Ruth might, just might, be among this line strengthened his determination. When studying the women as he passed, some raised weathered, wrinkled faces to meet his inquisitive stare with hard, defiant eyes, while others, mainly the younger ones, smiled cheekily back at him. Jim responded, grinning from ear to ear, enjoying this attention, the sound of their giggles reaching his ears as he sauntered further down the harbour side.

But there was not to be a first sighting. No sign of anyone Ruth's age, they were all a lot older than Jim expected. To clear his nostrils from the smell of fish, Jim decided on exploring the ancient cobbled streets of this bustling, thriving port, finally chancing upon the twisting stone steps rising up to the old Abbey itself.

On reaching the very top, Jim halted, gasping for breath and while resting, he gazed down upon the many ships moving steadily out from the safety of the harbour to where the wind whipped sea tossed them rhythmically further and further out into the vast expanse of the North Sea until lost from sight. Deep in thought, the chimes from the Abbey clock brought him back to reality. Jumping up, he ran down the steps and hopped onto the back of a cab and hoped it was heading close to the market. His luck was in, jumping off at the top of the bank and running the rest of the way. On arrival he was pleased to see a smile on Albert's face. The beast had done well so it would be a happy ride home for the pair of them.

It proved a cruel drag for the horses before finally reaching the flatter moorland tracks, but once there they made good time, Jim taking over as driver and telling Albert all what had happened, as Albert sat back to enjoy his pipe.

Chapter 54

On their arrival at Gallows Howe, the horses were bathed in sweat and breathing hard. In fact, to help ease their load, Jim and Albert both jumped off to walk alongside the cart on the steep uphill gradients and only about an hour of daylight remained when they arrived to gather up their own horses and head for home. Jim made sure the animals had a good drink after their hard day before returning them to the stable. Joshua was on hand to take the pair from him and stable them up for the night.

"Thank you. The horses have done really well for us today and hopefully we'll be back again next week to do the same. By the way, my name's Jim," and he held out his hand. Joshua took the proffered hand in a firm grip but dropped his gaze and quickly walked away. Jim, slightly embarrassed wondered what he'd done to bring about such a rebuttal.

On the way back home, Jim became wrapped up in his own thoughts until he said, "Albert, how long have you known the stable lad?"

"Oh, since he was born. Growing into a fine, strong man and good with horses. Why, what's on your mind, Jim?"

"Well, when I took the horses back, I told him they'd done us proud, especially around these hills and he never answered, he just lowered his head, shook hands, turned and walked away and I just wondered if I'd done anything wrong for him to be like that."

Albert smiled across at him. "No, you did nowt wrong Jim. Joshua has been mute since he was about ten years old. You'll mebbe not remember, a few years back we suffered terrible floods. I remember it well as it wasted most of our crops. Fields just stood in water. Anyway, after days of rain, the river below Gallows Howe burst its banks and the story goes that Joshua and his mother had an argument, Joshua ran out in a fit of temper slamming the door behind him and headed to the swollen river. Well, as any mother would, she raced after him shouting out in the storm for him to come back. Josh didn't hear, or didn't listen and lost his footing near the river. His mother jumped in to save him, which she did, somehow managing to push him onto the bank but the current proved too strong for her and sadly she was swept away while Josh could do nothing but watch. His father Jacob found him still sat on the bank staring into space and he's never been the same since."

"That's terrible, Albert. I really am sorry. I didn't realize."

"Not your fault, Jim. You weren't to know. Besides, you'll see him again next week as we have some more stock ready."

They both lapsed into a comfortable silence, the still of the night broken only by the sound of the steady clop of hooves and the crunch of the wheels and just as the greyness of dusk descended, they arrived back at the farm. After feeding up was done it was completely dark and Martha had a dinner put before them and a fire going to take the chill of the evening away.

"Have you managed okay today, Jim?" Martha asked.

"We've had a really good day haven't we, Mr Styles? D'you know that's the first time I've ever seen the sea. I ran up the steps to the old Abbey and looked down on the town to see all those fishing boats. Well, I couldn't believe it. I just stood and watched 'em all sail out to sea until they were tiny specks. But I s'pose I'll need a few more visits to find Ruth. There were hundreds of young girls gutting fish down by the bridge, so she could be there."

"Now, I've told you before, don't you go getting your hopes up young man. It'll be like looking for a needle in a haystack and she might not even be at

Chapter 54

Whitby. She could be anywhere."

"Aye, I realize now it might not be as easy as I thought but if I keep looking, I will find her."

"Well, if effort's anything to go by, I'm sure one day you will."

"Right, well I'm off to bed, Mrs Styles, it's been a long day. I'm more tired wi' travelling than I am working." A grin flashed across his face, the cheeky features now filling out and also losing their paleness and becoming more weather beaten. Martha watched him go. He had arrived at this farm a young boy. She knew one day he would leave as a man in the not too distant future.

Albert could see what she was thinking and came across to the old range, drawing his chair nearer the fire and reached out for her hand.

"I know what you're thinking" he said, "and yes, he's bound to leave us sometime, but let's not worry about that right now. We don't know what the future holds for us, never mind Jim. But we have some more stock ready to move next week and prices are up, so things are looking good." Albert got stiffly up from his chair and gave Martha a kiss on her brow.

"I'm off up to bed now, Martha, cos we have another hard day tomorrow."

"Aye, and the way you got out o' that chair, you're not getting any younger. You will have to take things a bit easier now Jim's here."

"I know, but I don't want to leave it all to him," and he turned toward her once more, an earnest look on his face, "but I've been thinking lately and I must admit Martha, he's got something in him that he might just take to the land. And who knows, we have a little bit put by, we might be able to take things easier and eventually hand over to Jim who would pay us a rent. What do you think o' that?"

Now it was Martha's face that lit up as she smiled up at her husband. "Now, that would be grand, wouldn't it, but I'll believe it when it happens," and went back to her sewing as she heard the door close and Albert's footsteps take the stairs.

She sat awhile staring into the fire, as thoughts swirled about in her head at what Albert had just said. Would that ever be possible? Not knowing the answer, she placed her sewing down by her side and began to pray quietly.

She prayed for all their futures but, in particular, she was praying that if God had any spare goodness to pass down, then to make sure it came young Jim's way, because he surely deserved a break.

Chapter 55

Ruth had taken Dan's advice in asking Jacob if he needed any extra help at Gallows Howe and he was only too pleased with an extra pair of hands. Just two days a week until Dan recovered which gave her time to look after him. Dan was now back walking with the aid of a crutch. A much better one than the one Ruth had crafted. Lord Darley's Land Agent had called to see him shortly after the accident, making the excuse of enquiring after his health, but Dan knew his job would be in jeopardy if the man thought he could not manage to look after the estate.

Dan sat with him and they discussed the situation while Ruth made them both a cup of tea and to save embarrassing questions as to who the girl was, as he noted the man casting inquisitive glances in her direction, Dan said, "We are managing pretty well really. It so happened my brother's daughter was on school holiday and able to come and look after me for a while, which couldn't have worked better. Ruth is looking after the livestock really well and the moor birds will take no harm until I am better. That will give me time to recover as the leg is mending well now."

This appeared to satisfy the man and it was quite true, Ruth had become quite adept at seeing to the animals, relishing the time she spent with them, especially Dulcie, often out early morning and enjoying the responsibility of looking after things. She did not enjoy milking the goat as much. Dan showed her how but found this difficult as every time she sat down next to the goat it would begin nibbling her hair, so, finding an old cap of Dan's, pushed her hair up inside to keep it safe. When Dan walked outside into the bright sunlight and saw her, he burst out laughing.

"It's not funny, Dan Parkes. Maisy keeps pulling my hair out in big chunks. I had to cover it with something," but she also found herself laughing alongside him, while Maisy continued to chew anything she could find.

As time passed, Ruth realized the change in herself. She found herself laughing more, the spark of adventure and learning that had once burned bright in her eyes sparkled again. Her confidence at the cottage and also in her job at the village, where she did the housework for Jacob grew stronger. Sometimes when things got too busy for Joshua, she would help out in the stables as the horse renting had turned into a thriving business, with more and more people arriving daily, many with young families, and settling in the dale due to work created by the mining industry at the nearby village of Roston.

Ruth had adapted to this way of life, loved working with the animals, especially the horses, and the kindness shown to her by the people she met overwhelmed her, so different from her past life.

The dark memories still remained with her of these times, but with every passing day they receded, but she could never, deep in her heart, totally rid herself of the deep-lying fear that her whole new world could, or would, all suddenly fall apart.

Chapter 56

Albert and Martha had enjoyed a good year on the farm. Profitable. They were breeding good stock, prices were up and the young beasts were selling well and Albert thought it time to sit down and have a chat with Jim about his future. When evening approached and when work was finished, they sat by the fire talking, Albert broached the subject cautiously, saying, "Jim, I think the time has come when we should all sit down and have a discussion about your future."

Concern spread across Jim's youthful features as he said, "What's up, have I done anything wrong, Mr Styles, 'cos if I have it wasn't intended."

"No, far from it, Jim. I think maybe you are ready to take on more responsibility around the farm. You've learnt well and come on a treat. What I'm trying to say is that Martha and I are not getting any younger and if you are thinking of staying on to work the farm then we should have something legal signed up that if, or when, anything happens to us, as we have no family to take the farm on, you will become the sole owner of the farm. How does that sound."

Jim, not usually one to be lost for words, suddenly found he couldn't speak for the lump that had formed in his throat, his eyes moistening, having to wipe away the tears with the back of his hand. Eventually, after a few moments gathering his thoughts and realizing just what this meant, the ever-ready smile began twitching at the corners of his mouth. He answered, "I don't know what to say, Mr Styles. You know I like it here. If you think it would work and it's the right thing to do, then I am not walking away from an opportunity like this." His brow furrowed, deep in thought. On looking up, he said, "you know what I'm going to say don't you?"

"I think I do, Jim."

"There is only one thing that would drag me away from here and that's Ruth."

Martha leaned forward and placed her hand on Jim's knee, saying quietly, "but who is to say that, if you did meet up with Ruth, that she might even find the idea of wanting to stay here with you quite acceptable."

"Well, if it were to happen like that, then it would just be a perfect world, wouldn't it?" and the cracked front tooth came on full display. Then suddenly, the big, burly figure of Judge John Durville at his law offices in York burst into Jim's thoughts.

"Have you anyone in mind, Mr Styles?"

"No, not off hand. You see, Martha and I have never had any need of lawyers, never had the money either, even if we had needed 'em. Only papers either of us has signed was when my parents handed the farm down to us and our wedding certificate," he said with a smile.

"Well, I might just have the man for us. I knew him at the Orphanage and he told me if I was ever struggling with anything, he would help me if he could," and with that he rushed up the stairs and found the card the Judge had given him, having kept it to get in touch when he found Ruth. He came back down and handed it to Albert.

Albert read the proffered card. "Judge John Durville.

Commercial and Business Lawyers. Offices. 15 Hargrove Court, York along with his phone number written on the back."

"You know him well, Jim?" Albert asked.

"Yes, he was good to me and Ruth. Ruth worked for him for a long time, then I don't know what happened. All I know is she ran away because of some trouble at the house but it wasn't Ruth's fault. He told me so. That's why he gave me the card to let him know if I ever found her. I've kept it ever

Chapter 56

since." Albert, a certain sparkle now lighting his eyes, said, "this sounds good news, Jim, just the man for us if we can contact him. I shall write a letter first thing tomorrow if you can carry out a job for me. I have taken on a contract with the mining company to supply pit props, just for the drift mines at present up on the moor top, but who knows what the future holds. They are not happy with their current suppliers and we have a surplus of wood on this hillside above the farm and with our own stationary engine and saw-bench in the barn, plus our own labour, we should be able to make some money from it. I'm not sure how long the mining will last, but if we can make a bit from it, then it's all to the good."

"So that's what you've been doing on the saw-bench all this time. I wondered what all those short, heavy posts were for. You must have been busy Mr Styles as we have a barn full. When do we start supplying?"

"I have a load to go first thing tomorrow. That's if you are ready for it, Jim."

"More than ready. I'll get a good start in the morning."

"That's settled then," said Albert." I'll feed up and then write my letter. That'll be harder than a day's work for me, 'cos writing doesn't come easy to me, but I'll manage and if you'll take charge of the wagon and horses that gets us under way."

Up at the crack of dawn, a beautiful red, grey mottled sky cast a pinkish tinge to the tree tops, informing him of a glorious day ahead. Jim strode into the stable, both horses acknowledging his entrance with a snort and a sharp toss of their heads, the comforting warmth and smell hitting him as soon as he opened the door. Jim started to talk as soon as he entered, the horses used to the sound of his voice. "I'll feed you well today. It's going to be a hard pull up onto that railway line whichever way we tackle it. I want no slacking from you, Tanner," he said stroking her neck. Jim knew Tanner well enough now and kept a keen eye on her, knowing she slacked off if you let her. She was a striking white Galloway but was getting on in years now. Albert had started the farm with her many years ago but the old horse was now beginning to feel her age. "Farmer needs all the help he can get today," he said rubbing her nose affectionately.

Dragging the harness from the saddle racks, he hefted the barfins up and around their necks and then the saddles to carry the shaft chains and as the sun broke over the moor top, they were pulling hard up the moor track with Jim urging them forward. By mid-morning they approached the track snaking around the very top of the valley, twisting its way through bogs and cuttings, passing the calcining arches and the huge chimney billowing smoke into the clear blue sky.

Ahead lay Jim's delivery point, but there seemed to be an enormous amount of activity taking place at the head of the new drift this morning. Drawing nearer, he realized something serious had taken place. Bodies were laid out on stretchers, others sat at the trackside, arms and heads heavily bandaged.

"Whoa Farmer, Tanner, whoa." Jim shouted, hauling back on the reins, bringing them to a halt, the pair glad of the respite. Jumping from the wagon Jim ran across enquiring as to what had happened.

One of the men, still dazed told him "there's been a fall further into the tunnel, the props broke up and there's still a couple of miners trapped. We can't get to them as the access is filled with rubble and too dangerous."

Jim ran to the mine head. "What's happening? How many are in there?" he shouted at the dishevelled men stood before him, concern showing in their faces.

A reply came from one of the band of men crowded around the mine head. "Still two trapped, young 'un. We're just trying to sort a way for getting 'em out."

"How far into the tunnel are they?" Jim asked urgently.

"Five hundred yards, maybe more. The problem is the pit props. They're too weak. We've been at t'management for ages, but they've done nothing but cut corners for their own profit. Damn 'em, damn 'em to Hell!" His dirt stained face was ashen with anger, but also from fright.

"Is there still a way in to 'em?" Jim asked.

"Aye, but it's not safe."

Jim suddenly flung his coat off and dashed into the entrance.

"Come back, you fool, it could collapse at any minute." shouted the man.

Chapter 56

Jim didn't listen, shouting, "Someone follow me in. If I can reach them I'll need some help to drag 'em out if they're unconscious."

"You idiot," the man bellowed. "Wait, you'll need a light," and with that disappeared into the darkness to follow hard on Jim's heels. It was rough going and Jim was soon in a crouching position and already scrubbing his backbone raw on the roof of the tunnel. The man followed Jim, the light from the man's helmet providing some guidance. Now, the roof above got even lower and Jim dropped down onto hands and knees. Deathly quiet, the only sound the squelching of their movements as they wriggled and crawled, almost on their bellies now, through the slime and mud.

When stopping to catch their breath, the steady drip of water from the tunnel roof and their heavy breathing sounded loud in their ears. Now, up ahead they could see, in the faint light, the cracked and splintered props. Almost flat on the ground Jim shouted, "Hello," his voice sounding weird, hollow even, as it echoed up the tunnel. Nothing. He shouted again, louder this time. "Hello, can anyone hear me? Answer me if you can."

Holding their breath for what seemed an age, a faint agonized cry of, "Help," reached their ears from beyond the blockage.

Jim shouted back. "I'm coming in." He turned to the man behind him and said, "if I can move some o' this rubble, I can squeeze through this gap and mebbe get them out."

"You can't go in. It's too bloody dangerous, young 'un. Listen, you can hear the remaining props creaking with the extra weight. They could give at any minute." He was right. The props were beginning to groan.

"Then we haven't got much time have we." Jim turned to the man and gave his gap-toothed smile, teeth shining bright in the light from the miner's lamp. This was no time to argue and they began to scrabble rubble out with their bare hands until fingers bled, and all the while tightening them up for room in the narrow confines of the mine shaft. Once Jim thought it big enough to squeeze through, he said "I'm going in to try and drag them out, if you wait here to take over."

"What if it collapses. We'll all be killed." But Jim wasn't listening, his ears were picking up on the sound of the props and wondering how much longer he had before the earth fell in around him and the trapped miners.

He wriggled his narrow frame through, entering a black void, the fear now so thick he could smell it, taste it, feel it at the back of his throat. Forcing himself to stay calm and keep a cool head, Jim shouted into the blackness.

"Answer me, or switch your light on if it works." He waited a few seconds and a faint glow appeared ahead. A sense of relief swept through him, renewing his energy and forgetting his fear Jim forged ahead, shouting, "I'm coming," edging forward once more on his belly. Reaching into the blackness, a surge of hope swept through him as his hand fell on a boot. Grabbing hold of it he began to drag the man back toward the entrance where the other miner waited. The man screamed in pain but Jim hardened himself to it. He was not about to fail as he inched his way back to safety. He guessed the leg was broken by the feel of crunching bone in his shin. "Push with your hands. Help me for God's sake, you're too heavy for me to drag on my own," Jim urging the man on to greater effort.

"I can't. Too much pain in my leg. I'm going to faint."

"Try dammit, try harder or we'll all die." The urgency in Jim's voice and the threat of death worked, as Jim felt renewed effort from the injured man.

"That's it, come on, we're nearly there. I can see light again. One big effort and we're through." Two more brave miners had come to their aid and they hauled the injured man through the narrow gap and handed Jim a rope and a lamp.

Thankful for the light, Jim told them, "I'll tie this on then give the rope a tug. You're going to have to do the work," shouted Jim. "I'm about all in." Crawling back and weak with fatigue, he knew one last superhuman effort would see him back out to safety if only the props held strong.

Dragging himself along on elbows now scrubbed to the bone and grimacing with the pain, he reached out and tied the rope around the unconscious man's arm and tugged on the rope. It tightened immediately and he was quickly hauled out into the light. Jim followed and began to squeeze through the opening when the creaking grew louder, until suddenly there was a massive crack as the pit props could take no more.

"Run," he screamed as he felt the weight of rocks fasten his legs to the

Chapter 56

floor. In blind panic he kicked and fought until he felt movement around his legs, then scurried after the fleeing miners. But Jim's luck had run out. A rock hit him hard on the back of the head knocking him unconscious. The last miner turned, saw what had happened and ran back to Jim, not knowing if he was dead or alive but, bravely, dragged him out to safety. A split second after reaching the open air, the whole mineshaft crashed in upon itself, followed by a sound like muffled thunder, and a billowing cloud of dust and debris burst forth from the gaping mouth of the mine as if fired from a gun.

Somebody gathered Jim in his arms and laid him gently down in the surrounding heather. He was still alive but had taken a nasty knock to the head. The miner who followed Jim in for the rescue, surveyed the haggard faces of the motley, dishevelled crew in front of him and knew it was down to the bravery of one young man that they were all safe and no deaths. Jim heard someone shout, "The Doctor is on his way." That was the last thing he remembered before passing out.

Chapter 57

Ruth was just busying herself clearing the dishes from the last meal before going out to help Joshua when hearing a sudden commotion out in the yard. Dashing out she heard the man on horseback yelling for help. There had been a collapse at the mine and they needed a Doctor urgently. All were safe, but some needed medical attention.

Ruth shouted for Joshua. "Josh, do you know where Jacob has gone?"

Joshua made the sign of the cross and Ruth quickly translated to the man that Jacob would be at the church.

"Joshua, harness the trap up. I'll gather Jacob's medical bag and things together while you do that. If you will stay here and look after the yard I'll go with Jacob. I might be able to help. Go now, please, Joshua." He read the concern on her face and hurried across to the stable. When Ruth came out with the medical supplies the trap was all ready and waiting for her. Gathering her skirt up she swiftly jumped up onto the seat and with a quick crack of the whip alongside the horse's neck, they were away. She had learnt to drive a horse and trap well over the last six months on her journey to and from Dan's cottage. Pulling up outside the church she shouted for Jacob. He came running out wondering what all the commotion was about, concern on his face.

"Jump in, I'll tell you on the way." She had no intention of letting go of the

Chapter 57

reins, and Jacob didn't ask, realizing Ruth had become a very efficient horse woman these past few months. Trying desperately to keep the horseman in sight, the trap rattled across the uneven ground as she related what little she knew to Jacob as they hurtled along. Soon they passed the highest point and began the steep descent of the rough moorland road to the mine head. There was still plenty of daylight left to attend to the injured, but they would soon need somewhere indoors if they were badly injured. Many people were milling around, but nobody seemed to know what to do.

There were five miners that needed attention, the others were just scrapes and shock really, so while Jacob saw to the more serious broken limbs, Ruth tried to bathe and wash the minor cuts and abrasions, chatting all the while to help keep them calm. As she carried out these tasks, she couldn't help but think how her life had changed. She came upon this community as a frightened young orphan girl and now here she was, aiding a preacher come doctor to dress the wounded. She worked quickly and efficiently, remarking how lucky they all were to still be alive.

"Aye, lucky indeed. If it hadn't been for that youngster delivering pit props, the two trapped inside the shaft would o' died for sure."

"Do any of you know where he's from?" Ruth asked.

"I think he's local as that's his cart over there with the two horses. He landed just as it happened. I suppose someone should let his parents know, they'll be wondering where he's got to."

"Has anyone seen to his team. Fed them, or watered them?"

"I dunno love, there's been that much happening, they might have been forgotten."

"I understand," said Ruth.

Now able to leave Jacob to tend the lesser injuries, she ran over to the pair of horses still harnessed to the cart, standing patiently, but the pit props were all unloaded and in the back the address of a farm scribbled on a piece of paper and the name Styles.

Ruth hurried back to where Jacob was treating the young rescuer. He was laid on his side now, head heavily bandaged and still unconscious.

"Jacob, I see this young man's horses are still harnessed and his parents will be wondering where he is. Do you think I should drive them back home? It shouldn't take long and you could follow in the trap to pick me up"

Jacob didn't stop working but asked the name.

"Honeybee Nest Farm, Roston and the name is Styles."

"Ah, that'll be Albert Styles. I did hear he'd taken a youngster on to ease his work load a little. Yes, that would be good if you could do that Ruth. If you follow this track back along past the chimney and kilns then you drop down the moorside to Roston East, you'll see the farm sign on the gate. Do you think you can manage a working pair like that? They are big horses."

"I've handled Dulcie well enough, haven't I?" she said, a satisfied smirk crossing her elfin features.

"I should know better than to question your horsemanship, Ruth. Carry on but be careful. It does get steep, and rough, toward the valley base. I'll follow as soon as I've treated this young fellow."

Ruth couldn't believe her luck. Not only allowed to handle a working pair like this, but also to be trusted to do so was quite an honour.

She ran over to the cart and quickly jumped up onto the wooden seat, gathering the reins as she did. "Well, I don't know your names horses, but we shall just have to learn as we go. Forward," and she flicked the reins smartly across their withers and they pulled away with a steady plod that reminded her very much of Dulcie.

Jacob was right, it was rough going and the old cart pitched violently from side to side as they made their way down to the base of the valley and within less than a half hour, she spotted the farm sign and the horses drew to a halt outside the stable door. The farmhouse door flew open and Ruth was greeted by a worried looking older woman.

"What's happened, young lady? Where's Jim? We were expecting him back hours ago. Has he been in an accident?" "Yes, a bad fall in the new mine shaft and men were trapped. I work for Jacob at Gallows Howe. I don't quite know what happened as we've been too busy tending the injured but, by all accounts, I think your driver was very brave, scrambling into the collapsing shaft and rescuing two workers." The woman grabbed Ruth by

Chapter 57

the shoulders.

"D'you know if Jim is all right, or is he hurt bad?"

"No, Jacob was pretty sure he would be okay, but he has taken a terrible knock to the head and Jacob, the Doctor was treating that when I left." Glancing up the moorside, Ruth was relieved to see the advancing horse and trap heading their way.

"Ah, here he comes now. He'll be able to tell you more." Martha ran across to Jacob. By this time Albert had joined her after seeing the pair of horses arrive back with a different driver, a concerned look on his face. Jacob explained about the accident and Albert replied with a shake of the head. "That's typical o' Jim. Jumps in with never a thought for himself, or safety for that matter, allus as brave as a lion. How is he? Is it serious, Jacob?"

"He's taken an awful knock, but he is a tough young man. They've taken him to the nearest dwelling along the line for the night and I will call and see him first thing in the morning." Jacob put a comforting arm around the sobbing Martha. Addressing Ruth, he said, "Would you help Albert stable the horses, while I see to Martha."

"Course I will," and walked over to unhitch the horses with Albert.

Jacob's arm was still around Martha's shoulders as she said, "I'm okay, Jacob. Really, I am. It's just I couldn't bear anything to happen to that little feller. He's come through so much and just when life seemed to be picking up for him, this happens."

"Don't worry, Martha, a few days and he will be back under your roof as fit as before. Although he may carry a nasty scar for the rest of his life."

"As if he hasn't been scarred enough in his short time on this earth."

"Scars on the surface heal much quicker than the deep emotional scars that some of these youngsters carry, but I'm pretty sure he will soon recover from this, God willing, no worse for wear, but perhaps a little more cautious."

Martha looked doubtful at the kindly vicar. "I am not sure I carry the same blind faith as you, Jacob, but I will pray for him, you know that."

"I know you will. Now settle in for the night as Ruth and I still have a long journey back home." As he walked back to the trap, Albert was lifting Ruth onto the front seat of the trap.

"Thank you for taking care of Jim after the accident Jacob. I don't know what we'd do without your expert knowledge, but what I'd like to know is how you found anyone as good as this to handle horses as confidently as this young lady." A smile spread across Ruth's face at such a compliment and especially someone as experienced as Mr Styles. At that moment she felt ten feet tall.

"Well, Ruth arrived to care for Dan Parkes, the gamekeeper, after he broke a leg. He's now on the mend and Ruth spares me a couple of days a week until moving on." Jacob stared directly at Ruth and said, "I'm hoping she has a change of heart and stays on because we shall all miss her very, very much."

Albert realized Ruth had made quite an impact at Gallows Howe and began to wonder just how much Jacob really knew about her. Albert had known Dan Parkes all his life and never heard of any young friends or relations in the vicinity. But, he thought, he may just be reading too much into it. He would fathom it out later when Jim recovered.

"Well," said Albert looking directly at the beaming Ruth, "no question you are a girl of strong character and will make your own mind up when the time is right. No doubt I'll see you again young lady and thank you for bringing my horses back safe and sound. Take care both of you and goodnight." Jacob cracked the whip and once on the open road they made good speed as dusk closed in around them. Ruth's mind was still on the injured miners, especially the young hero. That's just what my Jim would have done, she thought, and then smiled as his image floated into her mind. But, so high was she with excitement, she could not imagine anything more dramatic than the events that had taken place today, and now, after the steep pull back onto the high, wild moor, they hit flatter going and the horse gained speed, the wind whipping through her hair, the space and bleakness exhilarating in its vastness. So much so that, as they sped for home and a warm fire, she just hoped that this way of life she had stumbled upon could last forever.

On arrival at Gallows Howe, Jacob asked, "Would you rather stable Jenny up, or pop in the house and put the kettle on for a meal?"

Chapter 57

"What a silly question, Jacob," she said laughing and grabbed the reins from his hands. "You heard the farmer, confident with horses, he said."

Jacob took this slight young girl in his arms, giving her a bear hug as he lifted her down. "He did that and he was right."

Jacob watched as she led Jenny to the stable, witnessing the change in her, could see how she was growing to womanhood. He knew he and Joshua would miss her terribly if she did decide to move on. Not just for the work, but for her never-ending optimism that she brought to life. Here he was, a man preaching the word of God every Sunday. Do what's right and right will come of you. And here was a child who, he wasn't sure as yet, he believed had suffered cruelty from a young age, but it still had not embittered her. Where had she found this inner strength, the determination to pull through. It had not come from God. Or had it? Oh, how some of us older ones could learn from this. Shaking his head, he walked inside.

By the time Ruth had finished outside Jacob had a meal ready for the three of them and after reciting grace, Ruth enquired as to how bad Jacob thought the injury was to the boy from the farm.

"He was very lucky, Ruth. By all accounts he arrived just after the collapse of the mine and as soon as he heard two miners were still trapped inside, and before anyone could stop him, he disappeared inside, somehow managing to drag them out, one by one. Very, very brave but also very foolish. He could so easily have died in there alongside them. But God was with them all and his goodness brought him and the men out to safety."

Ruth glanced enquiringly across at him. "I really do admire your faith, Jacob. You honestly believe that God saved them, don't you?"

"I do, Ruth. I believe he watches over every one of us. Everything that happens, happens for a reason. God works in mysterious ways. We may not know the reason at the time, but it will become clear as day as we move further along the road of life."

Ruth thought for a while as she didn't want to argue with Jacob, especially in his own house and her just a girl, but she couldn't let this pass. It bothered her.

"So," she said, watching him earnestly, "you mean to say that if someone else other than this boy had driven the wagon to the mine, those miners would still be safe."

"My answer would be that God saw to it that Jim was on the wagon today and God gave him the strength and courage to do what he did. Albert told me the decision was made only the night before, believing Jim to be ready for more responsibility."

"Ah, but what if it had been me on the wagon. I wouldn't have had the strength to do that."

"But it wasn't you. It was Jim. God had you in mind to help me with the injured." She smiled across at the older man.

"You always have an answer, don't you? I hope I will also learn to have an answer to everything as I get older."

"You will not be able to answer everything, but you will grow wiser."

Ruth reached across the table and held Jacob's hand.

"Thank you for showing me such kindness, Jacob. I had almost forgotten what it was like to be wanted. I can't believe how my life is changing. Now, after such an exciting day I am going to my bed." She stopped and turned before going to her room. "You know what, Jacob, when I heard of the boy who saved those men, that's the sort of thing Jim would have done. The Jim that I knew. He did things without thinking." As she said this, she gave a shake of the head and a smile played at the corner of her lips as thoughts of him crept into her mind, although if truth be known he was never far away from her thoughts ever.

"Goodnight, Jacob," she said wistfully. The old man acknowledged with a wave of his hand.

As Dan's leg was now on the mend, when Jacob had suggested it made more sense for her to stay the night after working all day, Ruth readily agreed and soon added a few personal touches to her meagrely furnished room. A washstand and mirror stood along the low wall and a brightly coloured picture of the Almighty stared down from a thunder and lightning background which hung directly above her bed, giving it a slightly sinister feel Ruth thought but, as it was a favourite of Jacob's, it made no difference to her. The most important part for her was the tiny window, allowing her

Chapter 57

a view out across the moor to the church in the distance, which is where she loved to sit and read whenever time allowed.

Chapter 58

John Durville awoke, rubbed the sleep from his eyes and drew the curtains back to a glorious morning, the sun blazing across the room. He looked at the bedside clock Damn, he had overslept. Washing and dressing in great haste, he rushed downstairs to grab breakfast. He really did need to be on time at the Orphanage as things were taking shape.

The builders were doing a great job. The roof had undergone major repair, plus new bunks and windows were fitted in all dormitories for the children. Work was now going ahead for the kitchen and toilet areas. All the original staff had gone and, in their place, John had acquired the services of a headmaster of great standing, William Hopper and his wife Harriet. John had great faith in these two people. Strict, but very fair and the children were responding by learning well.

This project of transforming the old school from its former dilapidated state had reignited John's zest for life, for after the death of his wife, Miriam, his only son going to the devil and Ruth and Bella running away, he had taken to the bottle. The misery of these tragic losses hit him so hard that suicide crossed his mind more than once, believing he had nothing left to live for. What eventually pulled him out of this trough of dark, sinister depression was the thought of Ruth and Jim, and other children in the same predicament, who had known nothing else but to fight hard just to stay alive

Chapter 58

and here he was thinking about ending it all. Disgusted with himself for being so weak, this thought was uppermost in his mind until one morning, he roused from slumber knowing what he had to do. The renovation of the Orphanage and the running of it.

Grabbing the early morning post, he noticed one letter that appeared to be a childish scrawl, maybe written by a child. His heart missed a beat as he ripped it open to read.

Dear Sir

My name is Albert Styles and I live at Honeybee Nest Farm, Roston. I need advice on my property. I don't know anyone who can help, but Jim who works on the farm with me said you would know what to do.

A Styles

He checked the post mark. It was over a week since it was posted. This must be the place where young Jim had found work and it sounds as though he is still at the farm. He said he would get in touch and he's kept his promise. My goodness, this was great news. John tried to remember how long ago it was since he left and he couldn't recall exactly but it was a pleasant surprise.

John's mind began to shift into work mode, considering all possibilities upon what matters Mr Styles would need advice on. But, more importantly, why? And for the life of him he could not come up with a solution, so all he could do now was look forward to seeing the chirpy youngster's cheeky grin again and also, he may have news of Ruth.

Livelier than he had been for months, John wrote a swift reply saying he would be there the following day, but then realized he would arrive before the letter. What the Hell. It doesn't matter, I'll send it anyway. Signing it with his full title, Judge John Durville, so there could be no mistakes, he hailed a cab and made straight for the Orphanage to check with William that the work was ongoing, that there were no hold ups or shortage of materials, or more importantly, nothing affecting the children's education. He also had the builders' payments to put in order before leaving.

After months of pestering and badgering local businesses, the council, in fact anyone willing to listen, plus his own money, the funding hit the target. John could now see his dream could become, no, would become a reality.

There was one more important job he needed to do before making his journey to these rural villages amid the moors and that was try and make contact with his son Henry. He could not forgive him for what he had done but he also could not give up on his own flesh and blood without one last try. He had never heard a word from him since the day he threw him out.

Finding his address from the market trader, Harry, Jim's former boss, who appeared to know all and every bit of seedy information going, at a price, told him of his whereabouts and John now made his way through the stinking back alleys of rubbish and litter to his door.

He almost walked away, as he struggled to find the strength to face up to his son, but finally, swallowing hard, he rapped on the door twice. No answer. He knocked again. Nothing. Trying the door, it creaked open into a narrow hall with peeling wallpaper and the cloying smell of damp and rotting food. John heard snoring from the front room and on opening the door, peered into a room with the curtains still pulled shut. Dark and dingy as it was, he still saw enough to make his heart bleed. How could he have done this to his own son. Henry lay sprawled on the bed, fully dressed, amongst unwashed bedding, with stacks of plates, wine bottles and glasses piled in the sink.

"What do I do," thought John. "Do I wake him or leave him to die in his own squalor?"

It only took a second to decide. He grabbed the sleeping figure and shook him by the shoulder. Henry mumbled something unintelligible before his head lolled to one side. John shook him harder and a vague sign of life appeared as Henry's eyes flickered open, bloodshot and unseeing. No recognition at first and then finally, realization that it was his father staring down at him.

Dragging himself up onto one elbow, he managed to splutter out, "Father, what are you doing here? What do you want and however did you find me?" His speech was stumbling and slurred.

Chapter 58

John's shoulders slumped as if he could take no more. He looked, and felt, a beaten man. "Is that all you have to say to me Henry. Can you not see how far you have fallen through your own stupidity? Look at you, living in this…this slum, stinking and unwashed."

Henry's bloodshot eyes began to focus, as he shouted, "No, this is not my fault. You brought this upon me. It was all due to you father. You threw me out, remember. All because of that slut you hired."

John spoke earnestly. "No, it was not my fault, or Ruth's either Henry. The blame lies entirely at your door. You must understand and, somehow, take responsibility for your own downfall. The time has come to stop accusing everyone else. I accept my part in letting you down as a father and blame myself for being too engrossed with my work, just giving you everything you asked for instead of my time. I realize that now," he said with a shake of the head. "But that is in the past. I can do nothing to change that, but we can still turn it round Henry, if you are willing to try and work at it."

"No, this is all I have left now, father. I hope you are proud of yourself."

The Judge grabbed him by the lapels of his jacket, lifting him clear off his feet, those black eyes boring into him. John had not been hard enough before but, damn it, he would be now if it meant he could save his son from sinking further. A look of horror crossed Henry's face.

"Now you listen to me young man for once in your life," John hissed. "I am spending money at the Orphanage to help give the children there a chance of a good education and a better start to life. I need someone to do the job of caretaker when I am absent. I have just seen George, the foreman in charge of building operations, this morning and he is willing to take you on trial for two weeks. It is Thursday now. I am travelling toward the coast early tomorrow but should be back by Saturday. Call at my house, fully washed, tidily dressed and sober Saturday afternoon. If I am not back, speak to George and make sure you eat properly as there is plenty in the house. Is that clear?"

Henry rubbed the side of his head which still carried the sign of Ruth's attack with the poker.

"I…I don't know, father." Henry tried the sympathy route as he spotted a weakness in his father. He could see his way back in. "I get these awful headaches, and they are getting worse, from when that little wretch struck me on the side of the head. I sometimes cannot think straight."

John had let go of him now and he slouched down on the bed.

"Remember, this is a chance for you. There will not be another, because the way you are heading, illness or death are just around the corner. Hopefully I will see you late Saturday."

Outside in the cold light of day, John did not know if he had done the right thing but knew in his heart he had to try. Now, he could give full thought of what lay ahead, and consider the meeting with Mr Styles and what possible cause could he have for contacting him. His curiosity fully aroused, he made preparation for the journey to the country tomorrow, when he would hopefully see that bright-eyed young ragamuffin, Jim, again.

Chapter 59

Jim opened his eyes, lifting his head from the pillow and wished he hadn't. Hammer blows pounded inside his skull as if threatening to burst out. He settled back down, content to study his surroundings. He didn't recognize this room. It certainly wasn't the bedroom he was used to. At a loss to know where he was, or what had taken place, his memory not functioning properly, playing tricks, his vision fuzzy. Jim tried casting his mind back to trigger a recollection of events which had brought him to this strange room. It definitely wasn't the Orphanage, for which he was very much relieved, but it wasn't the farm either.

The curtains were drawn but the strong sunlight filtered through, so he knew it was daylight and then he noticed the doorknob slowly turn, the door quietly swing open and a short, rotund figure with a rolling sort of a gait, walked over to the bed.

"Ah, there now, you've finally returned to the real world then, young fella. How do you feel? A bit tender, I guess. But you are looking a lot better." A kindly face topped by a white bonnet smiled down at him as she arranged the bedclothes gently around him.

"Where am I?" asked Jim. His voice sounded weak, croaky.

"I've been looking after you 'till you get better. You were brought here to Railway cottages after the accident two days ago and Jacob wouldn't allow you to be moved 'till your senses returned."

Jim's face crumpled with worry. "I've been here two days? Hell, I'll be in trouble with Mr Styles. He expected me to deliver props for the mine. He'll not want me back now. I must go and explain but I can't remember what happened. He'll go mad."

With that, he flung the bedclothes back and swung his feet to the ground, almost slumping to the floor due to the thumping pain in his head. That's when he caught sight of himself in the mirror opposite, his head swathed in bandages and stained in blood. Arms and body heavily bandaged. He raised a hand to touch the side of his head, but the woman quickly reached out, gathering him in a motherly way and gently eased him back into the comfort of the bed.

"Shh, don't worry now." Her voice was no more than a whisper, "Albert and Martha have called to see you. They know all about the accident and can't wait to have you back safe and sound. Now, you lie still and I will bring you something to eat. You must be starving, poor boy."

"Please, tell me what happened. I can't remember anything, although I did have a dream where I was trapped and someone screaming at me to get out."

"That was no dream, Jim, that was the pit fall. You are a hero, young man." She beamed a smile at him. "You saved two men from certain death, one of them my very dear husband, for which I will forever be grateful to you. He is now recovering in Whitby hospital with a broken leg and concussion."

Jim gave a long drawn out sigh. As long as Albert and Martha knew where he was, then everything would work out, and he drifted off to sleep. The next time Jim roused, the headache had cleared and Jacob sat on the edge of his bed, having just checked the wound.

"No lasting damage, Jim. You'll have a nasty scar for a while but, with a mop of hair like yours, it will soon cover up. In fact, it can be your badge of courage, so wear it with pride."

As Jacob began to pack his bag ready to go, Jim said, "I don't remember anything like that happening, but the lady of the house told me I saved her husband. Is that right?" "Yes, that's right. But don't worry Jim, your memory

Chapter 59

will return. Sometimes after a traumatic accident and a blow to the head, the mind can shut it out for a long period of time and it is only the terror of the pitfall that you went through that is blocking the mind, saving you from some horrific nightmares and stress. You may still experience these as your memory returns but will be in a much fitter condition to handle it. Everything else is still clear in your mind, Mrs McCloud told me. I will inform Albert he can collect you tomorrow when most of the bandaging can come off."

"Thank you, Vicar, or should it be Doctor," and Jim held out his hand to thank him, the gap-tooth smile more radiant than ever with relief. Jacob knew now he would make a speedy recovery as after having a quiet word with Albert, he had a feeling that two young orphan children were in for quite a shock in the very near future. But he would not interfere; just let nature take its course. Unless, that is, things were not going to work out without a little help.

"Good day, Jim," and Jacob left the room whistling the tune, 'What a Friend we have in Jesus.'

Chapter 60

Ruth rose at the crack of dawn on Monday morning, made breakfast for Jacob and Joshua, donned her cape as the weather had turned colder in the early morning and entered the stable where Dulcie waited for her.

"Morning Dulcie," she said as if speaking to a person. The big horse tossed her head back and whinnied her recognition, gently nudging Ruth's pocket for a titbit which she duly gave her, before the big horse followed her dutifully out of the stable to the stone mounting steps.

Once mounted, she set off on her journey back to Dan's cottage which she did now every few days. Ruth began to wonder if she would ever bring herself to leave the security of this small hamlet. She had grown accustomed to its people, the gentle, unhurried way of life and had already saved a little money from her wages that Dan and Jacob paid for her work. Thinking about her limited options of finding work on the coast, she was not sure she had the courage to do what had gone before. There was no choice before, forced into it by circumstances and the behaviour of others. Now, if given the chance and opportunity to settle, she would much rather stay here, working with and alongside the animals, enjoying the freedom the great outdoors offered right on her doorstep. Even the fear of her former life catching up with her receding with every passing day. Only when catching

Chapter 60

sight of the sombre set of gallows did the shadow of guilt cloud her features and cause her uncertainty, but suddenly, she realized, with a gasp of pleasure, this morning she had passed by without giving it a second thought.

This always proved the happiest time for Ruth, riding the moors, the sun just beginning to peek above the horizon, casting a golden glow across the rugged face of the moor and would soon dispel the chill of a North wind. Her face, now possessing a healthy tan and framed with a mane of golden hair long enough to touch her slight shoulders, had regained its youthful vitality. During these past few months, her true beauty was becoming apparent, maturing into a beautiful young woman that was attracting admiring glances from the young men scattered around these dales. Oh, it didn't escape her notice and it lifted her spirits, while shyly accepting this seemingly harmless adulation from a distance.

As more and more working men heard of the job opportunities and plentiful work due to the mining industry just over the hill from Gallows Howe, the population of Roston and surrounding areas continued to grow. Optimism was high as some of the old ramshackle buildings were renovated to take on a new life in providing cheap, rented accommodation for these new settlers and their families as they searched for a better life, clear of poverty that appeared to be afflicting many parts of the country.

But now there was talk, maybe just idle gossip Ruth thought, that the mining had reached its peak as foreign imports were beginning to infiltrate, supposedly producing better, cheaper iron ore, placing pressure on the production at Roston.

The village street was just beginning to come alive as Ruth rode by the church and the lone peal of a bell rang out clear across the moor. A chill North wind was blowing, bringing the nearby fields of golden corn alive in a rhythmic, swaying dance of pure beauty, but surely such a light breeze could not be enough to ring the bell thought Ruth. Riding closer, but staying mounted, she peered through the high windows to check if Jacob was there. All quiet. Not a sign of anyone.

"Wait here, Dulcie," she ordered and Dulcie nodded her head in acknowledgement. Sliding easily down the side of the great horse, she stared up at the old tin tabernacle and, as Jacob had mentioned to her, with his congregation growing, they would soon be in need of the much-heralded new stone church to shelter his growing flock, instead of the draughty old building they were used to during the cold months of winter.

Ruth climbed the steps and tried the door. Why, she had no idea. Curiosity maybe, but something continued to draw her in. A feeling deep inside, luring, persuasive, persistent, urging her to enter the inner sanctum of the building for some reason. She quietly accepted that Jacob and many others gathered comfort from attending prayers and singing hymns, but the only memories Ruth had of religion were of the handsome young Salvation Army man preaching at the market and then when it reared its head in her time at the Orphanage with Miss Wade. A shiver ran through her at the memory of how harsh the old woman had treated her.

But this time her curiosity was aroused. The big, wrought iron catch lifted with a loud click and the door swung open easily. Pushing through the heavy red velvet curtains that helped to seal against the draughts, the interior of the church was bathed in a beautiful green, blue haze due to the early morning light filtering through the stained-glass windows. Heavy oak pews lined each side of the building and holding centre stage, the impressive carved eagle, wings outspread holding the Holy Book. Beyond this, Ruth presumed would be the choir stalls and at the very head of the building, a roughly hewn cross with the body of Jesus Christ nailed hand and foot, a crown of thorns circling his head. A prayer below stated 'Suffer little tchildren to come unto me.'

Ruth did not quite understand this saying. Why should little children suffer? They were not old enough to do wrong to anyone. But she knew from experience, they did suffer.

Settling herself in the front pew, she had no idea why, she allowed the silence and calm serenity of the old church envelop her and Ruth lost track of time. How long she sat, she did not know, but something held her fast, unable to move. Although not understanding her situation on why her limbs would not obey her, she felt no fear.

Staring quietly up at the forlorn figure of Jesus, Ruth felt the warmth of

Chapter 60

teardrops slide slowly down her cheeks, and only then realized she was crying, but for no apparent reason. And now she couldn't stop the steady trickle of tears streaming down her pretty face. Again, she tried to move, to run outside, but couldn't. Her limbs proving lifeless as time stood still.

Eventually, she sensed a comforting presence close by her side rather than felt and turned to find Jacob sitting quietly there. Gently wrapping her in his arms, he whispered, "I knew Jesus would find you dear child. You will never, ever be afraid or lonely again." Ruth flung her arms around him and the strength, the love and the compassion this man offered flowed through him into her as she continued to sob into his chest. And all the while he held her tight.

Finally, the tears subsided and Jacob gazed deep into those red rimmed eyes which had born so much unhappiness and cruelty in such a short life and asked, "Ruth, are you ready to share your grief with Jesus?"

A whispered, "Yes, I think so, Jacob," from Ruth, and in the sanctity of this building, this old church, Ruth related to Jacob her life story, holding nothing back. Her mother's death, her father maybe hanging from the gallows, the Orphanage, then gaol and Bella's horrible death. No one in the whole world knew about Bella. Or Henry. Not even Jim. After running out of words, Ruth's shoulders sagged and she slumped back in the pew, spent.

"I've never told anyone this before, Jacob. Please don't tell anyone else about what happened as I live in fear of someone hearing about my past. If Henry is dead then I could be hung like my father. Every time I see the gallows,

I imagine my body swinging from a rope around my neck." She buried her head once again into his chest, her arms wrapping tightly around him for comfort, her eyes tight shut as if trying to quell the frightening vision of her body swinging ungainly and lifeless at the end of a rope from the nearby gallows.

"Your secret is safe with me. A trouble shared is a trouble halved and you have no need for worry or guilt. You have done nothing wrong. You have only done what you had to do, what you were forced to do to survive, and no one could say different. The time has come to not condemn yourself.

Jesus will not condemn you dear child. His arms and heart are open for you. He will take away your suffering if you will only allow him to. That is what the saying means, 'Suffer little children, to come unto me.' You need suffer alone no more Ruth, just open your heart to Jesus."

Ruth remembered a long gone feeling of confiding troubles in her mother at home after some minor upsets had made her feel sick with guilt, but once talked over, nothing seemed insurmountable. This is how she felt this very minute, the millstone of guilt that had weighed so heavily on her young shoulders, eased. Ruth felt an inner peace never experienced before and, eventually, emerging once more into the bright sunlight, she suddenly arrived back into the real world and realized that Dan would be wondering what had happened.

"My goodness, Jacob, what time is it? I must get back to Dan, he'll fear the worst. He's a terrible worrier you know."

"Now, I am not sure who worries the most, you or him," he said with a smile. "Dan will be fine, he'll understand."

"Are you sure? He's been so good to me over these last few months. Thank you for being patient, Jacob." Then, a questioning look spread across her tear stained face. "Are you not curious as to why I entered the church this morning?"

"God works in mysterious ways, my child. You will tell me in your own good time, I'm sure," he replied as he lifted her onto Dulcie's back.

"I'll be back to help out on Friday, Jacob," and although her eyes told of her suffering and still red from the tears shed, she gave Jacob a smile that reached the very depth of his heart and he was pretty sure her personal turmoil was over. Oh, she would have more as she made her way in life, but he was of the strong belief that with God's help, and maybe just a little bit from himself, especially now he had learned of Jim's whereabouts, she would come through strong. Now, almost out of sight she turned and gave a cheery wave and he watched her disappear into the distance. Jacob turned away and headed back to the village, light of heart knowing God had reached out to her. 'Suffer little children,' he thought. How true a saying.

But he was also really quite pleased with himself as Ruth never noticed

Chapter 60

him slip out of the side door where the bell ropes were housed and was able to offer comfort just when she needed him.

Chapter 61

After three days confinement, although still heavily bandaged, Jim made his welcome return to the farm and on first sight of him, Martha rushed out and flung her arms around him, tears of relief welling up in her eyes.

"Steady on, Mrs Styles, I'm still a bit sore but I'm glad to be back."

"Oh, sorry, Jim. I'm just so relieved to see you. Now, we'll soon have you better once you are back home."

Jim realized that is just how he felt, that he was back home. A feeling of contentment swept through him. All the years of resentment and anger previously experienced, he realized, were born from a feeling of envy, or jealousy even, of witnessing other children with homes to go to and, most of all, loving parents to share their troubles with. He now also had someone with whom to share his troubles, someone he could talk to. This could be his family, a link missing from his life, a home with Mr and Mrs Styles.

"You know, when I came round and found out how long I'd been unconscious, I worried that you might think I'd run off somewhere and just left. I would never do that you know. Not without telling you..."

"We know you wouldn't, Jim. We heard later in the day what had happened when the young girl from Gallows Howe brought the horse and wagon back. Sweet little thing. Don't know where Jacob found that one but she certainly

Chapter 61

could handle horses. Wouldn't stay though, not even for a cup o' tea. Said Jacob was following on and would pick her up. Now come inside and I'll fix you up with some dinner."

"That's good 'cos I'm starving. Mrs McCloud looked well after me, but not the same as here." He gave his crooked grin that he now knew brought the mothering instinct out in Martha. He then turned to Martha a serious expression clouding the bright eyes. "They told me I saved her husband's life but the last thing I remember is arriving at the mine head. Nothing else until waking up in Mrs McCloud's house."

"Well," Martha replied, "Jacob thinks that after a while, when the mind settles down and you're fit enough, your memory will return as good as ever." She didn't say she had her doubts as she thought of young Joshua's experience, he was still mute years after the event of his mother's death. But she supposed Jacob knew much better than her on these things.

With that Albert walked through the door after feeding the stock, his eyes lighting up on seeing Jim sat at the table.

"Well, we have the wounded hero back with us," he said, a smile cracking the hard-weathered features, immediately wrapping his arm around the young boy's shoulders.

"Have you missed me, Mr Styles?" He shot an inquiring glance at Albert. "How have you managed without me?"

"Oh, Jim, d'you know, I never noticed you were missing till someone told me."

Jim looked devastated until he realized Albert was joking and their laughter echoed around the kitchen until tears rolled down their cheeks. Eventually they reached out to hold each other's hands across the table and Albert became serious.

"The good Lord never blessed us with a son, but he has now. We know we cannot replace your natural parents, and would never try to do that, but this accident of yours has made us both realize just how much we have come to rely on you, not just for the work, but it is as if we were meant to be together as a complete family."

After a while Jim spoke. "You know, I never knew my parents or what happened as to why I should be on my own. Whether they died, or if they just abandoned me. As I get older that's the hardest part. The not knowing. I would see other children with mothers and fathers, playing together, enjoying life, where I would be hungry and lonely in the Orphanage. It didn't seem right but I had to make the best of it. And now look where I am." Even when swathed in bandages, his face had the ability to light up the room. "Here with you and Mrs Styles as my mam and dad." Smiling he got up and hugged both of them. "Now I'm going to bed as I want to try and get well as soon as possible so I can start helping again and also, I've got to keep searching for Ruth," he said earnestly.

Chapter 62

John Durville rose at seven am sharp, immediately beginning to pack an overnight bag. He was not sure what was expected of him, or how long he would be away, but didn't envisage more than one night away. A bright sharp morning welcomed him as he stood at the roadside waiting for his cab.

"Morning, Judge." John had made sure it was his regular cabbie taking him to the railway station as the journey could be a long one.

"Morning, Jackson. Thank you very much for turning out early for me." The last time John had visited anywhere close to that area was when he first realized his wife Miriam would soon suffer badly with her arthritic body so he booked a holiday on the coast in a faint hope that it would help. Although enjoying the change of scenery and the bracing sea air, the long travel within the cab had made it difficult for her and made no significant change to her health, so the journey was never made again. But now things were different, John would make the journey by rail to the nearest village and then find a local cabbie who would surely know where the farm was.

Fifteen minutes later they pulled up outside the station and giving Jackson the usual tip, John waved him farewell and entered the covered area for his ticket. Once inside the carriage, John heaved his case up onto the small hammock like luggage rack above his head and returned to the window, peering out at the winding row of carriages spread out behind this impressive iron giant as the fireman threw coal into the boiler to build up a head of steam for the journey ahead. Billowing clouds of grey-black smoke plumed upward from the short stub of a funnel, followed by a shrill blast of the whistle from the signalman and the huge wheels began to turn as it ever so slowly chugged out of the station, gathering more momentum every second. John reflected on how these steam trains had changed travel across the whole country, as many more railway tracks were opening up, criss-crossing the country, linking remote areas that, before this, had only the faithful horse to rely on.

Alone in the carriage, John peered out of the window and watched the trailing cloud of smoke disappear into the clear blue sky and the snaking line of carriages following in a mesmerising pattern of uniformity until the station disappeared from sight. Sliding the window up and securing it with the broad leather strap, John settled back into the comfortable, upholstered seat to enjoy, hopefully, a stress- free journey. This and the motorcar are surely the future for travel in the years ahead, he thought as he listened to the rhythmic beat of the track and he now took time to ponder on the meeting ahead.

A couple of train changes allowed him to stretch his legs before nearing his destination, the scenery changing from the flat, urban sprawl of York, to rugged moorland countryside, where agriculture dominated. The train rattled over the many bridges and viaducts, before cutting through deep gorges gouged out of the hillsides by the thousands of navvies who worked on building the tracks, as it wound its unrelenting way to the coast. John could only marvel at the brains behind the engineering and architecture that had gone into the design and building of this revolutionary way of travel.

After a comfortable journey, the whistle blew loud and shrill, the train slowing to enter the final bend into the station of Castle Moor. Once the train halted, John grabbed his bag and jumped down onto the platform quickly surveying the surroundings. Remote, yes, but stunningly beautiful in the strong sunlight. Easy to see where its name originated, the mound of the site where the castle once stood still evident at the base of the village.

Chapter 62

From there, stout stone houses straggled high on a backbone of moor, either side of the fiercely rising dirt road that led to Gallows Howe and the highest point above sea level.

Chapter 63

John was quietly disappointed as he watched the train pull slowly away from the station to continue its journey toward the coast, but he well knew he had other more important matters to sort, rather than train journeys. Firstly transport. Definitely not too much activity here, only a lonely horse and cart drawn up just outside the station, into which a farmer busily loaded his merchandise. John wandered over and asked for directions on how to get to the mining village of Roston.

"You on foot?" the man enquired.

"I am," replied John. "I have travelled from York and I need to be in touch with a family who reside in the village of Roston." He rummaged in his pocket and found the address that Albert had so carefully written.

"It is Mr Albert Styles and he gives the address as Honeybee Nest Farm, Roston."

"Oh, yes, I've heard of the place. Don't know it meself, but I heard the farms are doing well up there due to the mining. Population up there almost doubled, they say, bringing money into these here dales, you see."

"I see," said John. "Can you help me get there, or tell me of someone who can?"

"If you jump on board, Squire, I'm going to Gallows Howe, a little hamlet just a bit further up on the moor top. They do hire horses and such for

Chapter 63

travellers, or they'll tek you there themselves for a small charge. If you are ready then, Squire, jump on."

John threw his case in the back and jumped up alongside the man, who had the reins in his hands ready to go.

"Move on, Bella," the farmer shouted as he flicked the reins. The sudden mention of the name Bella brought memories of the two girls back to John. What had happened to Ruth after all this time? Where was she? Could she possibly have made it to Whitby to find work, he wondered? All these unanswered questions ran through his brain. But then he brightened, as he realized Jim may have good news of her.

The iron hooped wheels of the old cart crunched over the rubble dirt track, weaving its way between the houses lining each side of the steeply rising road, a couple of small shops advertising their wares and a public house that seemed to be doing a good trade even though it was just the middle of the day. Soon, as they passed the last house, they were facing open moorland again, apart from a few small fields, or garths, cultivated and within easy access of the road. The Judge's eye followed the ridge overlooking the rolling moorland down to the base of the lush green dale where small farmsteads dotted the hillsides, as if sheltering in the lee of the steep valley sides. Then, in the distance, as they travelled higher, the spire of the old tin church at Gallows Howe rose from the moor spiking the clear, blue sky. As the road levelled out, John took note of the rough stone dwellings, some still in a state of disrepair, but much building work appeared to be in progress on the most needy. Taking in the beautiful, bleak surroundings, he began to wonder how ever anyone could make a living out here but, somehow, this little corner of rural England appeared to be thriving.

"And this I take it, is Gallows Howe." It was a statement rather than a question but the farmer answered him anyway.

"It certainly is. Whoa, Bella!" He pulled up at the side of the road, leaving John just a short walk along a cart track to the nearest building which appeared to be stables, with stone living quarters off to the rear. "You should be able to get all you need here. Food, information or horses, all available at reasonable prices. Jacob's a preacher man, so I don't think he's about to rob anyone." This said with a smile.

John reached into his pocket to pay. The man waved it away. "No, no need for that, Squire. I was coming up here anyway as I live at the next farm. Find Jacob or Joshua, they'll see you all right," and with a slap of the reins he was on his way.

Chapter 64

John strode out along the pot holed track, mopping the sweat from his brow, the sun high in the sky and as he neared the stable, Joshua came out leading a horse to the old water trough at the side of the street. He waited as John approached with outstretched hand, Joshua taking it in a firm grip.

"Good afternoon, my name is John Durville from York, Judge John Durville and I am travelling through to a business meeting with a Mr Styles residing at Roston. Do you happen to know of him?"

Joshua gave the sign to say he couldn't speak, but to follow him. John, realizing the problem, did as he was bid. After tying the horse up at the trough, they walked across to the dwelling which also served as the office. Jacob, seated behind his desk, head lowered in concentration on his writing, heard the familiar creak of the outer door and immediately rose to his feet and offered his hand in greeting as Joshua ushered the visitor in.

John introduced himself, then asked Jacob for the same information.

"Of course, "Jacob answered, "I know him well, from a good, hard working family and has lived there all his life. A farmer, as most folk are in this neck of the woods. Honey Bee Nest was handed down to him from his parents. At present though the wind of change is blowing across these dales with the mining taking hold such a strong hold. It has changed lives dramatically, many leaving agriculture, finding they can make far more money working underground, but some say it will fade in the near future. They may be right, who can tell? But, yes, Albert trades here quite often when travelling through to the coast and about.

Have you come far?"

As Jacob talked, John was busy surveying the house and surroundings, the church in the distance, alongside the tall sombre spectre of the gibbet.

"I've just arrived by train from York and I was advised to come here by a farmer who kindly gave me a lift here on his wagon, and for which, I must add, would not take pay. He did say, and these were his very words, that 'you would see me right.' You appear to have respect among your kinfolk, Jacob and not just because of your profession."

"I have ministered here for many years and, as you can see, it is a close-knit community. There have been many hard years but we are now beginning to see the fruits of our labour."

"Well, I can see religion has found its way out here but an odd combination if you don't mind me saying with the gallows close by."

Jacob eyed him steadily, weighing his visitor up carefully before stating, "the people here have taken to religion in this part of the world quite readily and a new church is planned for the future as every community or gathering needs a shelter. These very same people, well before I arrived, performed their own services and they were held come hail, rain or snow on the open moor. Whatever the weather they would attend and listen to the preaching's of God. Although our following is Church of England it was that great orator, John Wesley, who rode through these desolate dales in the late 1700's that inspired the rise of religion, particularly Methodism, in the area. And as you can witness it is still growing. Now I admit life is certainly lived quite differently from what you will be used to in the city of York, but as you will have gathered during your lift here from the station, life is not all about money."

John realized his words had angered – no, not angered, upset the minister and he was, quite mildly, admonishing him.

John was instantly contrite. "I'm sorry, I spoke out of ignorance, and, yes,

Chapter 64

like you say, rural people appear to live a very different life to the city life I am used to, so please bear with me on certain issues that I am not sure of. And, I must admit, it is only recently that I have opened my eyes as to just what is happening in the poorer, deprived areas of many towns and cities." John proceeded to tell Jacob about the conditions in the Orphanage; how the children were treated, and how he was now trying to do something about it.

Jacob held out his hand, contrite. "I apologise also, if I appeared slightly sharp with you, John – may I call you John – I did not mean to be, but sometimes even ministers can speak out of turn." John took the proffered hand again, but this time in mutual agreement.

"Now, down to business. Will you be wanting a horse to travel to Roston on your own or would pony and trap suit you better. I could take you there myself as I have patients to see in that part of the world."

John began to warm to the pleasant nature of this man.

"That would be splendid. I would enjoy your company if that is possible and if you could regale me with your knowledge on some of the local history along the way, as my education is limited, mainly to the inside of courtrooms, you understand."

"So be it. Now we shall have a bite to eat and a drink before we set off and I shall have you there shortly."

After enjoying the hospitality of the house, Jacob called Joshua for his pony and trap and they were soon on their way, the road rising still higher and higher as it meandered its way over the rolling hills, passing the ancient stone monument of Ralph's Cross placed centuries ago, Jacob explaining, anyone with a little money to spare would place it on top for the hungry traveller, or so tradition has it.

The little pony had found it hard going and was blowing hard by the time it reached the crest, but now they veered left, and the road dropped steeply, plunging down into another completely separate valley, the winding snake of the ironstone railway line clearly visible skirting the rim of the dale. Off in the distance, the enormous calcining stone chimney, stood like some ancient obelisk, looking strangely out of place in these rural surroundings.

Martha spotted the trap approaching along the farm road, shouting to Albert in the nearby building that they had company arriving. Albert rushed out, wiping his hands on his trousers, ready to greet his visitors. Jacob jumped down from the front of the trap, grabbed Albert's hand warmly before introducing him to John.

"Albert, I would like you to meet Judge John Durville who has travelled all the way from York to meet you and he just happened to call in at the village for directions and here we are. Now, I have a couple of patients to see at Railway Cottages, John, so if I could call back and pick you up in about a couple of hours, would that be okay with you?"

"That will give us all the time we need, Jacob," John replied, as they stood and waved the pony and trap away.

Albert was the first to speak. "I'm very pleased to meet you, Mr Durville. Jim's told me a lot about you. Not often do we get people of your standing visiting but you are very welcome. I wasn't even sure my letter would reach you or not, but I'm very pleased it did," the pleasure showing in Albert's countenance.

"Cup of tea on the go gentlemen," Martha shouted from the house.

"Well, how about that for good timing, John," Albert remarked as they made their way to the farmhouse. "Come in, come in," and Albert ushered John through to the kitchen, John having to duck his huge bulk under the low stone lintel to enter, before taking a seat at the table. John was quite taken by the friendly, relaxed nature of these people and after introductions were made to Martha, she fussed over the two men like a mother hen, busily setting the table for dinner.

"Please give Jim a shout, Albert, will you, he's just fettling a building roof. I gather you and Jim know each other, Mr Durville?"

"Call me John, Mrs Styles. Yes, we met in difficult and strange circumstances and, I must admit, we did not see eye to eye early on. My fault entirely, a selfish person only thinking of work and never taking the time to find out just how other walks of life are struggling due to poverty and especially how the young, often orphaned children, are treated. It is absolutely shameful in this day and age. It was Jim and his young friend

Chapter 64

Ruth who initially opened my eyes to their plight of how and why they are on the streets, through no fault of their own. I am now trying, in some small way to help others by bringing proper education into the system for these very children."

As John finished talking, Jim walked in, his injured head clear of bandages, a broad grin cracking his features in greeting.

John showed his surprise at the change in Jim. Gone was the small, cheeky chap he remembered. In his place stood a confident young man, still with the shock of tousled black hair, the chipped tooth and the same sparkling gaze as intense as ever.

"I wasn't sure if you would remember me, sir, but I said to Mr Styles it's worth a try. And you've come. I can't believe it." He shook his head in disbelief.

"Not sure if I would remember you! How could you think that? Don't forget it was down to you and Ruth that my life changed, and for the better I might add. If it hadn't been for you two, I would still be buried under with my work, thinking of nothing else, where now, I am beginning to see the transformation at the Orphanage. And also, don't you forget I owe you a big favour for helping me in my hour of need."

John looked across at Martha and said, "You really have someone special here, Mrs Styles," and he went across and gave Jim a big bear hug that brought tears to Martha's face. To cover her embarrassment, she rushed off to the pantry and returned with plates piled high with sandwiches.

"Come on men, pull your chairs up and have something to eat."

Once all were seated and eaten their fill, John broached the subject of why he was here. "I understand from your letter you may have some business I can help you with, Albert; is that correct?"

"Aye, that it is, John. You see, Martha and me are not getting any younger and Jim here has shown that given a few years, he'll be able to farm this place on his own. And we thought, as we have no family, when out 'appens to us it would be best if it were all legal like and in Jim's name."

"And are you agreeable with this, Mrs Styles?" "I am that, fully agreeable, Mr Durville." "And you, Jim?" he asked with a smile.

"I am. I can't really believe how it's happened. I never realized anywhere like this existed. And now, me, working with stock, ploughing fields, travelling to Whitby. Think o' me roamin' them streets in York just a couple o' years since. I was going to say it's like a dream come true, but I couldn't 'ave dreamt it because I didn't know about places such as this."

John smiled across at the lad and said, "Right, Albert, if you have the deeds, I have all the necessary paperwork. All we need is a witness and I hope Jacob will be back for me tonight and who better to ask than a preacher."

Once all the paperwork had been scrutinised and whilst waiting for Jacob's return, John asked Jim if he had any further news of Ruth.

A troubled look crossed the boy's features. "Not as yet, sir, but I'm still looking. We travel to Whitby and down this valley now quite a bit, trading stock and if I keep asking, I'm sure I'll find her, 'cos we used to talk of heading for the coast for work, you see."

"I understand, Jim, but it is a tall order as she could be anywhere. Now I cannot stay more than a day this time but when everything is taken care of in York and I fancy a few days holiday, I'll be back and in the meantime, I will keep my eyes open for any further news."

"Where will you stay?" Martha asked. "You know you would be very welcome here, John."

"No, I couldn't possibly put on your hospitality, Mrs Styles and I have approached Jacob who will be able to rent me a room, so that's what I'll do."

"Splendid," replied Albert and just then they heard the clatter of a pony and trap pull up outside.

After all the necessary paperwork was signed and witnessed, John thanked Martha and Albert for their hospitality and such good food, then he and Jacob made their way back to Gallows Howe across the moors, the darkness gathering like a cloak around them.

Chapter 65

Ruth arrived back at Dan's cottage to find him standing at the mounting block, looking out for her.

"Ruth, where've you been. I was just beginning to think something had happened. You're later than usual. I've got us some tea on the go." Dan was almost back to fitness, doing light work and only a slight limp betraying his accident. He reached up, his hands gripping her round her slender waist to help her dismount. She placed her hands on his shoulders and he lowered her to the ground. She felt his breath on her cheek as she slid down and it was then he noticed her tear stained cheeks. Suddenly the concern showed in his face. "What's wrong, Ruth, you've been crying? Has someone upset you?"

"No, really, Dan, it's nothing," she replied, trying desperately to force a smile onto her lips. "I said to Jacob you would be wondering where I was. I just got delayed but it's nothing really, nothing at all. Come on, let's stable up and have some tea. It's getting late."

Ruth, now developing into a young woman and although inexperienced with the opposite sex, knew that if she and Dan went on living like this, their friendship blossoming as the weeks passed, something was bound to happen and they could soon become more than just friends. The thought excited her, but also frightened her. In her quieter moments, when out with the animals, or out riding on Dulcie, she tried to imagine how it would be if she and Dan ever became lovers.

Lovers. Even the word excited her, wildly excited her, having learnt many things due to witnessing the coupling of animals since working and living out here with Dan, although she still found great difficulty in relating the same situation to a man and woman relationship; but it did not stop her imagination from running wild. This was definitely not something Miriam ever taught her. She smiled as these visions now came vividly to mind, loving the way it made her body tingle, becoming alive with new sensations.

Frighteningly alive.

Only with immense will power did she manage to push such thoughts to one side, and also, by reminding herself how lucky she was to have fallen into such a way of life by accident and have Dan as a good friend. She realized it was becoming more difficult as their friendship grew, but she determined not to be foolish as it could jeopardize her position and with it her future. She would not destroy this chance of happiness for anything. And another thing, whenever her mind wandered into such exciting thoughts, it often brought the roguish features of Jim to life, along with a stab of sadness that settled like lead around her heart. Sometimes so strong, it pushed everything else out. Where was he? Was he still looking for her?

Ruth cast her mind back to the time of their forced parting. Surely, he would have tried to find her if he'd really wanted. The last memory of Jim was that awful day when caught for stealing. My goodness that seemed a lifetime ago. Maybe Jim had forgotten her, wouldn't remember who she was? Uncertainty clogged her brain as to what he may be doing now. But she was happy to keep the thought there of him searching for her. I mean really, how could he find me, even if he wanted to? There was no way he could get any news about her, and if he did, the only news would be that she died trying to escape from a murder. She thought back to that horrible time with Bella and her legs almost gave way in a faint. But only Jacob knows the true story and my secret is surely safe with him.

She busied herself by stabling Dulcie and feeding the few chickens that Dan had acquired, this always drove any depressive thoughts from her mind,

Chapter 65

before going to the cottage and joining Dan for a meal.

After they had eaten, Ruth stood by the small window, gazing out onto the orchard as she loved to watch the sun sink steadily behind the line of trees, casting long shadows and a golden glow across the tidy garden. Dan came to her side. Standing close, she could smell the masculinity of him. She sensed a difference in his mood. She wasn't frightened, but a sliver of excitement crept through her slight frame as he grasped her hand in his.

In serious mood, Dan asked, "Now, are you ready to tell me what upset you, Ruth. I know you well enough now and I hope we are good enough friends for you to talk to me if there is a problem. Are you wanting to leave? Is that it? 'Cos if you do, and I've been meaning to say this for a while and I've never been able to muster up the courage in case I didn't like the answer..." Dan took a deep breath, then rushed the words out as he turned her toward him, the serious grey eyes searching hers as if they could give him the answer he yearned for. "...I'm not very good at explaining what's on my mind, but I must tell you, I don't want you to go, Ruth. I'm a selfish sod, see. Just thinking about me when I should be thinking about how you feel, stuck out here in the middle of nowhere. Not much of a life for a young girl is it? But you know I would miss you terribly if you left, Ruth."

"Dan, what brought this on? What makes you think I want to leave? Why would I want to leave? This is the first time I have found real happiness since I lost my mother. I once thought I was settled in York, but that didn't work out. I am happier here than I have ever been in my whole life."

Ruth's eyes sparkled as she took in this information blurted out by Dan and decided to tell him exactly what happened.

"I'll tell you the reason why I was upset, Dan. As I rode alongside the church on my way back here, you know what," Ruth's face became serious as she recalled her experience, "as I passed, the bell rang out. There wasn't a breath of wind, well, only a slight breeze and no one about. Can you explain that?" The excitement shone in her eyes as she went on in a quiet voice. "I entered the church and everything was so silent, a feeling of calmness came over me. I sat at the front staring at Jesus on the cross and thought of His suffering and for some reason, I still can't explain it, I couldn't move. I tried as hard as I could to stand up and walk out, but I couldn't. That's when I began to cry. No other reason, I just couldn't help it. I don't know how long I sat there before realising Jacob had entered and sat down beside me and stayed with me until I finally stopped crying. That's why I was late and why I was upset. Nothing to do with wanting to leave. Do you think God had something to do with it, Dan?"

He reached out for her, relief on his face, catching her round the waist and swinging her off her feet, "Oh that's the best news yet, Ruth. I'm not sure that God had anything to do with it. My guess would be it was more to do with Jacob. But whoever it was, I don't mind, if it means you'll be staying a bit longer." His face was close, she could feel the warmth of his breath on her cheek, his heart beating strong against her chest.

"Yes, you'll not get rid of me that easy, Dan Parkes. I have a lot to talk over with Jacob, but with his help I may be able to settle here. You see, Dan, there is a lot you don't know about me. Even though I am young in years, I feel older, surviving many awful experiences in the past. I have to live with many secrets due to those early years."

"I don't care, Ruth. "Just let's take it as it comes, eh?" and suddenly his lips were on hers, his stubbly chin rough against her fair skin taking her breath away, wrapping his strong arms around her. Ruth, although taken by surprise with this sudden turn of events, responded naturally and quickly, wrapping her arms around his neck. Never having experienced anything close to such an intimate gesture, not even a peck on the cheek from anyone, let alone a full- blooded passionate kiss on the lips, brought her emotions to the surface. Sparks flew before her eyes, a sudden rush of colour rushed to her cheeks and, eventually, when Dan put her down and held her at arms-length, her legs would not support her.

"Wow, Dan Parkes, that was certainly some kiss," she said, trying to back away and put some distance between them so she could somehow gain control of her senses.

"You enjoyed it then?" he asked, his eyes locking on hers. He continued to hold her at arms-length. "Oh, Ruth, I've been wanting to do that ever since I saw you. Ever since that day you saved my life."

Chapter 65

"Now Dan, we must be sensible, not get emotional." Ruth's head had stopped spinning and she lifted Dan's hands from her shoulders. "You must realize, this changes everything. I'm not yet fifteen, just a young girl and don't think you can take advantage of me just 'cos you are stronger. Now this has happened I have my reputation to think of. We will have to talk this through. You see everyone believes I'm your niece but they are soon going to realize that I'm not and then what do I do?" Her eyes searched his for an answer.

"Well, we could live in sin. Wow, how good would that be?" a broad grin spreading across his face at the mere thought of it.

Ruth's mouth dropped open, a look of shock on her face but she knew that Dan Parkes had kindled a spark deep inside her with that kiss that was exciting to her. "Never." This said with a finality she did not feel. "No, we could never do that. How would I explain that to everyone, especially to Jacob? Oh, Dan, why did you have to go and do that? This changes everything. Nothing's ever going to be the same again. I think we must tell the truth and face the consequences."

"Does that mean you are not mad with me and will stay here?"

"No, I'm not mad with you. How could I be mad with you after a kiss like that. She smiled at him as he cast her a wicked look. "But," and she wagged her finger in his direction, "I can't commit to anything like that for a long time as there is someone else, or was, a long time ago." It was beginning to seem as if from another life but, she had to admit, the feelings she held for young Jim still held strong. So strong she had to push them from her mind so she could concentrate on what to do now.

Dan's face lost its glow. "Someone else you say. How can that be? You've never mentioned anyone else before."

"Well, I did tell you I had a friend at the Orphanage but I never had the need to explain before until now, have I? As for staying here with you under the same roof, it changes things, but I think I know what I am going to do Dan. I will ask Jacob if I can rent my room at Gallows Howe for the week. That might be the best."

"Then you'll be staying close." He reached out for her, but she was quicker than him and laughing, she skipped out of the door.

"I'm going to check on Dulcie and go for a walk. Come on, Nip, let's see what's happening down by the river." The little Spaniel jumped up in delight and followed her outside. Ruth fervently hoped her emotions had settled back to normal by the time she returned.

Chapter 66

The silver disc of a harvest moon lit the last few miles of rough track for John and Jacob to arrive safely back at Gallows Howe and as Joshua was on hand to stable the horse, the two men entered the house. Drawing their chairs nearer to the smouldering fire, John said, "You appear to have quite a close-knit community here, Jacob, and thriving, but one thing that puzzles me in this day and age, is why the devil do you keep something as grisly and outdated as the gallows as a landmark to endure every day?"

Jacob laid back contentedly in his chair before answering. "Good question, John, but the answer is really quite simple, and behind it lays a story. The last person to die upon these gallows had done nothing more than steal a sheep. Can you believe that? Not only did they hang the unfortunate man, they left the body swinging from the gallows overnight and some miscreant or vagabond was desperate enough to hack the right hand off the corpse." John sat listening intently. "Next day they cut the body down, buried him in a pauper's grave out on the moor. No gravestone, no marker. Not a sign that he ever lived, apart from the story that sprang from the severed hand.

Legend has it that the hand hacked off a dead man at Gallows Howe and placed on or around the house the thief is going to rob, he can take all the time he needs to ransack the house of all its valuables and the occupants will hear nothing, never a thing disturbing their slumber. It became known as the 'Hand of Glory'. Such a hand was found in the village from which the legend was born. Whoever carried one of these grisly limbs with them would be protected by its power when carrying out their illegal deeds. Legend or truth, I am not sure, but the fact is, when our eyes rest upon the gallows it reminds us of the evil still among us. In just the same way as you rest your eyes upon a church, it brings to mind the good deeds that can, and will, be done."

After listening intently John broke into a smile and replied, "I can see now why you are such a respected preacher, Jacob. You hold your audience well. What a marvellous piece of local history. Now, if you will forgive me, I must retire for the night. All this fresh country air has tired me out and I need to be ready for away early tomorrow morning. As you can well imagine, sat in an office can be incredibly boring and after our two maids left, in such terrible circumstances I might add, Miriam lost the will to live. I think it broke her heart, she had grown very attached to both, especially Ruth." A sadness swept over John's features and he suddenly appeared an old man, the memories flooding back to haunt him. With his voice barely a whisper, as if talking to himself he said, "If it was not for my ongoing work at the Orphanage, I could easily have followed her."

Jacob's heart went out to this man. One would have thought he had everything in life. A beautiful house in the better part of York, a prosperous business, maids to call upon for their every whim, but when Jacob glanced at John in unguarded moments, he instantly recognised the look of a lonely, troubled man. But his heart also gave a little jump on hearing the name Ruth.

Now he was almost certain this was the same Judge John Durville who featured in Ruth's past life but he would never think of divulging her secret. He had given his word, he would tell no one.

He sat on well into the night, his mind pondering for a solution but in the end, he admitted defeat and muttered to himself, 'So be it Lord, I leave it entirely in your hands.' Then, as an afterthought, added, 'but please try and make it sooner rather than later.' He then retired to his bed.

Chapter 67

Ruth rose early. The weather had deteriorated suddenly and it had rained for the past few days. A quick look out of the window showed the river swollen as if ready to burst into the surrounding fields below the cottage. Crimson shards of light were shooting across the lightening sky as she dressed. It wasn't her day for working at the village, but she felt an overwhelming desire to catch Jacob before he left on his rounds and explain how things had changed between her and Dan and ask him if it was possible for her to move in full time at Gallows Howe.

Dan lay fast asleep as she ran out to mount Dulcie and set off for the ride across the moors that she looked upon as home. Ruth realized she could run faster and be at the village well before riding there but there was something about the soft, slow thud of hooves that soothed her spirit, so therefore it became her ritual to ride there.

Arriving early, she greeted Jacob and Joshua who were up and about. "Morning, Jacob, morning, Joshua, are you ready for breakfast," Ruth asked with a smile, well knowing the answer.

Jacob's face lit up. "That would be splendid," he said, "but you must have your days mixed up, Ruth. You usually work the weekend." He began carving the bread set out on the table. "But it is fortunate you came. We have a guest this morning, Ruth, so if you could do an extra plate, that would be good."

"I certainly will," and she hurried through to the kitchen to boil the kettle and begin frying their eggs and bacon. As she left Jacob couldn't believe her timely arrival and glancing Heavenward murmured "Thank you God, you certainly work quickly sometimes."

Through in the kitchen, singing softly to herself, Ruth busied herself with plates and cutlery, quickly setting three places at the table. With the tea made and wondering idly who the guest was and where he was from, she walked back into the living room with a tray of cups. Her eyes lifted and found herself staring at the unmistakable figure of Judge John Durville. As recognition dawned on him, he started up from his chair.

"Ruth, Ruth Brennan. It must be you, surely?" The tray crashed from Ruth's hands, her legs turning weak, the shattered crockery scattering across the floor, her hand shooting to her mouth to stifle a scream. Josh and Jacob rushed to her side, easing her down into a chair before she fell.

Ruth, as white as ghost, her voice barely more than a whisper, but carrying a fierceness in its delivery, she turned to Jacob. "What have you done to me, Jacob Thrall. I trusted you with all my heart and all my troubles. So much for your God. I will never trust you, or your God, or anyone else ever again," and she turned to flee from the room. But both Jacob and Joshua grabbed her and held her as she tried to beat her fists against them both, such was her rage.

"Ruth, I did not betray you. I would never do that. Please listen to us for a minute." Jacob was on his knees by her side begging, pleading with her.

She sank back in the chair, turning away from them all, defeated and broken. "Everyone deserts me eventually. Even your all-loving God, Jacob, when he knows the full truth," and, head bowed to her chest, she broke down, covering her face, weeping silently into her lap.

She realized it was too good to last, although at one time she had dared to hope but, in a way, it would be a relief for it to be out in the open and she would suffer the consequences.

Ruth began, "I didn't mean to kill your son, sir. It was an accident, you must believe me," she said through her tears, looking beseechingly up at the huge figure of the man as she spoke, "but when I was alone, he attacked me.

Chapter 67

I was frightened at what he was going to do. I had to defend myself."

Jacob knelt by the side of Ruth's chair, taking her small, shaking hand in his, as Joshua stood, close to crying himself, understanding the pain and torment she was suffering.

Jacob said, "Ruth you must believe me. I did not know John was coming. We only met yesterday. I had no idea that you knew each other."

John strode forward. "Please can I be allowed to speak with her, Jacob." The beetle brows were drawn together in worry at the distress caused to Ruth.

"Of course, John. We will leave you to talk," and Jacob ushered Joshua outside.

"Ruth, I'm so glad to see you again," he said as he pulled a chair up alongside her. "First things first. You did not kill anyone, Ruth. Henry is still alive and, hopefully, he is now hard at work at the Orphanage as we speak. So, you have no need to worry on that score. In fact, it was a very good lesson for him to realize he cannot treat people the way he did without repercussions. And honestly it was only by chance I called here as I had business at a farm at Roston.

Jacob had nothing to do with it. You must believe that."

"Oh, sir. I'm so thankful he's still alive." Relief instantly flooding through her. She closed her eyes as she said, "I still carry the image of him laid in a pool of blood. I didn't think anyone would believe me, so that's why I ran away. I didn't want Bella to come but she insisted. She was so desperate that I couldn't think of any other way out. I did my best for her, sir. I really did. I pleaded with her to go back."

"You poor child. No one should have to suffer torment such as this. I know you would do your utmost for her, as you did for Miriam, or for anybody, Ruth. Now, I know this has been a big shock to you, but I may have some good news to come out of all this. I hope you are ready for what I am about to say." Ruth was still deathly pale with shock, but she managed to return his smile.

"An old friend got in touch, asking me to transfer some property into another name for him at Roston and that is how I came to be at Gallows

Howe. For transport." Ruth sat quietly, taking in every word that John told her. "While I concluded the transfer of the property, who should walk in but a tousle headed ragamuffin with a chipped tooth, who told me he was still looking for his friend from the Orphanage who used to work for me. Do you know who I mean?"

Ruth's heart suddenly began to beat much faster as she stared wide eyed at John as he related his story. "You mean Jim, don't you. Jim is just at Roston?"

"You remember him then? He is that, and a typical farmer's boy. In fact, he is so good at the job... well I'm not saying any more as I think the two of you will have a lot to talk about when you meet up, Ruth. Now, Jacob assures me there is a beautiful walk down by the river and the rain appears to have ceased for a while, so I will enjoy that before I leave. Jacob is going to arrange transport for me to the station as I have unfinished work to do in York."

"This can't be happening to me. All this time, I thought I had killed a man until a few minutes ago, then you tell me he is alive. Then you say Jim is only a few miles away in the next valley. And looking for me you say, to meet up again. Sir, you've made me so happy, I must tell Jacob."

"Of course. If a pleasure cannot be shared, it counts for nought." But before she did, Ruth thought it may be best if she had a word with God before Jacob and with that, running as fast as possible along the old stone footpath, she again entered the sacred old building and once inside felt the same comforting feelings clasp around her heart once more. Striding purposefully to the front of the church, she knelt dutifully before the cross. Bowing her head, blond tresses brushing her cheeks, she began to pray.

"Dear Jesus, I have never prayed before in my life, so I am not sure just what to say, or how to say it, but I thank you for making it possible to meet up with Mr Durville again and I am so glad his son Henry is alive. I may not swing from the gallows now like I had imagined. And thank you for the knowledge that Jim is just a short distance away and that he has been looking for me all this time. I know that Dan will be upset. He kissed me the other day you know, but I suppose you know all that. Jacob tells me you see everything, but I don't know how you do that.

Chapter 67

I did mention to Dan there was someone else. That is if they still wanted to see me and with your help, I think Dan will understand. Please don't leave me alone again Lord, as I feel I need you more now than ever before. Amen. Now, if you will excuse me, Lord, I must rush to find Jacob as I have something important to discuss with him."

Chapter 68

John Durville arrived back home in good spirits after his meeting with both Jim and Ruth and found it so inspiring that they had come through so much turmoil and strife and finding, no, not just finding, making their way in life after such difficult childhoods.

Work was going well at the Orphanage and with the old building weatherproof and well heated, the decoration began to transform the dull, damp rooms into bright areas for learning. Henry must have taken heed of his warning, appearing to have pulled himself together and was on hand to greet his father.

"Morning, Henry, you are looking more like your old self." Henry was back to being the elegant, well-groomed man before he slid from grace, apart from the now permanent disfigurement.

"Morning, father, I hope you had an enjoyable weekend out in the wilds with your country friends."

John ignored the sarcasm and answered, "thoroughly enjoyable and very friendly people I may add. Nothing too much trouble. Now, down to business. I see you and George, the foreman, have met and he has set work for you to do." At this minute George made an appearance. "Ah, George, good morning. I must say you and your men are making this place unrecognisable from the state it was in. I can now finally see it as a place

Chapter 68

where children can be properly educated and cared for and hopefully set them toward a better future and a better life."

John was soon discussing further plans with the builder, wandering through the rooms the smell of paint strong in their nostrils. It was while planning this future work that John began to relate to George of his trip to the country and of the unexpected joy of finding Jim and Ruth both having suffered bitter experiences at this establishment when under the former management.

Henry, in the adjoining room, listened intently. On hearing Ruth's name mentioned he became even more alert, realizing now that his father had stumbled upon her, hiding somewhere out in the countryside. A sly smile crossed his features. He knew if he bided his time, his chance to get even with that little bitch for disfiguring him, would come. All he needed now was her exact whereabouts.

Henry knew the days would be long and boring but had no other options at present, so was thankful to sit down for dinner later that day. After eating, Henry brought the conversation round to his father's trip.

"And did you find plenty to interest you among the yokels of the moors, father?" Again, this cutting reference to people Henry thought were below him angered John but he kept his temper in check.

"Very entertaining and magnificent scenery, Henry. Jacob filled me in with all the local history of the surrounding area. Fascinating."

"Hmm, I'm sure," replied Henry not really interested in the history, more on where he had visited. "Are they still living in mud huts and the past, or has time moved on a certain amount for them?"

"I'll grant you, there is not much money about but the ironstone mines at nearby Roston are booming and bringing a better future for the community and also a better chance of jobs for the local people."

"I suppose that is all there is for them really, slaving away in the fields, or like rats never seeing the light of day down a mine, then praying for a better life at church every Sunday."

John had had enough. He threw down his napkin and got to his feet, "Henry, your attitude is totally unacceptable. I now realize why you had to leave home. A few hours of your company and you have dispelled all the good feelings and joy I received from Jacob and his friends at Gallows Howe. We never did see eye to eye and we never will. Now if you will excuse me, I have work to do." And with that he stormed out before saying something he would regret.

Henry relaxed back in his chair, a smirk of satisfaction across his already smug features. He now had the snippet of information that would lead him to the evil little guttersnipe that had so disfigured him, destroying his life.

Rising from the table, he shouted goodbye to his father who, either didn't hear, or possibly chose to ignore him, as the office door was almost wrenched from its hinges when it slammed shut, such was his rage.

Henry didn't give a damn, biding his time on sauntering back to the flat, and decided this could be a rare opportunity to call in a favour from an old sporting friend of his, who once fell into what could have become a rather embarrassing situation, but with Henry's connections, and money, they had somehow managed to keep it hidden from the public eye.

Now, he thought, would be a right time to call in that favour. Henry knew his friend, Jocelyn, liked nothing better than a wild ride across the moors with his pony and trap, often following the local hunt when they were running. Well, he might have to venture further afield this time, but then, what were old friends for, but to help out in times of need?

After a brief meeting, Jocelyn made no effort in hiding his annoyance with the proposal but could see no way of getting out of it, but forcefully reminded Henry he must be back mid-afternoon as he had an appointment which must be adhered too.

"Don't worry, Jocelyn, I shall see you are back in good time. Once I have directions, you can drop me off and return home." Agreeing to meet at the flat on the hour, Henry returned home and quickly threw a few items into a small case, just on the off-chance things did not work out as planned, his expectations rising by the minute.

True to his word, Jocelyn arrived prompt on the hour and they were soon making their way out of the city and into the countryside beyond. It proved a sullen, silent journey as the men, although acquainted, could

Chapter 68

not be described as close friends, only ever brought together through sheer necessity.

After days of heavy rain roads were waterlogged but the cloud had lifted briefly and Henry settled back to enjoy the journey. After a good hour's ride, the little pony gained some respite from the fierce climb up and over the moors, eventually dropping down to follow a long, straight road, where the lush valleys ran for miles on either side when they spotted a lone figure walking toward them by the roadside, possibly on his way to work in the fields, Henry thought.

"Stop here, Jocelyn, I'll ask this man for directions. He is sure to know."

Pulling up alongside Henry greeted the man in cordial fashion. "Good morning, my good man. I wonder if you could direct me to a small village called Gallows Howe in this vicinity?"

The man was dressed in his Sunday best and Henry changed his view, surmising he was more likely to be on his way home from attending church. They must be quite a God-fearing lot out here as Henry could not see any likely buildings.

"Aye, I can that." He turned, pointing in the direction of the road. "You are in walking distance of it, young man, but it's just out o' sight ovver t' next moor end. Keep on this road and you'll soon see the old gallows and church on your left. That's Gallows Howe. If you have to go further, be careful, as the river is about to burst its banks." The man doffed his cap to the pair of them as Henry offered his reply.

"Thank you kindly," but the man had already turned and begun to walk on.

"Well, I think this would be as good a place as any for us to part company, Jocylyn, wouldn't you say?"

"By the look of those clouds, it looks as if I am in for a rough ride home, as another storm is brewing by the look of that sky." Henry glanced skyward. Angry black clouds rolled in at the head of the dale and the distant rumble of thunder reached their ears and Henry felt the first drops of rain spatter his face.

"You could be right Jocelyn, old friend. You could be right," he said, unfurling a long coat out of his case. Jocelyn did not hear him as he quickly swung the trap around and whipped the little horse into a gallop, leaving Henry to continue his journey by foot in whatever weather came his way.

Chapter 69

Ruth had finally found Jacob after leaving the chapel and blushingly, tried to explain, much to Jacob's amusement, how things had become a little bit more complicated, as Dan's feelings toward her had suddenly changed.

She said, "you knew from the start I wasn't Dan's relation didn't you?"

"Well, I hadn't heard in all the years I have lived here, of Dan having any relatives close by but it was a plausible story."

"I'm very lucky you have a spare room. I'll miss Dan and Dulcie though. In fact, all his animals, his garden. Everything really."

"You'll still be able to visit him, Ruth."

"Not be the same though," she said thoughtfully and a little sadly, realizing another chapter in her life was closing, that she had no control over and was having to move on. But this time, she could see a future beckoning and with a much lighter heart, she began to lead her few meagre possessions from the cottage into Jacob's house.

She occupied the same small room, but it was quite adequate and she had made it more homely with a few wild flowers picked from along the riverside that very morning and placed in tiny vases dotted around the room. The same picture adorned the wall above the bed, but Jacob had put a brightly coloured bedspread on for her, helping to lighten what was a dark room.

But it did look out onto the church, the open fields and the river in the far distance down in the valley. At present not much further could be seen, the rain continuing to hammer down and the river levels were continuing to rise and close to flooding.

Ruth was hoping that Joshua had been able to get word to Jim that she was at Gallows Howe but she had no way of knowing if he had. All she could do was wait. She kept herself busy and spent many hours helping Jacob write his sermons for preaching on Sunday services. She was only just adding the finishing touches for his sermon this very night and had become accustomed to the ways of the church, attending now most Sundays but tonight she had decided not to go as if Jim did call, she didn't want to miss him, and Sunday would be the best day for him.

Jacob poked his head around the door. "Did you manage to finish my sermon, Ruth?" he inquired.

Ruth jumped up from the chair. "I certainly did. Do you want to read it before you go?" She frowned, saying, "For this one Jacob, I've tried to explain my feelings on how we should try and find Jesus ourselves and not leave everything up to him. That sometimes he may just appreciate a little help from us. Does that sound okay?"

"I'm sure it will be right. I have no need to read it before and, if it isn't, I'm old enough to improvise. I must admit though, you are turning into a very fine wordsmith and scholar, Ruth Brennan."

She beamed as he dashed out of the door. Ruth had grown to love and admire this man, a father figure to her now, with boundless energy, who gave so graciously of his time for others, even though suffering so much in the past himself. In her quieter moments, Ruth sometimes thought that the cruelty and hardships she had endured had certainly made her stronger but she also realized that everyone had their own cross to bear, no matter what age it came to them. Looking back, she was old enough now to realize there would always be someone suffering somewhere, because it was a cruel world, but, she thought, the very young should never be part of that world; and that was something she would add to her prayers on a night.

Chapter 69

It was now late evening and relieved at not having to make the trip back to Dan's on a night such as this. Watching the village folk, shoulders hunched and huddled together, as they walked through the now driving rain toward the comfort of the church made her smile. At one time the sermon would have gone ahead outside, even in a storm such as this, or so Jacob had informed her. Religion, it seemed, relied on suffering in silence, discomfort, or long, boring sermons. She hoped hers didn't sound boring.

Breathing a sigh of regret, she listened for any sound outside, hoping against hope that Joshua had got a message through to Jim. She was definitely not expecting anyone else to call on a night such as this.

Building the fire up and settling down with a book, the room soon became cosy and after a while, she cocked her head on one side and listened intently, sure she could hear the sound of footsteps outside. Her heart missed a beat, thinking it could only be Jim and she ran to the door just as the stranger was about to open it. Startled, she stepped back. Stood in the dark of the porch, Ruth didn't recognize him immediately and before she had time to slam the door, he swaggered further into the room, the lamplight highlighting the still prominent deep scar on the right side of his skull, a scar he would carry for the rest of his life. The realization that this man had actually found her made her sick to her stomach, a feeling of nausea sweeping over her.

"You!" she gasped. Her eyes widened with fright. "How did you find me? Your father must have told you where I was."

"As a matter of fact, he didn't, but I listened in on a conversation and I have struck lucky, haven't I? All on your own for this next couple of hours in this God forsaken place. Just enough time to pay you back for what you have made me suffer you worthless little trollop." His words held such venom that had built up and eaten away at him for the past couple of years or more. His eyes narrowed, staring unblinking with a devilish intensity, undressing her in a gaze that travelled up and down her young frame, just as he had the first time that he set his eyes on her.

Ruth, regaining her senses, ran across the far side of the room, putting as much distance as she could between them. He shrugged the sodden coat from his shoulders, letting it drop to the floor, arrogantly strolling after her as she slid behind the table, her eyes spotting the half open knife drawer.

She tried playing for time. "They will be back from church any minute, so do not think I am on my own."

"Oh, but I know they won't return for quite a while," he replied, "I have sat patiently in this torrential rain, watching every one of those stupid followers trudge across the moor to say their prayers. And that is what I suggest you do now. Say your prayers as I make you pay for ruining my life."

Before Ruth could make a grab for the drawer or escape his clutches, quick as lightning, he shot around the table and grabbed her wrists, shoving her roughly up against the wall, his lips searching wildly for hers as she wrenched her head from side to side in a determined bid to keep him from kissing her, almost retching as his stinking, drink fuelled breath hit her face.

"How dare you," she screamed. "Get away from me. Please leave me alone, I beg you."

"You can beg all you want, but there will be no escape this time by your scheming little plea of ignorance. I bet you are up for it now, just ripe and ready for the taking." Lust now controlled his whole being. All his longing and pent up hatred he would take out on this young virgin girl. Ruth could already taste the blood in her mouth from where he had savagely bitten deep into her inner lip.

Fighting with the strength and energy that only fear can bring, she screamed and fought and kicked out at him with all her might. Eventually, his strength proved superior, wearing her down as she fought tooth and nail to ward him off but, in the end, gasping with exertion, she began to weaken.

She saw the room swim dizzily as he swung her violently off her feet as if she were no more than a discarded package and she fell to the floor, her head making a loud smack on the flagged floor. Stars shot through her skull, a searing pain firing up through her shoulder, then the weight of his body landing on top of her, knocking the wind from her heaving lungs. With her head still spinning after hitting the floor, she still had managed to keep her senses about her.

"You evil bastard," she spat out, fear fuelling her rage. "I wish I had killed you when I had the chance." Fighting as hard as she could, she continued to

Chapter 69

scream for help. "Lord, where are you? Help me now." He laughed in her face.

"There is no one here to help. If you are still a virgin, then it will not be for much longer. She felt the coldness of his fingers on the soft warm flesh of her thighs as he forced his fingers nearer and nearer to their zenith, the thought of possessing her, overpowering.

With lungs fighting for air and muscles screaming for rest, Ruth could see the end and felt the shame of what was about to happen. The belt buckle was undone as he could now hold her two hands with his one. She heaved and strained and gave one final effort, but she was no match for him. His strength was proving a vital factor, as her own strength waned, her chest heaving with effort, her breath forced out through her bleeding lips in ragged gasps, but she would fight him off with every ounce of energy she had until the bitter end.

Suddenly, as her head turned to one side, warding off the kisses that Henry was trying to smother her with, she watched in disbelief as the door opened and Joshua stormed into the room. He took one look and grabbed a knife from the half open drawer. Henry had not heard or noticed anything, so intent was he on tearing the clothes from Ruth's body.

"No, Josh, no!" Ruth's scream tore through the silence of the little cottage. But either he did not hear her or did not care to.

The knife in Joshua's hand flashed once in the lamplight, before plunging deep into the attacker's back. The eyes, once filled with lust, now opened wide in disbelief, a last breath rattle escaping from his slack mouth, hot against Ruth's cheek before his head slumped forward. The body suddenly became limp, lifeless, a dead weight on top of her. She fought quickly to crawl out from underneath the body, then trying urgently to gather her senses, her shoulder screaming in pain, grabbed Joshua roughly by the collar. He stood, as if in a trance. Ruth slapped his face hard in a desperate bid to bring him back to reality.

"Listen to me, Josh," she hissed. "Listen. We need to get him out of here before your father arrives back. Do you understand?" Joshua, in a daze, nodded. Blood was now beginning to soak through the dead man's shirt.

They dragged the corpse out into the rain lashed night. Gasping for breath, their gaze suddenly fell on the tall, grisly silhouette of the gallows as if standing in judgement of their evil deed, its eerie presence chilling them to the very bone. Snatches of singing drifted from the church to where they stood. Everyone from the community would be there. Ruth realised she and Joshua had very little time, maybe an hour at the most, before someone would return.

Rushing out to the stable she grabbed one of the horses, quickly draping a halter around its neck, before dashing back to the cottage. Joshua had already found some old sacking and wrapped the body in that. Dragging the body feet first to the waiting horse, with great effort and hearts pounding madly, they lifted the corpse up, Joshua's brute strength invaluable as he finally managed to drape the dead carcass over the horse's back.

The storm was now at its ferocious peak, the rain peppering their skin like millions of needles as if trying to peel the flesh from the bones of their unprotected faces, the wind tearing at their meagre clothing like mad clutching, demons. They made the journey to the fast-flowing river, but were terrified of getting too close, as the torrent of water was uprooting trees from the river bank as if they were mere saplings, hurtling them past in a crashing torrent and crescendo of noise. Ruth could see the horror in Josh's eyes, as he once again relived the nightmare death of his mother on that traumatic night of his childhood so many years go. His eyes stared, unseeing, frozen to the spot. Ruth rushed to him beating at his chest, trying to stir him into life.

"Josh, please help me," she screamed at him. "I can't manage on my own. You've got to help." As she shook him, his eyes blinked once, then he slowly came to life. He lifted the body off the horse and carried it closer to the river on his shoulder. In the last few steps he dropped the heavy load and kicked it down the bank with his foot, watching the ungainly bundle roll toward the river. Suddenly, it snagged on something and stopped rolling, and, for a second, so did Ruth's heart.

Seizing a broken-down branch, she tried to prod the body toward the torrent, but because of her injured shoulder she hadn't the strength to push

Chapter 69

the body in. Josh was staring wildly at the water when Ruth pushed the stick into his hands. "Push now, Josh. With all your strength, push."

He dug the end of the branch into the sacking and pushed with all his might, until finally the strong current surged higher to reach out and snatch the grisly bundle from the bank side and they both watched, almost fainting with relief as it disappeared from view.

With not a second to waste, Ruth shouted, "come on Josh, we haven't much time left before everyone returns from church and we have to clean up yet."

Jumping on the horse's back, Joshua hauled Ruth up behind him then galloped at full stretch back to the cottage where Josh rushed to stable the horse, while Ruth replaced everything knocked over in her fight against Henry and just had time to check everything was in its place before changing into dry clothes.

Joshua did likewise and they were both calmly sitting reading with just a few minutes to spare. The door swung open and in strode Jacob like a drowned rat, shaking water from his wide brimmed hat.

"My goodness it's been many a year since we have seen a flood like this." He entered and backed up to the fire, hanging his coat up to dry. "Now I know it is a truly awful night but I believe it has brought some good news with it."

He turned toward the door and Ruth and Joshua followed his gaze as Jim walked into the room. Ruth's emotions, so high, they were almost at breaking point anyway, rushed over to Jim and wrapped her arms around his neck, immediately breaking into tears.

"Well, I'll take it you recognized me then, eh? Or do you greet all fellers like that?" the gap-toothed smile lighting Ruth's world up, his arms wrapping strongly around her as if he would never let her go again.

"Oh, Jim," she said as she smothered him with kisses. "I've missed you so much. I've needed you so much. I thought I would never see you again. I have so much to tell you."

Jim held her close in his arms and when the kisses stopped, he whispered in her ear, "I knew I would find you, Ruth. I just knew it. We were meant to be together and I would never have stopped searching for you. Never, as long as I lived!"

After their emotional meeting up, they turned to see Jacob studying Josh carefully. Eventually, wandering over to where Josh sat, he asked, "are you all right, Josh, you are looking pale, as if you have had quite a shock."

Josh looked earnestly in his father's eyes and answered quietly, "I'm fine, father, never felt better, but I suppose I am just really shocked at this sudden turn of events." Jacob's mouth dropped open in surprise. Expecting the usual sign language, Jacob's emotions got the better of him and it was his turn for tears. Tears of joy and relief to hear these first words uttered by Joshua since his mother's death all those years ago.

"Josh, I cannot believe it. After all this time you have found your voice again. The Lord be praised." After a pause for this to sink in, he said, "you know, Josh, I always knew God would finally bring your voice back. Josh flung his arms around his father in a massive bear hug and in that instant stole a quick glance across the room at Ruth and winked. She winked back as if to say, this is our secret Joshua. Another secret that I suppose we will have to live with for the rest of our lives.

Still hugging Jim close, as if frightened of losing him again, Ruth was dizzy with excitement and happiness. Once again, she gazed deep into those sparkling eyes that had entranced her, oh such a long, long time ago now and Ruth recalled the words of wisdom Jacob had whispered to her in the church and one of his favourite sayings.

"Remember, Ruth, God works in mysterious ways."

Yes, she thought, he certainly does.

About the Author

John Watson lives with his wife Ann in the small, rural village of Castleton, set amid the North York Moors. A bricklayer on leaving school, John and Ann ran their own building business for more than forty years. Now well and truly retired and with many of his earlier sports behind him – apart from still enjoying the competitiveness of table tennis - he decided to recapture the passion held for writing in his schooldays.

A Journey of Hope is his first novel, beginning among the slums in the City of York, before moving on to capture the spectacular area where he lives and which he knows so well.

Also by John F. Watson

Inheritance

The year is 1911 and Ruth Brennan, reunited with Jim from their orphanage days together, now looks to the future with a new found confidence. But first, she must banish the haunting memories from her early childhood if she is to find true happiness.

As Ruth battles with her own demons, Joshua Thrall learns that he must leave Freda, his first true love and as the horror of the 1st World War begins, Josh, along with close friends Barney and Pete, they decide to leave the hardship and poverty of the countryside to fight for King and Country.

A hard, emotional story of love, romance, family conflicts and bravery set around this close-knit rural community with the rugged, stunning scenery of the North York moors as its backdrop.

'Inheritance' is a sequel to 'A Journey of Hope.'

Printed in Great Britain
by Amazon